Tears slid from Bernie's eyes.

She knew how much he needed her, how desperately she needed him. But he wanted her without condition, and she wanted him with reservation. And she didn't seem to be winning.

Mark felt angry, confused, frustrated – but he couldn't do anything to hurt her. He sat up and pulled her into his arms.

She held him, absorbing the security he offered, wanting to believe it would be all right. "I want to make love with you," she whispered. "I'd like to lay with you right now. But . . ."

His clamouring heart plummeted. He wanted to make love to her with a desperation he hadn't known in so long. He wanted to know her – really know her in the only way physical bonding could reveal her. But . . . the deadly word fell like a hammer.

To Lorraine, my sister and friend,
who was once Sister Michael of the Angels

Other novels by Muriel Jensen

Silhouette Sensation

Love and Lavender
Fantasies and Memories
The Duck Shack Agreement
Strings
Side by Side
A Carol Christmas

MURIEL JENSEN
The Miracle

Silhouette Sensation

First published in Great Britain in 1991 by Silhouette Books, Eton House, 18-24 Paradise Road, Richmond, Surrey TW9 1SR

© Muriel Jensen 1991

Silhouette, Silhouette Sensation and Colophon are Trade Marks of Harlequin Enterprises B.V.

ISBN 0 373 58324 9

18 – 9112

Made and printed in Great Britain

Chapter One

Mark Costello looked across his new oak desk at the latest applicant for office manager of his commercial photography studio. He tried to be open-minded. So one side of her head was shaved, the hair on the other side was pink. He could appreciate self-expression.

"Can you type, Miss..." He glanced down at her name, the only thing she'd written on the two-page application. "Moon. Mojave Moon?"

Slumped in the chair across from him, the young woman in her late teens chewed a large wad of gum and nodded. "Yeah. Like the desert. No, I can't."

"Take dictation?"

"No."

Mark looked up as his brother Tony and Hal Cummings, his brother-in-law, walked past carrying a spotlight on a folding stand. Tony glanced at the young woman in the chair, then looked at Mark with a roll of his eyes and a barely suppressed laugh. "Have you had experience answering the telephone?" Mark asked.

Mojave straightened out of her slump and crossed one denim-clad knee with a colorful patch on it over the other knee, visible through a hole in her jeans. "Like, who hasn't?" she asked.

He had to grant her that one. "I meant in a professional capacity," he explained.

She blinked heavy-lidded blue eyes under thick, glittering eyeshadow. "Huh?"

Doggedly Mark tried again. "Do you enjoy working with people?"

Mojave nodded halfheartedly. "If they stay out of my space."

Cecelia Costello, Mark's mother, came through the open front door carrying a thriving philodendron in one arm and a fat fern in the other. In a long gray coat and sturdy white nurse's shoes, she came to an abrupt halt several feet behind Mojave, her eyes glued to the unique coiffure. She looked at Mark over the girl's head, her eyes widening.

"Mom," he said firmly, "those go in the back bedroom where Tony and Hal are putting the equipment."

Ignoring him, Cecelia came around to stand beside Mark and frowned down at the girl. "Sweetheart, you're going to freeze your brain." She studied the girl a moment, then asked irrepressibly, "Or am I already too late?"

Mark stood, pushed his mother toward the back of the house, then helped Mojave out of her chair and toward the door. "Thanks for coming by, Miss Moon. I'll keep your application on file, but I'm looking for someone..." How could he put it tactfully? Someone with a pulse? With hair on both sides of her head? With a better tailor?

Mojave stopped at the door and nodded. "Got the picture, Pops. You'll, like, tell Unemployment I came by?"

He smiled. "Fer sure."

Mojave slouched away, the snap of her gum still audible after she crossed the street. Mark closed the door with a groan.

"So, 'Pops.'" With a laugh, Tony quoted what he'd overheard. "Did you hire her?"

Mark turned to find his brother sitting on a corner of his desk. He went to his chair and fell into it, shaking his head. "Aren't there any more normal women? All I want is an attractive, articulate female to answer the phone and keep clients and models happy and occupied while I'm working. Is that so much to ask?"

Tony swung on his perch to face Mark. "What was wrong with the hooker? I kind of liked her."

Mark remembered the previous applicant, who'd worn a leather mini, fishnet stockings and a slightly tubercular look, and gave his brother a tired grin. "She was a cab driver."

Tony laughed. "That's a new spin on an old theme."

"She could type at least." Mark's grin widened. "Lucky Mom missed her. Is the van empty yet?"

"One more load from Mom's should do it. Any more applicants today?"

"One more." Mark glanced at the notepad attached to his telephone. "Bernadette Emerson. If she isn't suitable, I may have to put Mom in this chair. I've already had a couple of calls from prospective clients."

Tony nodded. "I'm not surprised. When one of the country's foremost photojournalists decides to settle down in his hometown to do commercial photography, he's bound to have everyone at his doorstep."

Mark looked at Tony levelly. "You coerced the clients who called today into coming to me."

Tony opened his mouth to deny it, then saw the look in his brother's eye. Mark had a gift for seeing to the heart of things. "How'd you know?" he asked.

Mark put his feet up on the desk. "The three of you played football together. I may have been four years behind you, but I remember your friends. When I told you I was coming home, you promised me that you wouldn't hover. And you promised not to let Mom take over."

Tony laughed in self-deprecation. "That might have been rash of me. You can't blame her for being excited that her favorite child has come home after twelve years."

"It's only been eleven, and Angie's her favorite."

Tony shook his head. "Our little sister's out of favor. She bought bottled spaghetti sauce."

Hal materialized from behind them to sit on the other corner of Mark's desk. Blond and slender, a contrast to the Costellos' dark, thick-shouldered good looks, he moved into their conversation easily, like a third brother. "She's gone back to school to get her CPA, and Mom thinks that means she's less devoted to the boys and me."

"She's a brat," Cecelia said as she marched across the living room and out the door. She'd shed her coat, and her short, stout body moved with surprisingly graceful efficiency in a dark blue sweat suit. "Marinara in a bottle! I ask you!"

"Where's she going?" Tony asked Mark.

Mark grinned. "Probably back to her car. I'll bet you ten bucks she brought lasagna for lunch."

Hal got to his feet. "I have to go. Can you two handle the last load from Mom's, or do you need me to come back after work?"

Mark walked him to the door his mother had left open. "No. We'll manage. Thanks for coming to help," he said, clapping his shoulder. "I owe you a family portrait or something."

Cecelia walked past them carrying a foil-wrapped oblong pan. She shook her finger at Hal. "You should have been firmer. I told you that."

Hal paused to give her a quick kiss. "I want her to do this, Mom," he insisted. "You stop picking on her. See you later."

Cecelia rolled her eyes at his directive, but patted his cheek with the same affection she showed her sons. She turned up the walk to the house.

Hal shook his head and grinned at Mark. "Everything's so simple for Mom. I really envy her that. Her thinking is just forty years out of date. See you tomorrow."

Mark walked back up the path, wondering if coming home had been such a good idea. It had seemed so a month ago, when life had felt so empty. The pain in his heart had dulled to a throbbing ache, but he couldn't seem to find his feet again. There'd been no pleasure in his work. He'd lost the art that once stood out in every photo he took. He knew it was because he'd lost the compassion, the caring.

But he still had to support himself. It occurred to him that he'd done that successfully with commercial photography before he'd risen to national attention with his chronicle of world events. He could do it again. Then he'd had to decide where.

The pull of home was strong. The year before he'd almost run there for comfort, but he'd been too angry, too hate-filled, destroyed. His family would never have understood the darkness that had lived in him then. It was still there, but he'd learned to control it.

He'd grown strangely comfortable with the emotional pain, but he had to do something about the emptiness. He was from a loud, opinionated, song-filled family. An elbow to rub against was like breath in his lungs. So he'd come home.

He stopped at the foot of the porch steps and looked up at the big old two-story he'd bought to be his home and studio. It wasn't Victorian, it was just old. It had no gables, no interesting angles, just a square solidity that seemed to embody everything he needed. He'd live upstairs, where the big windows looked out onto the ocean on one side and the busy streets of Seaside on the other, and work downstairs, where bushes crowded the windows and he could control the light more easily.

He waited to feel at least a small thrill of professional excitement. But there was nothing. He started up the steps. It was too much to ask at this point. He'd never be the same Mark Costello he'd once been; he'd accepted that. But the man he'd become had to get on with his life.

Tony met him at the door. "You were wrong about the lasagna," he said with a broad smile. "Mom brought manicotti. You owe me ten bucks."

BERNADETTE EMERSON CHECKED the note in her hand against the house number. A swell of excitement rose in her. Behind her, the ocean churned against a broad beach and sea gulls hovered over a solitary old man tossing them bread crumbs.

To her right the Promenade stretched for a quarter of a mile, lined with beautiful old houses where the rich once summered. Some were elegant, some cozy, some whimsical. They offered a glimpse of a romantic past, and she couldn't help but be touched by it.

To her left, the Promenade spilled onto the famous Seaside Turnaround, a spot that marked the end of the Lewis and Clark Trail. On weekends kids cruised there, visitors walked to watch the ocean and residents stayed away. It also marked the end of Broadway, a long, midway-like street filled with fascinating shops and restaurants dispensing wonderful aromas. In the summer it was thick with tourists, but now, with a late September breeze in the air, traffic was light.

Bernie walked quietly up the porch steps, thinking how much she wanted this job. Freedom was everything she had thought it would be—exhilarating, inspiring—but she had to think practically. She had to eat, pay the rent and save money to buy a car.

She smiled at a small balding man on a ladder hanging a carved wooden sign. Pictured on it was an old box camera, and tall block letters that spelled GOOD IMPRESSIONS. "Mark Costello, proprietor" was in smaller type.

Bernie still couldn't quite believe she was applying for a job to work with Mark Costello. The clerk at the employment office had boasted about the hometown boy who'd become a renowned name in photojournalism. Bernie was a little overwhelmed to find herself on his doorstep.

The front door was open. Hardwood floors stretched dustily to a large oak desk. There was nothing on it but a telephone, and there was no one in the chair behind it.

"Mr. Costello?" she asked, peering into an open door off the living room. There was a blue velvet Victorian chaise, and two potted plants rested on a window seat. She tried the next room. It was filled with cartons, lights on tall stands and other things she presumed were camera equipment but couldn't really identify.

She peeked into another room and found a spotless kitchen redolent of oregano and cheese. She sniffed appreciatively, then went back to wait in what was apparently intended to be the office.

Her new black heels bit her toes uncomfortably as she headed for the chair that faced the desk. Before she could sit, the telephone rang. She wondered if someone would answer it in another part of the house. It rang a second time and a third. She picked up the receiver on the fourth ring, spotted the notepad attached to the base of the phone, and routed through her purse with her free hand.

"Good Impressions," she said cheerfully as her fingers closed over a pen. "May I help you?"

"This is David Boardwell," a brisk voice said. "Of Boardwell Imports. I'd like to talk to Costello about doing a Christmas brochure. Can we get it done in time for a late October mailing, and what's it going to cost mc?"

Bernie scanned the empty rooms again and perched on the edge of the desk. "Mr. Costello's with another client right now," she fibbed. "But I'll have him return your call. Where can he reach you, Mr. Boardwell?"

MARK STOPPED IN THE DOORWAY, a box of film in his arms. A strange woman was sitting on his desk, trim calves visible beneath a red wool skirt.

"He's with another client, Mr. Boardwell," he heard her say in a sunny, professional voice. "But I'll have him return your call. Where can he reach you?" Could this be Bernadette Emerson, he wondered, and could she be as competent as she appeared?

He put the box down and walked into the room.

"Of course, Mr. Boardwell," she said, writing quickly. "Thank you for calling." She cradled the receiver and leapt gracefully off the desk. Then she turned around, saw him and screamed.

Mark reached out to steady her arm as she sank back against the desk, a hand over her heart.

"I didn't know you were there," she explained with an apologetic little laugh. Then she straightened and offered her hand. "I'm Bernie Emerson."

Bernie was startled first by his youth. He could be no more than thirty-five. Young, she thought, for a man of his accomplishments. Then she looked into deep, dark eyes that caught and held her attention. Vaguely she noticed a broad forehead, a strong nose, a square chin, and thick dark brown hair, but his eyes drew hers back. The expression in them was curiously at odds, she thought, with his wide, open smile—as though he felt one thing and tried hard to convey something else.

Trained to look beyond the obvious, she focused on the dark turbulence. Sadness, she wondered, or anger? Before she could decide, humor rose to hide whatever it was.

"Any relation to Ralph Waldo?" He teased, shaking her hand. "I'm Mark Costello."

She smiled, liking his steady grip. "No. Any relation to Abbott and . . . ?"

He laughed softly. "Good telephone manners *and* a sense of humor?"

She looked surprised. "Is that an unusual combination?"

Mark thought back to the other women he had interviewed and drew a breath. "You have no idea."

"I took a message for you . . ." She tried to hand him the slip of paper. Mark walked around her, ignoring it.

Her hair was short and dark, and on both sides of her head. Her wide hazel eyes, free of makeup, had a sparkle of warmth and enthusiasm. She wore a simple white blouse tucked into the red skirt.

"Mr. Boardwell called from Boardwell Imports," she said, turning in a small circle as he continued to walk around her. "He wants to talk to you about a brochure."

Mark stopped and took the note without looking at it. She had an air of elegance, he thought, of money and breeding. An heiress on a lark, he wondered? Runaway princess? "Can you type?" he asked.

"Fifty words a minute," she replied. "I know that's not executive secretary material—"

"Dictation?"

"Rapidly in person. A little slower off a Dictaphone."

He had to concentrate to prevent his excitement from showing. "You interact well with people?"

"I love them," she replied with believable enthusiasm.

This couldn't be happening to him, Mark thought. She was too good to be true. "Married?"

She smiled a little. "No."

"Kids?"

"No."

No. She looked too sure of herself to have ever been married, too serene to have ever had children. He remembered something the employment office had told him when they'd first called about her. "I was told you were a teacher."

Her calm expression didn't change, but she angled her chin in a slightly defensive gesture. "That's right," she said. "But summers I worked in an office."

A touch of color rose in her cheeks. Mark concluded that she had stretched the truth a little there, or told him some variation of it. It didn't matter. He'd heard her in action, and he liked her. Still, he couldn't resist teasing her. "You lied to a prospective client."

She laughed huskily, her color deepening a little. "I thought, 'He's with another client,' sounded better than, 'He left the front door open and is nowhere to be found.' "

Mark studied the color in her cheeks and wondered how it fit with the air of calm elegance. The woman was an enigma. "You're hired," he said. "When can you start?"

"Tomorrow?" The phone rang and she grinned. "Now?"

"Please." He shooed her toward the phone as he headed for the kitchen. "I'll get you a cup of coffee."

Mark tipped the fragrant brew into a cup. Bernie Emerson wasn't beautiful, but she wore her simplicity as though it were a mink, and it gave her a quality that couldn't be achieved with makeup and designer clothes.

Probably running from a powerful father or a dull society boyfriend, Mark thought. Whatever her problem, he was selfishly glad she had it. He hoped she'd be unable to solve it until he had Good Impressions on its feet.

I HAVE A JOB! Bernie sat behind the large desk and experienced a sensation that was startlingly familiar, yet undeniably different. There was no sea of young faces staring back at her, just a large room, still bare of furniture, and a broad front window with a view of the Promenade and the ocean.

The fear that sometimes gripped her at night, the crisis of confidence that made her long for the old familiar life were gone. She'd found a tiny apartment and a job to pay the rent. Next she would start saving for a car, something old but dependable that got good mileage. Then she could think about getting a dog. Or maybe a cat. Loneliness was the one thing about her new life she hadn't anticipated and hadn't learned to handle.

But she wouldn't think about that now. She'd leapt the hurdle of employment and felt invincible.

The sounds of industry and an occasional curse came from the back bedroom as her employer set up his studio. Trying to find something to do, Bernie located a mop in the kitchen and began to clear away the dust on the office floor. She was on her knees, mopping under the desk, when the front door opened. She looked up, a smile on her face, ready to greet a prospective client. Her eyes widened as two full-grown dalmatians raced toward her, knocking her on her back and kissing her into submission before running off in search of other prey. From the studio came the sound of clawed feet losing traction on the hardwood floor, a loud, descriptive curse, then the chink of metal striking metal and glass breaking.

A short, plump woman in a long gray coat and white lace-up shoes hurried to offer Bernie a hand up. "I'm so sorry, sweetheart," she said, dusting off Bernie's skirt. "Oh, and this is good wool, too." She made a sound of distress. "The dry cleaner will rob you blind."

"I don't think it's stained." Bernie tried to reassure the woman who was beating at the hem of her skirt with both hands. "It's just dusty. Really. It's all right."

Unconvinced, Cecelia straightened, her eyebrows coming together as she noted a smudge on the sleeve of Bernie's blouse. "Oh, and look at that!"

Before the woman could start beating her arm, Bernie flicked the dust off with her fingertips. "There, see? No problem." She offered her hand. "I'm Bernie Emerson."

Cecelia looked her full in the face for the first time—and stared. "Are you here to buy pictures from Marco?" she asked.

Bernie frowned. "Marco? Oh, you mean Mr. Costello? No, I—"

Cecelia's eyes narrowed slightly. "To pose for them?" She seemed to consider posing less reputable than buying.

"She works here, Mom."

Bernie breathed a small sigh of relief when her employer materialized with the dalmatians in tow. The dogs' tails wagged crazily as they nuzzled at Mark's hands. He patted them absently and smiled. "Bernie, meet my mother, Cecelia Costello. Mom, this is Bernie Emerson, my new office manager."

Cecelia finally took Bernie's extended hand. Her grip was so firm Bernie had to hold back a wince. Lively dark eyes studied her carefully from head to foot, then came back to her face. "You did something right, Marco," she said. "Surprise, surprise. How old are you, sweetheart?"

"Mom..." Mark protested.

"Twenty-eight," Bernie replied.

"Where did you go to school?"

That was tricky. Bernie had to think a minute. "Lots of places. The longest was St. Boniface High School near Seattle."

Cecelia took hold of her arms. "Catholic?"

Bernie threw a smiling, disbelieving glance at Mark, who had a hand over his eyes. "Yes."

Cecelia's eyes narrowed. "Do you still go to church?"

"Every Sunday."

Cecelia drew Bernie to her in a choking hug. "It's a miracle. Dear God, it's a miracle!"

"That's it, Mom." Mark took a firm grip on his mother's arm and led her toward the door. "Thank you for keeping the dogs for me, and thanks for bringing them over. If you step one foot inside this office again during business hours, I'll send that picture I have of you in a bathing suit to Mr. Fontanini."

Cecelia hit him in the stomach with her purse. "Thank God your father didn't live to see the day you threaten your mother." She smiled at him. "Are you coming for dinner?"

"I have work to do. I'll just grab something and eat here. Thanks, anyway."

"You could bring Bernie." Cecelia smiled around her son's shoulder at his office manager. "She looks like she could use a good meal. She's a little pale, a little—"

Bernie felt an instant warmth rise in her chest at the idea of dinner with people talking and laughing together.

"Mom," Mark said patiently, "I'm sure Bernie has her own plans."

The warmth sputtered and died.

"You can't bully everyone like this," Mark went on more quietly. Bernie pretended to be busy at the desk. "She's Catholic, she still goes to mass and she's pretty. But she's not for me, okay? There is no one else for me. Get that through your head and stop embarrassing me and yourself."

Cecelia smiled around Mark's shoulder with no sign of embarrassment. "I'll be back to fit the drapes," she said to Bernie. "Bye, sweetheart." She poked a finger in Mark's chest. "And you—" she glowered at him. "—you *need* a miracle."

Chapter Two

White-chocolate macadamia frozen yogurt. Bernie rolled the last spoonful of it on her tongue while she watched the evening news in her tiny living room. The scrumptious flavor didn't quite dispel the loneliness, but it eased it a little. Eating what she wanted was one of the new freedoms she so enjoyed. She knew that having twelve ounces of frozen yogurt for dinner was silly. She loved the decadent feeling of having done it anyway.

As she looked through the slim pickings in her closet for something to wear to work the following day, she wondered what Cecelia Costello had made for dinner. She recalled the wonderful aroma in the kitchen at Good Impressions and could almost taste the Italian food. She probably made her own pasta, Bernie speculated, and grew basil and oregano on her windowsill.

Curiously, the thought brought a lump to her throat. She pushed it firmly aside and concentrated on the contents of her closet. She would have to do something about it at the first opportunity. She'd found some great bargains at the thrift store, but three skirts, three blouses and a pair of sweatpants wouldn't go far when she had to appear well-dressed and groomed five days a week. And the shoes. She studied her one pair of black high heels and wondered if she'd ever get used to walking in them. Pulling a white-and-yellow cotton blouse out of the closet to press it, she remembered Cecelia's sensible shoes and smiled.

Putting water in the iron, she tried to remember her own mother. Janet Emerson's picture still stood in a double frame on Bernie's bedside table, next to the photo of Bernie's father in his military uniform. But she felt as though she'd lost the essence of the woman long ago. She'd been kind and caring, but she'd been gone since Bernie had been ten. Even the memories had faded.

Bernie wondered if that was why Cecelia had made such an impression on her. She laughed softly at the thought. Mark Costello's mother would make a strong impression on anybody.

I'm probably gravitating toward a mother figure, Bernie thought with self-deprecation. *Someone strong and brave, who'll insulate me from the world and take care of me.* "Stupid!" she told herself. "This is it. Freedom. You have what you wanted. You're on your own."

She put the iron down and listened as the apartment rang with silence. It was in every corner, it enfolded her. At night she sometimes felt as though it would deafen her.

Her mind played back the sounds of evenings as they used to be—filled with the voices of friends. She felt a sharp pang for the old life. When she'd planned for freedom then, she'd known it would be difficult. But somehow the excitement of controlling her own life, of one day having the family she wanted with an intensity too strong to deny, had blinded her to the reality of living alone. She sometimes thought she'd have never made it through the past few weeks if it hadn't been for the children she watched in one of the local schools' after-school day-care programs.

Okay. She put the blouse on a hanger and carried it back to the closet. It would be quiet around here tonight. But tomorrow she would go to work where the telephone rang, where her employer swore in the background and where dogs knocked you down. Tomorrow had possibilities.

THE SKY THREATENED RAIN as Bernie walked the mile to Good Impressions. "Please don't." She smiled at the sky. "I'll look like a wet chihuahua and probably get pneumonia, and I'm sure I'm not entitled to sick days yet."

The phone was ringing as she walked in the door and she ran to it, shedding her shoulder bag, preparing to dig through it for her pen. But a few amenities had been added since she'd left the previous evening. Near the phone was a holder filled with pens and sharpened pencils and a steno pad beside it. On the desk was a blotter and an appointment book opened to the dates for the following week.

The caller wanted several photographs of North Head Lighthouse for a promotional brochure on the Washington peninsula. "I need eight-by-ten prints by a week from Monday."

She looked up to find Mark walking into the room with two mugs of coffee. "Eight-by-ten prints of the North Head Lighthouse by a week from Monday?" she repeated, looking to him for confirmation.

"Black-and-white or color?" he asked quietly, putting her cup on the desk.

She repeated the question to the caller. "Color."

Mark nodded.

"Yes, we can do that," she said into the phone, then took down his number and a time when Mark could call him back.

He pulled her chair back as she came around the desk. "Good morning," he said. He noted her pink cheeks. "Did you jog to work?"

She pulled her coat off and looked around for a place to put it. "In a manner of speaking," she said. "I don't have a car. That coffee smells wonderful."

He took the coat from her and hung it on a hall tree near the front door—another addition to the office. He came back to the desk frowning as she sat in her chair. How could someone get along without a car? "Where do you live?"

"Beyond the high school," she replied.

"That's a mile or better." He sounded horrified.

She smiled. "It's good exercise."

"What do you do when it rains, or you have to buy groceries?"

She tucked her purse under the desk and pulled her chair in. "I carry an umbrella, and I don't eat much."

He continued to frown. "Without a car, you're forced to live in a very narrow space."

Her smile became enigmatic. "I'm used to that."

Mark looked into that smile, wondering what it meant. Before he could come to a conclusion, she opened the appointment book. "Would you explain to me how you'd like jobs scheduled? Can you do more than one in a day? Do you need an entire day for outside jobs? Shall I—"

He came around the desk to lean over her, flipping a few pages back. "I've already scheduled the first three days of next week. You can see how I've done it . . ."

Mark spoke for several minutes and Bernie somehow absorbed his instructions, though she didn't really hear the words. She sat quietly, experiencing . . . was it awareness? . . . for the first time in ten years. She knew it was normal, simply a part of the daily interaction between men and women. But it was new enough to make her uncomfortable.

She breathed in the musky scent of Mark's after-shave, noted with startling interest the length of the sweater-clad arm over her shoulder and the long, slim but strong-looking fingers pointing to the book. His other hand was on the back of her chair and she felt the knuckles of it against her shoulder blade. If she turned her face a fraction of an inch, she'd be looking into his eyes. She was careful not to.

"...and always save Fridays for processing," he was saying, "unless the client insists—then check with me first." He straightened.

"Got it." She expelled a soft breath and took a sip of coffee, trying to act casual. "What can I do between phone calls?"

Coffee cup in hand, he strolled to a new beige four-drawer file cabinet. "You can file this stuff, if you have time." He indicated a stack of three cardboard boxes. Then he nudged another one several feet over. "That one's just old papers. I'll take care of it later. Just take your time. Relax and enjoy the job." He gave her shoulder a fraternal pat as he walked past her into the studio. "I'll be shooting some pottery for a Cannon Beach artist this morning. Holler if you need me."

Bernie drew another breath and drank more coffee.

Cecelia arrived mid-morning, yards of loosely woven light yellow fabric over her arm. Bernie smiled, pleased to see her. "Hello, Mrs—" she began, but Cecelia silenced her with a shushing gesture. Then she pointed toward the closed door of the studio. "We don't want Marco the Magnificent to know I'm here. He'll make me leave."

Bernie nodded conspiratorially. "Want some coffee?"

Cecelia nodded. "Please. And a ladder. I think there's one in the service porch off the kitchen."

Obediently Bernie maneuvered an eight-foot aluminum ladder against the front window according to Cecelia's instructions. She tested its steadiness. It wobbled. "Mrs. Costello, I don't think—"

Already halfway up the ladder, Cecelia smiled down at her. "Call me Cecelia. Did you say something about coffee?"

The woman had already hung one panel by the time Bernie returned with the coffee. She reached down for it, balancing nimbly, while holding onto the drapes laid over the small shelf at the top of the ladder. "Thank you, Bernie. Now, you go back to work."

"Cecelia," Bernie said doubtfully, "let me—"

"What are you doing?" The demand was made from across the room as Mark emerged from the studio, empty cup in hand.

Cecelia, one hand on the thick wooden curtain rod, rolled her eyes at him. "I'm chinning myself. What does it look like I'm doing?"

Mark slammed his cup on Bernie's desk and came to the foot of the ladder. He looked up at his mother implacably. "Come down from there."

"Mark," she began reasonably, "I'm—"

She got no farther. Bernie watched in fascination as Mark reached up and swung his mother to the floor without apparent effort. He leaned over her, his eyes angry. He was a foot taller than she was. "You are sixty-nine years old. You don't belong on top of a ladder."

Cecelia raised both hands in exasperation. "So the next time you take Dot and Dash to the vet, you can take me, too, and have me put to sleep!"

He wanted to laugh. Bernie watched him battle the smile manfully. He might have lost the struggle if he hadn't looked up and seen the amusement in her eyes, the sudden clamping of her teeth on her bottom lip. She looked back at him innocently.

"You stood there and let her do this," he accused, the amusement in him losing, the anger firming.

Bernie caught the humor in Cecelia's eye and shrugged, smiling. "Maybe you could have us both put to sleep."

Mark closed his eyes for a moment, then opened them and pointed to her desk. "Go back to work." To his mother, he said, "I'll climb the ladder, and you can supervise. That's your strongest quality, anyway."

As he turned to do so, Cecelia shook her fist at his back and winked at Bernie.

While Bernie filed the correspondence and photographic prints contained in the first of the three boxes, the arguing continued. It was antagonistic, but with an underlying affection and a peppering of humor that made it almost pleasant to listen to. Cecelia was relentless, and Mark, despite his back talk, was endlessly patient.

They broke for lunch at one. Cecelia had brought an antipasto plate and hot rolls. Bernie remained at her desk while Mark and Cecelia argued over setting up in the kitchen.

"Bernie," Mark called from the kitchen doorway. "You're welcome to join us, or you can go out for an hour, if you'd prefer."

She looked at him uncertainly, wondering if she'd be intruding if she accepted his invitation.

"There's enough for six people," he coaxed. "Come on."

Cecelia placed three plates on a small table, which already held a platter filled with sausage, marinated vegetables and cheeses.

Bernie helped herself to a slice of sausage and made a loud "Mmm!" of approval as she savored the spicy succulence.

"My sister Theresa's recipe," Cecelia said. "The woman can do anything," she frowned, pouring blood red Chianti into three glasses, "but she lives three thousand miles away in New York."

Cecelia took her place at the table and raised her glass. "To little Paolo."

Bernie turned to Mark in question.

"Newest member of the family," he explained. "My brother Tony's baby."

Bernie hesitated over the wine, then took a small sip. The flavor was so strong she couldn't quite withhold the wince.

"Chianti takes getting used to," Mark said, passing her a heaping plate Cecelia handed him.

"I'm not used to alcohol," she said. "Except for a very little sherry once in a while."

"That's good," Cecelia said heartily. "No one wants a drunken woman."

Mark was mildly surprised. He'd imagined her with a champagne glass in one hand and some blue-blooded polo player on the other arm. One moment she had an air of worldly experience and the next she seemed so innocent for a woman approaching thirty that he wanted to ask her why.

The telephone rang and she ran out to answer it.

"She's a beautiful girl," his mother said, nibbling on an olive.

He nodded agreement. "Yes. Very pretty."

"And untouched," she added. "You can see that."

Mark gave his mother a dry glance before biting the cap off a fat mushroom. "There are no more virgins, Mom."

She raised an eyebrow. "You think you've despoiled every one?"

He expelled a little sound of frustration. "Mom . . ."

"She's untouched. I'm telling you."

"As though it's your business. Or mine."

"It might be someday."

He looked at his mother steadily. "No, Mom. It won't."

"God puts a miracle right in your lap," she said quietly. "And you look the other way."

Pain and anger erupted instantly, despite all the months of conditioning. He pushed away from the table, the scrape of his chair a loud and jagged sound in the quiet kitchen. He drew a deep breath to stop himself from shouting. He finally spoke with quiet bitterness. "He took a miracle away. Nobody gets two."

"If you'd think of yourself as blessed," Cecelia said, "instead of cursed—"

"Blessed!" He did shout then, overcome with a frustration so strong he almost couldn't stand it. He knew what she was doing. This little woman who had the kindest heart in the whole world, the gentlest touch and a generosity more vast than the universe had set out deliberately to shake him up. She'd seen the emotional armor he wore the moment he came home, and she'd started to chip away at it. She just didn't know there was a monster inside.

From her chair, Cecelia reached back to pat his arm. "I love you, Marco." There was a quiver in her voice.

He turned his hand to catch hers. "I know, Mom," he said.

Bernie walked in at that moment, a smile on her face. "I just spoke to your sister-in-law, Becky. She wants to know..." She stopped then, their grim expressions registering on her. Cecelia looked on the brink of tears, and Mark's eyes were dark and turbulent. Bernie backed out of the room. "I'm sorry. It can wait. I told her you'd call her back."

Mark drew a deep breath. "What did she want?" he asked.

"To know if you're coming to Paul's baptism."

The turbulence died in his eyes, as though the energy to sustain it had been snuffed. He ran a hand down his face and looked at his mother, who appeared to be waiting for an answer.

"I'll meet you all at the house afterward," he said.

Cecelia stood and pushed in her chair, covering the antipasto tray with the foil she had put aside. "He's your nephew," she said mildly. "You have to come to the church."

"I don't have to do anything." Mark took the tray from her and put it in the refrigerator.

"That's what you think, but you're wrong. Everybody has things they have to do."

"You're right. I have to take pictures." He put a hand on Cecelia's shoulder and pushed her gently out of the kitchen. "And you're preventing me from doing that."

When Bernie moved toward her desk, he gestured her back to the kitchen. "Finish your lunch," he said quietly. "I'll listen for the phone."

Bernie went back into the kitchen with its quiet early afternoon sunlight, feeling the tension that had invaded this warm and happy place. Feeling anxiety she didn't understand, she sipped at the wine and listened as quiet conversation drifted back to her.

"Marco, you have to stop this," Cecelia pleaded.

Mark's voice was exasperated. "Mom, we've been over and over it. It's my life."

"You're ruining it. I can't bear to watch."

"Then from now on, send lunch over in a cab." Bernie heard no response to his attempt at humor.

"Come to the church," Cecelia coaxed. "Bring Bernie."

"No. Thanks for lunch, Mom." There was the sound of a kiss. "Bye." The door closed firmly.

For a moment the office was so silent Bernie wondered if Mark had gone out with his mother. Then he appeared in the kitchen doorway and leaned against the molding. "I'm sorry about that," he said. "I'll see that you get hazard pay for this afternoon."

Bernie smiled at him because he looked as though he needed it. She didn't understand what had hurt him, but she could see that it went deep. "Families disagree. That's a fact you can't dispute. My mother died when I was ten and my father was a career soldier, always off somewhere. There were a lot of times when I'd have given anything to have one of them to fight with."

She saw his attention shift from his problems to hers. "I'm sorry." He came into the room to resume his seat across from her. "Who raised you?"

She shrugged. "Other families on the bases where Dad was stationed. There was always a friend's mother who didn't mind one more child around while he was away."

"Must have been lonely."

"Sometimes. But I saw a lot of the world."

Mark shook his head. "I'd guessed that about you," he admitted, leaning back in his chair. "But I thought you'd done it from the back of a Rolls-Royce."

Bernie laughed in surprise. "Why?"

He shrugged. "I'm not sure. You have a look of culture and experience. No, not experience," he amended. "You look too...naive to be experienced. Knowledge, that's it. Culture and knowledge. Like a Victorian lady in contemporary clothes."

She laughed again, trying not to betray nervousness. "Your business should be entitled Wrong Impressions, rather than Good Impressions."

He took the tease with a smile, his eyes still evaluating her. "I don't think so. I still have that impression about you, I simply misjudged what created it."

He was giving her the opportunity to explain, she knew, but she had decided at the outset to keep the details of her past to herself. "It's these shoes," she said, hobbling to her feet and carrying her plate to the sink. "That wise and cultured look is really bunion pain."

Mark pushed his chair in and grinned at her. "I don't mind if you wear pants and low shoes to work. There'll even be times when you'll have to come out on location with me, so you may as well be comfortable."

"Really?" She found that possibility intriguing and exciting.

He smiled at her enthusiasm. "When I shoot the lighthouse, for instance. Day after tomorrow. Wear jeans and a warm jacket."

"What about the phone?"

"The answering service can take our calls." His smile took on a teasing quality. "You'll be more valuable to me on the shoot."

She folded her arms and looked at him wryly. "Does this mean you're not having your mother and me put to sleep after all?"

"Nah." He put a hand at the back of her neck and pushed her into the office toward her chair. "I couldn't live without my mother, and after only a day and a half, Good Impressions couldn't manage without you. Get my sister-in-law on the phone, will you?"

He disappeared into the studio and closed the door. Bernie reached for the phone, a silly grin on her face. It had something to do with his admission that she was already valuable to his studio, and something to do with the tingle on her shoulder where he had touched.

"FIVE-THIRTY, BERNIE!" Mark shouted from the back studio. "Lock it up. We're out of here. Want a ride home?"

"Thanks, but I have to stop at the school first," she called over her shoulder as she crossed the office to turn the sign to "closed" and lock the door.

But the door opened before she could reach it, and the sound of deep laughter preceded the entrance of two men who carried a very large file box between them. She stepped back as they bumped into the room.

"I'm sorry," she said apologetically but firmly. "We're closed."

The darker-featured of the two men stopped in his tracks, staring at her in surprise. The other man, younger and very fair, walked into the now stationary box with a startled, "Oof!"

On closer inspection, Bernie noticed that the first man bore a strong resemblance to Mark. He shifted the folded-in handle of the box to his left hand and held out his right. "Tony Costello," he said with a broad smile. "Mark's brother. You must be Bernie."

She returned his smile as his large hand swallowed hers. "I am."

He indicated the other man with a jerk of his thumb. "The clumsy one's our brother-in-law, Hal Cummings."

Hal winked at her. "Their much maligned brother-in-law. That's what happens in this family when you're not Italian."

"As though you didn't deserve the abuse we heap upon you anyway." Mark appeared, rolling down the sleeves of a blue plaid flannel shirt. "What's up?"

Tony pointed to the box with his free hand. "Mom found more of your files, and we'd like to put them down. Where do you want this box?"

Mark pointed up. "You mind carrying it upstairs?"

Hal looked at Tony with feigned impatience. "I mind. Don't you?"

Tony sighed. "I've minded his presence in my life for thirty-five years. It hasn't helped. He's still here. Let's take this damn thing upstairs and go for a drink." He glanced at his brother as Hal began to lead the way toward the kitchen and the stairs. "If you promise not to bore us with details of aperture and exposure, you can come."

"I was going to take Bernie home," Mark replied.

"We'll drop her off," Tony offered, stopping to ask Bernie, "Where do you live?"

"Cleveland," she replied. Hal barked a laugh as Tony looked at her in surprise. Mark groaned. "She lives on Oregon Street."

Tony smiled vaguely at his brother, then at Bernie. "Strange sense of humor. You two should get along fine. We'll be back in a minute."

As they disappeared through the kitchen, Mark went to the hall tree for his jacket and Bernie's coat. He turned the "closed" sign on the front door and locked it. Then he tossed his jacket on her desk and helped her into her dull gray tweed. "You're weird, Emerson," he said. "You know that?"

She looked at him over her shoulder as she fitted her arms into the sleeves. Her grin held a touch of irony. "Story of my life."

He was beginning to really wonder what her story was. "You mentioned having to stop at the school. Which one?"

"Our Lady of Victory," she replied. "Right behind the church."

"Will you be long? We could wait for you and take you home."

She shouldered her purse. "Thanks, but I help with the after-school program, and some of the children stay until seven. But you could drop me off there."

Tony and Hal thumped down the stairs and led the way out to Tony's truck. Hal leapt into the middle seat and Mark followed him up to sit on the end. Bernie looked up into the full cab uncertainly.

Mark grinned and offered his hand. "We could strap you to the hood, but I think you'll be more comfortable in my lap."

She hesitated another moment. She functioned better, was able to behave more normally, when she saw these things coming and could prepare for them. But she'd had no idea that Tony's offer of a ride home involved the tight squeeze of a truck cab and not a roomy four-door sedan.

With considerably more aplomb than she felt, she handed up her purse. Tony passed it on to Hal, who protested that it didn't go with what he was wearing. Then she put her hand into Mark's, stepped on the running board, and ducked her head as he hauled her up into his lap.

She felt awkward, embarrassed. There was nothing to do with the arm trapped between them but put it around his neck. He placed his arms around her waist to hold her in place as Tony turned the truck around on the narrow street and headed for the highway.

She smiled down at Mark, trying to appear nonchalant. "I'll bet you're glad I don't really live in Cleveland."

Despite the fact that his arms were filled with a soft, mysterious woman, Mark had little trouble controlling his reactions. He'd locked sexual awareness away long ago and he'd acquired the formidable skill of isolating himself in the most intimate situation. He could hold a woman in his arms and be miles away, but still behave as though she were uppermost on his mind.

"Yes," he replied with an answering smile, "because this clunker wouldn't make it to Astoria, much less Cleveland."

Hal elbowed him. "Watch how you talk about Tony's truck. He'll make us all get out and walk."

Mark cast him a side-glance. "What do you care? You've got a purse. You can call a cab."

Bernie was very relieved when Tony pulled up in front of the school. Sitting in Mark's lap had been an awkward experience, made more uncomfortable for her by the fact that she'd rather liked it. He'd seemed completely unaffected.

Mark pushed the door open and she ducked her head and leapt down. She waved at Tony and Hal. "It was nice to meet you. Thanks for the ride."

"Any time," Tony replied.

Hal passed her purse to her. "Here you go. I like a front pocket, myself. And something a little smaller, possibly in a shade of—"

Mark turned to him. "Shut up, Hal."

Hal leaned around him and looked at Bernie. "He wouldn't talk to me that way if I was Italian. Nice to meet you."

Mark smiled at Bernie and pushed Hal back without looking at him. "See you in the morning, Bernie. Remember to wear something comfortable. We're going to walk in tall grass and climb over rocks."

"Right." She waved as the truck departed and turned her attention to the kids running toward her from the playground. Children. Being around them always made her happy.

Chapter Three

As Mark cleaned up the darkroom, he thought about Bernie. He didn't want to, necessarily, she just kept coming to mind. He liked things and people he could bring into focus, but he couldn't do that with her. She seemed to be composed of paradoxes. One minute she was laughing with his mother, the next she wore a wry, sad smile he couldn't begin to analyze. She could be serious and competent, then soberly tell his brother she lived in Cleveland. She was poised and elegant, but with a deep-down warmth one would expect of a clown or a plump, cozy matron. Yet she'd never been married and had no children. But she'd wanted to be dropped off at the school without offering any explanation.

Well, the mystery would dissolve eventually, he thought. It was difficult to keep one's inner self private during the enforced eight-hours-a-day contact of a work environment—although he usually did pretty well. Of course, he doubted she was hiding a monster inside.

A CARTON OF ORANGE SWIRL frozen yogurt in one hand and a hairbrush in the other, Bernie ran to the door of her apartment to answer the bell. It was only eight in the morning. Who could be visiting her at this hour?

Mark stood there in jeans and a thick blue parka. It was a damp, blustery morning and the wind played with the dark hair on his forehead. "Good morning," he said, then frowned into the carton in her hand. "What's that?"

"Orange and vanilla yogurt," she replied automatically, surprise making her frown at him. "What are you doing here?"

"We're shooting the lighthouse today." He continued to wince at the contents of the carton. "I thought I'd pick you up. Yogurt for breakfast?"

"It's an indulgence of mine." She stepped back to let him in. She wore the sweatpants she'd bought at the thrift shop, intending to use them for cleaning house, and an old black sweater she used to wear in the garden. She knew her appearance was less than elegant, and that her apartment might seem minuscule to someone who could afford better.

"Is this all right?" she asked, a little self-consciously, indicating her clothes. "I mean, we're not going to call on a client or anything?"

His dark glance went over her quickly and he nodded. "Fine. You don't have to look as though Ralph Lauren dressed you, you just have to keep warm."

She laughed softly as she turned to leave the room. "Good thing. He didn't have much to do with the reigning fashion where I've been."

"Where was that?" he asked before he could stop himself.

For a moment she looked alarmed, then she smiled before walking into the kitchen to dispose of the carton. "Los Angeles," was all she said.

He persisted, hoping she'd explain. "I thought Los Angeles was a fashion center."

She reappeared in the doorway with a carefully neutral expression. "We were more into survival than fashion. I'll just be a minute."

MARK GUIDED THE VAN over the Astoria-Megler Bridge that
connected Oregon with the Washington peninsula. Bernie'd
given him an explanation, he thought, but now he was more
perplexed than ever. Why would a pretty young woman be
more "into survival than fashion?" And who were "we"?

She sat beside him now, watching the rugged coastal
landscape with a fascination that was ingenuous. As the
road wound along the riverbank, they passed a heron
perched on a piling, his neck hunched into his feathers so
that he appeared to be all body and beak.

"Look!" Bernie said, pointing across him.

Mark leaned back to avoid her fingernail. "If I look," he
said, laughing, "we'll all be sharing that piling."

"It was a heron," she said, sitting forward so she could
look over her shoulder as they left him behind. "They look
so primitive, don't they? Like something left over from the
age of dinosaurs."

"Not many herons in Los Angeles?"

She settled back in her seat. "Pigeons. Buildings. All the
time I was there, I thought about the north coast of Oregon."

"You've lived here before?"

"Only for a month. My father was on leave and came to
Astoria to fish. I was about thirteen." She sighed, the sound
half nostalgia, half contentment. "He took me to Seaside
one night to go on the rides and play in the arcades. I fell in
love with the Promenade and the ocean. I promised myself
I'd live there one day."

"Took you a long time to get back."

She hesitated only a moment. "You know how life is."

Yes, he did. It did everything to get in one's way. He dismissed thoughts of himself, and concentrated on solving the
mystery of Bernie Emerson.

"I shot a series on the homeless in L.A.," he said. "I
spent two weeks in the seediest part of town, half the time

fascinated by the intelligence of some of the men I came across and the other half in mortal fear that one of them would slit my throat for the resale value of my cameras. But there was a little Mexican restaurant in an old brick building on Whittier Boulevard. They had salsa that could blow your head off, and—''

"Mungia's," Bernie said before she had time to think. She'd been caught up in his very accurate sketch of life there, in the unexpected pleasure of finding something in common with someone. She realized her mistake too late.

Mark glanced at her in grim surprise. "How in the hell do you know about Mungia's?"

The suggestion was that she was too good for a place like that. She'd always thought that attitude was what was wrong with the world.

She raised an eyebrow at him. "You take a good hand-rolled tortilla wherever you can find it."

He frowned at the road. "That neighborhood's a hell-hole for druggies, prostitutes, gang—"

"You found them interesting enough to photograph," she said quietly.

"That was my job."

"We had a print of your photo of a twelve-year-old girl dead on a Soweto street, hanging in my Comparative Governments class when I was in college. Our teacher said it should remind us every day what freedom really is."

Until that moment, Mark hadn't been sure she'd recognized his name. He and his photographs had made a lot of headlines, but he'd been virtually out of the news for the past year and a half.

"What made you turn to commercial photography?" she asked. "You saw inside people's eyes and recorded it for everyone to see."

Questions made him defensive. He stopped at a traffic light in one of the small towns on their route and turned to look at her. Her hazel gaze met his without apology. She was telling him that questions made her defensive, too. He accepted that with a reluctant smile.

"It was time to do something else," he said.

She nodded. "Me, too."

The light turned green and Mark drove on, realizing with a twinge of frustration that she hadn't really told him a thing, except that she'd needed a change. From what? What legitimate business could she have been conducting in that part of East Los Angeles? Though, who said it had to be legitimate? He was beginning to wonder if she'd made up her past as a teacher.

Neatly sidestepping his questions, she'd turned the tables on him and tried to ask him about himself. Clever. Maybe she'd been a shrink.

THE LIGHTHOUSE STOOD on the edge of a cliff, a red-domed sentinel with a railed gallery that surrounded the glass-enclosed beacon. The tower stood below the small visitors' parking lot, a quarter of a mile down a fir-lined road that rimmed the cliff.

Mark parked the van, then walked around it to open the sliding side door. Bernie leapt down beside him. "You wearing comfortable shoes?" he asked.

She raised her foot and twirled it. It sported an ugly black lace-up shoe with a gum sole. "It isn't high-styled," she said into his carefully neutral expression, "but you said the point was to be comfortable."

She was smiling eagerly, the wind whipping color into her cheeks and ruffling her short, dark curls. He had to smile back. He handed her a tripod, and put a small film bag over her shoulder. "You carry these."

He pulled a huge backpack out of the van and shrugged into it. Bernie reached up to pull the collar of his jacket out from under the strap. Her cold hand against his jaw jangled his nerves for an instant.

Her touch was soft, her movements competent as she drew his lapels together, laughingly telling him that Cecelia would be upset if she knew he was out in this weather with his jacket unbuttoned. She lifted her eyes to his and her expression seemed to freeze, as though her mind was concentrating on something else.

Bernie felt the smoothness of his jaw against her knuckles. His skin was as cool as her hands were, and she noticed it only absently until she looked into his eyes to share her little joke about his mother. There was a slight frown between his eyes, a sudden tension in them that was directed at her. It ran through the hand that touched him, down her arm and into her chest. She quickly lowered her hand, staring at him a moment before turning away.

Mark took a moment to zip his jacket. The perfectly ordinary action helped settle his nerves. He pointed up the road. "We'll follow that to the lighthouse, then come back and get the car and go around the cove for a different angle."

"Okay." Bernie fell into step beside him, the startled look gone from her eyes. "And you call this work? The great outdoors..." She spread her arms to indicate the rainy day beauty of their surroundings and lost her grip on the tripod. "Oops." She hurried to retrieve it and grinned at him sheepishly. "Sorry. This is all very exciting after a lifetime of barracks and big cities."

He smiled at her, equanimity completely restored. "It'll seem like work when we get off the road."

Bernie could not remember ever having had a more wonderful day. The sky and the ocean seemed to come together in a foggy gray. Pine and cedar covered the cliff side with their bristled green, their slender, spindly tops swaying high overhead. Birds called mournfully, surf crashed and the wind whined through the trees. The lighthouse stood at the edge of the cliff, a stalwart defense against the darkness and the fog.

Bernie felt caught up in the drama. The harsh wind and the vastness of the landscape intensified her sense of being free.

"What are you grinning about?" It was mid-morning and they sat on the edge of the road that ran above the one on which they'd walked out. Mark was adjusting the tripod when he looked down and caught her expression. Bernie sat several yards away from him looking down into the water.

She leaned back on her hands and looked up at him. "I was thinking about what a great way this is to make a living. I could have ended up working in an insurance office or a bank. Yet here I am, sitting in the grass while you do all the work."

The tripod adjusted, he slid a sheet-film holder into the camera, then pulled the slide out. "That'll all change in a couple of weeks. We have to do a newspaper insert for Kids' Kingdom. You'll earn your money then, believe me."

"That sounds like fun," she said, drawing her knees up and wrapping her arms around them. "What ages?"

"Older." He said it quickly, a little edge to his tone. "Eight, ten."

She laughed. "You have something against babies and toddlers?"

She realized her mistake instantly. He didn't turn to look at her, but she saw the grim set of his expression as he checked the light meter, the tension in him as he pocketed it and checked his subject one last time. She suddenly remembered his argument with Cecelia about attending his nephew's baptism.

"Too squally to work with efficiently," he said, then disappeared behind the camera.

He was lying. Yet it was obvious he preferred not to be around them. She considered several reasons why, then dismissed them. She decided that if she could keep her secrets, he should be entitled to his.

They drove around the cove, took more photographs, then stopped to pick up hamburgers and hot coffee. They ate as Mark drove back to the office. He glanced at his watch.

"What time's my appointment this afternoon?"

Bernie offered him the bag of fries that sat between them on the seat, then realized he didn't have a free hand for it. She put one in his mouth. "Two o'clock."

Her action was completely companionable, but Mark was momentarily startled by the tip of her finger between his lips. "We'll stop by your apartment to pick up a change of clothes for you. But we might be cutting it a little close. You can change at my place."

A dozen excuses sprang to Bernie's mind. *You don't have to wait for me. I can change and walk right back to the office. I can take a cab back.* They sounded naive and silly, and she was trying so hard to project a competent, experienced image. "All right," she said. She held the empty bag for him to dispose of his burger wrapper, then handed him his coffee.

"Pick something you can wear to dinner tonight," he said.

She turned to him, a french fry halfway to her mouth. It's upper half fell over limply while she frowned. "Am I going to dinner tonight?"

He cast her a quick, smiling glance. "You deserve some reward for following me around through the drizzle without complaint this morning."

She smiled back in surprise. "Who could complain about being somewhere so beautiful?"

"You were carrying camera equipment through grass and mud."

A grave detail occurred to her. "I don't have anything to wear to dinner." He glanced at her again with that half confused, half speculative look and she shrugged a shoulder, a little embarrassed. "No Ralph Lauren clothing in my closet, remember?" It was strange, she thought, that of all the things that could have tripped her up in this effort to start a new life, clothes were one of the biggest problems.

He looked back at the road as they crossed the bridge. "What about that black skirt and pink sweater you had on the other day?"

"Will that do?"

"Sure." Mark took the turn that led to her apartment. He pulled into her parking space, opened his window and turned off the motor, prepared to wait. He glanced at his watch. "It's one forty-five. Don't dawdle, okay?"

She was back in four minutes, hanging the skirt and sweater in the back, putting a grocery bag on the floor between their seats. Mark caught a glimpse of the black shoes she complained were uncomfortable and some white silky stuff he was too gentlemanly to investigate.

He looked up to see that she'd caught his glance into the bag. Her cheeks were flushed, her eyes distressed as she leaned over to fold the top of the bag.

Mark started the car, pretending not to notice her discomfort. The mystery of Bernie Emerson deepened. How could a woman who knew the bowels of East Los Angeles be embarrassed because a man caught a glimpse of her underwear—in a bag, no less?

THE NIGHT WAS DARK, the air redolent of salt and wood smoke. Old globe streetlights lit the deserted Promenade. Surf crashed in the dark distance.

"Up here." Mark put an arm around Bernie's shoulders to urge her up the side street where the van was parked. "I left a roll of film in the glove compartment yesterday. I want to get it while I'm thinking about it. Then we'll head back to the Shilo for dinner." Bernie turned, huddling further into her coat, very much aware that his hand still rested on her shoulder. "I'm starving. For someone who's only been in business a week and a half, your office is jumping."

"Wait until it's full of kids for the brochure. You're going to wish you'd gone into fire fighting or something."

"If it gets too bad, I can always hang curtains with your mother."

Laughing, he unlocked the van door and reached into the glove box. "That's something I'd really like to see."

The street was dark and quiet, the only sound that of traffic several blocks away. Holding her collar closed, Bernie looked up and down the street, suddenly feeling vaguely uneasy. She attributed it to the darkness and the wind and the new, unsettling experience of having a date.

Mark pocketed the film and closed the door. "All right." He took her hand and turned toward the lights of the Prom. "Let's get some food in you."

That was when she noticed the two figures silhouetted against the old globe lights. They stood with feet apart, arms folded, waiting. It was clearly apparent they were waiting for them. She felt Mark's sudden tension as he pulled her to a stop.

"Who are they?" she whispered.

"Just punks, I'd guess," he replied quietly, glancing over his shoulder. Bernie turned also, to find a man advancing on them from behind. Fear filled her like a cold draft of air.

"We need a car, buddy," one of the figures drawled as he walked loosely toward them. He held his hands away from his body in a gesture of helplessness. "But we're short of cash."

The man behind them said, "We need you to be a Good Samaritan and help us out."

As Mark's mind worked frantically to sort through his options, Bernie said quietly, "Isn't it interesting how people who don't live by it otherwise can quote the parts of scripture that suit their needs?"

Mark gave her a quick, surprised glance and uttered a small sound of confusion. They were trapped in an alley by three punks and not only did she not appear to be frightened, she was being philosophical.

The second of the two approaching from the Prom laughed throatily. "I think we could use a lady, too. What do you say, pal? Your van and the lady, and we won't do any chiropractic work on you."

Mark gave Bernie a sudden push toward the dark-windowed house on their right. "Go!" he ordered.

There was obviously no one home to offer assistance. She guessed she could probably disappear into the shadows if she were quick, but she was beginning to formulate a plan—and running wasn't part of it.

The two men on the Prom side stopped. "Oh, come on, man," one complained wearily. "Can't we make this easy?"

"Go, damn it!" Mark ordered again, when Bernie continued to stand there. He moved to the middle of the street, obviously intending to cover her retreat.

She backed up out of his line of vision, dropped her purse where she stood and let her coat fall on top of it. The cold air chilled her for just a moment, then adrenaline took over, warming her muscles, relaxing her joints, concentrating her power. Making her stronger than the fear.

Mark waited for the attack, circling, arms loosely at his sides. It came from the man approaching from behind who danced at him with a quick one-two punch. Mark dodged both and aimed hard at the man's gut. As the other two closed in, Bernie ran at them. They stopped, obviously more annoyed than concerned, one ignoring her completely in favor of Mark, while the other prepared to fend her off. Her sharp toe to his groin brought a pained grunt from him as he doubled over. Her knee to his chin snapped his head up and he went down to his knees with a look of astonishment, gasping for air.

The series of shouts and thuds surprised Mark and his assailant. They stood several feet apart in a state of suspended animation, watching as the slender woman felled the burly man, then turned, her skirt swirling around her knees, her hands poised for action.

Stunned and distracted, Mark took a right to the jaw, saw stars and went to his knees, as buildings seemed to tumble around him in the darkness.

A moment later he shook himself back to awareness to see Bernie chasing the two running men toward the lights of the Shilo Inn. "Get back here!" he bellowed at her. He immediately regretted it, as everything inside his head seemed to fly apart.

"Mark!" She was back, both hands on his arms, her eyes wide with concern. "Are you all right?" It was a moment before he could reply. Not only had his pride been destroyed by this slender woman, but every conclusion he'd ever made about her disintegrated. In the front office of Good Impressions, he was harboring a cold-blooded karate master.

Embarrassment and a small sense of betrayal made his touch and his voice a little rough as he shrugged her off.

"All right, what is it with you?" he demanded, dusting off his sweater. "This air of mystery, of untouchability. Who were you with before you came here? CIA? FBI?" He swept a hand toward the direction in which their two assailants had quickly fled. His voice rose. "Some ninja assassin?"

"The Sisters of Peace," she said, her fingers linked together. She lifted a shoulder and gave him a reluctant little laugh. "I was a nun."

Chapter Four

"A what?" Mark asked.

It was two hours later. The police had taken his and Bernie's reports and promised an investigation. Mark and Bernie now sat in a quiet corner of the Shilo restaurant. Beyond the wall of windows facing the ocean, the lights of the Promenade stood like candles against the black night. Bernie's pale face was outlined against it.

"A nun," she replied, holding his eyes for a moment, then looking down at the fork she played with.

So that explained the ethereal air, the quality of having experienced things, coupled with a mystifying innocence. But it didn't explain the karate.

"I went to Catholic school," he said. He remained silent a moment, while a waitress put a gin-and-tonic in front of him and a coffee nudge by Bernie's hand. "I never met a nun," he went on when she walked away, "who knew karate."

Bernie smiled and dipped a spoon into the dollop of whipped cream in her cup. "You never met one whose father had been a career soldier—who didn't know what to do with his little girl but teach her what he knew best. He trained commandos and special forces."

"Why didn't you tell me?" he asked. There was an accusatory tone in the question.

She looked at him innocently. "About having been a nun or about knowing karate?"

"Either. Both."

"Because I thought all you wanted to know about me was on your application form." She put the spoon to her mouth, then set it down on the table and looked at him. "And to avoid getting the look you're giving me right now."

He leaned back in his chair. "What look?"

"The look that tells me you consider me some alien form of life." She took a sip of the liquored coffee and decided she liked the taste. The alcohol spread warmth in her chest, a nice contrast to the coolly suspicious look on the face of the man across the table. They'd been so close to becoming friends, she thought sadly. "There's something about dedicating your life to God that makes people think you're different. They behave more normally toward you if they don't know. Am I fired?"

He grinned for the first time since the incident in the alley. "It's hard to fire someone who's probably saved you from having your ribs relocated up your nose. That was a little hard on my pride, you know."

She laughed. It was a relief to see him relax. "The skill has come in very handy for me more than once. I was assigned to a rough neighborhood in Los Angeles because I could take care of myself. We had a shelter for battered and homeless women. A few abusive husbands and pimps took exception to our giving their women an alternative."

Mark shook his head at her, still not quite recovered from the shock. "So that stuff about your having been a teacher—"

"Oh, that's true," she assured him quickly. "I taught fourth and fifth grades for six years. Then the school where I taught was closed and I was assigned to the shelter in L.A."

"What about the office experience you claimed?"

"That was true, too. When I taught school, I worked summers at the motherhouse in Mother General's office."

He studied her, his forearms folded on the table. "I'm trying to picture you in a black habit, and I can't. What made you choose the convent?"

Bernie's smile dissolved and she shook her head, as though to focus on a memory—or dispel it. "My father died in the bombing of the embassy in Beirut. I was seventeen. Though he'd been a soldier all his life, he thought of himself as the arm of a benevolent justice, as a peacemaker in a world gone crazy. He often lamented the absence of love and reason. The church had always been a major part of our lives and there I was, suddenly alone. I decided to dedicate myself to all the good and decent things he wanted to see in the world." She sipped at her coffee nudge and sighed thoughtfully. "At least, that's what I told myself. Deep down, I think I needed somewhere where I could feel safe, and the sisters had been there all my life—different orders of sisters in different towns, but always the same at heart—spiritual women operating in a practical way to achieve extraordinary things."

Mark wanted to ask her why she'd changed her mind, but didn't know how, or even if he had the right. He remembered enough about the nuns who'd taught him to know there were vows involved. No one gave those up lightly, particularly a woman with that kind of power behind her commitment.

She put her cup down and shrugged. "I had a long list of reasons for leaving the convent," she said, reading his thoughts. She winced and rubbed her temple. "They were very clear to me at the time, but now that I've been out a while the loneliness makes me forget."

"How long have you been out?"

"A month."

Mark leaned back in his chair, as though he needed distance from her. Bernie smiled wryly. "Are you afraid the sanctity of the convent still lingers in me and that I'll try to bless you, or that my freedom after years without a man might have me attack you?"

He struggled to swallow the laugh, but couldn't. "All right," he admitted, downing the last of his gin-and-tonic. "I've been out of social circulation for a long time. Ordinary women make me nervous. And here I am escorting one with a madonna face and a black belt in karate. You can understand my confusion."

She folded her arms on the table. "Of course. I just hope this won't change anything between us. I'll do a good job for you, and you don't have to worry about me praying over you or anything. I've seen how you feel about..." Bernie stopped, knowing she was getting into the personal territory she was trying so hard to assure him she wouldn't intrude upon. "I mean, I know you don't want..." She stopped again, afraid of making matters worse.

"I'm not a spiritual man," he said. The statement was made without qualification or apology. She couldn't believe it because she'd seen his work. No one could see that clearly without an eye for the power that existed beyond man, but this was not the time to point that out.

She nodded. "I gathered that," she said. "My spiritual life is a very personal thing to me. I won't try to impose it on you. I need this job, Mark. The money the order gave me when I left is just about gone and there are a lot of things I need to live from day to day."

He looked into her eyes and she couldn't decide if he believed her or not. "What, for instance?"

"A car," she replied. "A dog." She smiled in embarrassment. "Clothes that don't come from the thrift shop."

He raised an eyebrow. "You always look impeccable, if a little..." he probed his mind for a diplomatic word.

"Staid?" she suggested helpfully, grinning. "Dated?"

He laughed. "Well, maybe a little." Then he added more seriously. "But your elegance wears the clothes, and that's what's noticeable. Do you need an advance? Is that why you were having yogurt for breakfast?"

"No." She rested her chin on the heel of her hand and confided, "I've had it for lunch and dinner, too, because I love it. At the motherhouse, a cook prepared wonderful balanced meals for us, and at the home in Los Angeles we did the best we could with limited funds. It's such an indulgence to eat what I want, without having to justify it to anyone."

She leaned back as the waitress placed a large shrimp salad in front of her. Mark looked from his steak sandwich to her bowl of greens. "At least you crave healthy stuff."

She put the salt and pepper between them and glanced at him guiltily. "I won't tell you about my passion for chocolate-covered macadamia nuts. Fortunately they're too expensive to allow me to indulge my craving."

The initial shock he'd felt at her admission that she'd been a nun was dissipating. She was so genuine and open that he found it hard to keep a clinical distance from her. "You were the first qualified applicant the employment office sent me," he said, cutting into his steak.

"The only other job they had that I was qualified to fill was as a statistical typist for a brokerage firm." She made a face at him over a bite of shrimp. "That sounded boring and lonely. Loneliness has been my biggest problem since I've been on my own. I'm used to my fellow sisters scurrying around and more recently the company of the women and children who came to us." She sighed. "I really miss the children. Your studio sounded as though it had the potential for more contact with people."

He nodded wryly. "And dogs and meddlesome mothers."

"She's a sweetheart," Bernie said in Cecelia's defense. "Even when you're teasing her, I can see how much you appreciate her. I hope I'm like that when I'm older. Full of spirit and fun, with children I'm still fussing after and lots to do."

"So you're on the lookout for a husband?" he asked.

"No," she denied quickly, looking a little startled. She appeared to consider the question belatedly, then said again, "No. At least not for a while. I don't really know a lot about myself as . . . as a woman." It occurred to her that this conversation was becoming far more personal than she'd intended. Honesty was one thing, but intimacy was quite another. She finished briskly, "I have a lot of adjustments to make—a lot to learn."

Mark sensed her withdrawal and accepted it. He'd learned all he wanted to know about himself this past year, and he'd just as soon no one else saw inside him. Bernie was the perfect woman to have near at hand. She was capable, fun to be around, and firmly set on a path that required nothing from him but a paycheck. They were a match made in heaven.

"So how many bad guys can you handle at once?" he asked.

She shrugged airily. "Depends on how good they are, and how quick. Several, if I'm not taken by surprise. Then sometimes one's too many." She remembered how he'd tried to cover her retreat. "I'm not sure you'd have needed me. You've got the heart of a winner. That's all karate is—mind over muscle." She frowned at him suddenly. "How are you going to explain that purple jaw to your mother?"

He chewed and swallowed a bite of baked potato. "No problem. She'll presume I got fresh with a model and got what I deserved. Anyway, she stopped worrying about me when I went to Romania during the revolution."

Bernie nibbled on her salad while he finished his steak. He has little respect for his life, she thought. Something had undermined not only his faith, but his joy in being. Something to do with a child. She wished she knew a way to offer comfort, then reminded herself that she'd just promised she wouldn't interfere in his personal life. If she was going to keep this job and make her own way in the world, she had to be true to the promise.

She allowed herself a private smile while the waitress distracted him with a tray of desserts. She'd been in the spiritual-service business too long not to believe there was a way she could help him despite her problems and his. She simply had to bide her time.

The waitress put a plump and creamy piece of pie in front of her and walked away. Bernie gasped at Mark. "I can't eat that!"

He smiled. "It's macadamia cream pie."

"It is?" She looked at it—and stabbed her fork into the rich dessert. She rolled the decadent flavor on her tongue and closed her eyes.

"Sinful?" Mark asked.

"Unbelievably so," she replied, knowing she couldn't push the pie away now that she'd tasted it.

Reading the distress on her face, Mark laughed. "It's only the curve of your hips in danger, Sister Sunshine," he teased, "not your immortal soul. Enjoy. I promise to work it off you before it does any damage."

Bernie rolled her eyes at Mark. "You're witnessing a slide into temptation," she said in self-deprecation.

He toasted her with his coffee cup and a wicked smile. "And you thought adjusting to life on the 'outside' world would require effort."

"YOU'RE BOOKED SOLID next week," Bernie said, looking over the appointment book in wonder. "And for most of the following week."

It was Friday afternoon, and Mark leaned over her chair to check Monday's schedule. "Well, that's good," he said, straightening to pull on a leather jacket. "We can use the bucks. Here." He handed her a long envelope, then crossed the room to lock the office door.

Bernie opened the envelope and found a check for a substantial draw on her salary. She looked up at him as he came toward her with her coat. "But, I—" she began to protest.

"Are you busy Sunday?" he interrupted, holding her coat open.

Surprised by the question, she momentarily forgot her objections to the check and stood to let him help her into her coat. "Just mass," she replied.

He turned her to face him, his hands loosely, fraternally, on her shoulders. "Paul's being baptized." He sighed and closed his eyes.

Bernie nodded, remembering his insistence several days earlier that he wouldn't go.

"Tony and Becky would never forgive me if I stayed away." His dark eyes pleaded quietly. "Will you come with me?"

The suggestion that her company would somehow help him filled her with a warmth she hadn't felt since she'd left the convent. It seemed it had been an eternity since she'd been needed. She grinned. "As your bodyguard?"

He gave her an answering smile and pulled her toward the door. "As a buffer between me and the family. They'll be so excited that I've brought a woman with me, they'll forget to hover and pester."

Bernie thought that Cecelia seemed too dedicated to ever forget, but she kept that to herself. "Sure. What time?"

"One o'clock. Then dinner at Mom's. I'll pick you up."

"Okay. About the check . . ."

He flipped the lights off and opened the door. They stood for a moment in the thick shadows. "I thought you might want to buy a dress. And some pants and comfortable shoes to wear to work."

She opened her mouth to explain that she couldn't afford that large an expenditure out of her paycheck.

"I'll take it out of your next few checks," he said, forestalling her protest. He pushed her gently onto the porch and locked the door. "I'll take you home. I'm invited to Hal and Angie's for dinner."

"But . . ." she began to complain again.

He frowned at her as he unlocked the passenger-side door of the van. "Didn't you take a vow of obedience?"

She gave him a scolding glance as she slipped into the seat. "To the church, Mr. Costello, not to you." Her expression became vaguely troubled. "And anyway, I've been freed from it."

Sitting behind the wheel, Mark put the key in the ignition but studied her a moment before turning it. "Second thoughts?" he asked quietly.

She sighed and buckled her seat belt with a snap. "Mostly I'm convinced it was the right move for me." She glanced at him quickly, her hazel eyes unsure despite her words. "I guess I'll always feel a little guilty that I left a life of service to do something for myself."

"Lives of service aren't limited to those living in convents and rectories," he said with gentle reason. "My mother probably does more for her family and friends than someone formally dedicated to his fellow man."

Bernie smiled at the thought of Cecelia. "I know. I suppose the doubts are all just part of my adjustment. I miss my fellow sisters so much." She pulled one of her shoes off with a groan. "And these are instruments of torture."

Mark laughed and turned the key in the ignition. The car's engine roared to life. "So stop fussing about the check," he said, "and buy something comfortable."

OUR LADY OF VICTORY Church was small and simple. Mark and Bernie stopped just inside the rear doors and saw the family gathered at the head of the main aisle near the communion rail. Bernie recognized Tony, Hal and Cecelia, and saw two young women in deep conversation. One held a baby swathed in white and the other rocked a little boy astride her hip. Two little girls and another boy, hands joined, made a circle around their grandmother, chanting a song that seemed to delight her.

Bernie looked up at Mark with a smile, but saw that his jaw was set and the good humor that usually lit his eyes had been snuffed. He was watching his family with an expression that paradoxically combined antagonism and yearning. This was going to be hard for him. She didn't know why, but she knew it would.

She took his arm, offering comfort the only way she could without understanding why he needed it. He looked down at her in surprise, as though he'd forgotten she was with him.

"There's Marco!" Cecelia cried.

"Mark!" the women called simultaneously. Tony started down the aisle toward them, the children running ahead. With a hand on Bernie's shoulder, Mark led her forward to intercept the welcoming committee. She saw the three women at the head of the aisle exchange a glance.

"Hi, Uncle Mark!" A dark-haired boy of about five launched himself at Mark's legs. The two little girls, a redhead and a blonde, jumped up and down for his attention. As he knelt down to hug them, Tony pulled Bernie into his arm and led her to the front of the church.

"How'd you get him to come?" he whispered.

"I didn't," she replied softly. "He wanted to come. Well, he didn't want to, exactly..." She hesitated, knowing that Mark's feelings about this were none of her business, though Tony didn't seem to think so.

He squeezed her shoulder. "Thanks," he said. "I'll bet he wouldn't have shown up if you hadn't agreed to come along. Bernie, this is my wife, Becky." He extended an arm toward the tall, elegant blonde holding the baby.

She came to them with a bright smile and a hand extended. "So, you're the miracle worker," she said in a low voice, glancing furtively along the aisle up which Mark was making slow progress with the children hanging on him. "Tony and I couldn't believe it when Mom said Mark called yesterday to tell her he was coming. He needs a good influence."

Bernie laughed a little nervously. "I'd love to be worthy of your praise," she said. "But I really didn't do anything. Mark decided to come. I think he just brought me along because I'm new here and don't know anyone."

"We're just so excited that he's interested in someone." The small, dark-haired woman who'd been talking to Becky beamed at Bernie over her sleepy son's head. "I'm Angie, Mark's sister."

"He's not interested in me," Bernie corrected, touching the boy's downy dark head. "At least not the way you're thinking. I just work for him."

"That's a good start," Angie said agreeably. She indicated the child in her arms. "This is Cameron, by the way. You've met my husband and my mother?"

Hal, his arm around Cecelia, joined their circle. Mark's mother came forward to give Bernie an affectionate hug. "Don't you look pretty," she said, holding both her hands and stepping back to admire the new blue wool dress with its dropped waist and flared skirt.

"Thank you." Bernie smiled at the eager faces clustered around her, sensing their speculation.

"Mark gave me an advance so I could buy a few things," she said. "I needed clothes desperately." They couldn't care about her wardrobe problems, she was sure, but she kept talking, a little concerned about the interest with which they all studied her.

"Oh?" Becky looked interested. "Did you wear a uniform in your previous job?"

Politely they all awaited an answer.

She allowed herself a small sigh. Mark knew; there was no longer any point in keeping her past to herself. "You could say that," she replied. "I belonged to the order of the Sisters of Peace."

"It took me days to get that out of her," Mark said, coming up behind her. "And you guys have done it in five minutes." He gave Bernie's shoulder a consoling squeeze. "It's all right. Strong men have fallen under their interrogations. I'm sure there were Italians involved in the Spanish Inquisition, and that their name was Costello."

The family wore various expressions of surprise and disbelief, but Cecelia's hands were joined together over her generous bosom as though in prayer. She made a small sound that seemed to convey strong emotion and hugged Bernie again. Then she looked heavenward and closed her eyes. "Thank you," she said fervently. "Thank you."

Bernie looked at Mark in alarm.

He smiled. "Don't worry. She's just thanking Saint Cecelia. She thinks the saints brought you here, not me."

The priest appeared, a tall man with thick white hair and a booming voice. He wore a gold-and-white vestment that added to his demeanor of spiritual power. He greeted Cecelia and the rest of the family with the ease of long-standing friendship. He stopped in front of Mark and put a shocked hand to his heart. His eyes widened dramatically. "Saints be praised!" he exclaimed. "It's the prodigal!"

Everyone laughed a little nervously and Bernie held her breath. She was acquainted with Father John Greer and knew his outrageously honest, decidedly unsanctimonious approach could offend some.

Mark was apparently not one of them. "I haven't returned, Father. I'm just visiting. How are you?"

"Very well," the priest replied, shaking his hand. "And delighted to see you, whatever the circumstances."

Mark drew Bernie to his side. "I'd like you to meet Bernadette Emerson. She's new in the parish."

"I'm acquainted with Bernie," he said, giving her a bear hug. "She helps with our after-school child-care program." He looked from one to the other with interest. "You two an item?"

"We work together," Mark explained. "I just opened a commercial photo studio and she's my office manager."

"Well, if she handles offices as well as she handles children, you're destined for success. And speaking of children, where is little Paul?"

Becky produced the sleeping baby and Father John took control of the boisterous Costellos, urging them into place. Soon Tony and Becky and the baby in her arms, and Hal and Angie as godparents, were gathered around the marble baptismal font.

Cecelia, holding Cameron, and Mark and Bernie and the other children formed the second line. Mark finally had to lift five-year-old Anthony into his arms to keep him out of mischief. Bernie held the smaller girl so she could see, and anchored the other at her side.

"Why is he pouring water on Paulie?" Cece, four years old, wanted to know.

"Water means life," Bernie explained in a whisper, "because we can't live without it. When Father John pours water on Paul, it means he has a new life in Jesus."

Cece put an arm around Bernie's neck and watched with frowning solemnity. Janie, six, frowned up at her. "Wasn't the old one any good?"

Bernie smiled and tousled her hair. "Yes. But this one will be better."

Mark watched the byplay between Bernie and his nieces with a reluctant smile. He remembered her admission of how much she missed the children she'd come in contact with at the shelter in Los Angeles. It was easy to see why. Her natural warmth and easy disposition drew them, anchored them. She needed to find a good man and have lots of babies.

For one swift and painful moment he envied her the opportunity to start all over. Then he knew that even if he were given the opportunity, he wouldn't take it. That part of life—love and family—was over for him. Nothing, not even baptism from the hand of God himself would bring it back.

Bernie glanced up at him as she and the family crossed themselves in response to the priest's blessing. She saw Mark's distracted look and knew his mind was elsewhere. He'd missed it.

Dinner at Cecelia's was a spectacle of grand proportions, to which all the family and Father John were invited. Extravagant pasta dishes came and went, followed by vegetables and meats. By the time Angela sliced the cake and served spumoni, Bernie was full to bursting. She turned to Mark, who sat beside her with Anthony in his lap.

"If I eat one more bite," she groaned, "you're going to have to spring for another dress."

He laughed and ruffled the boy's hair. "Anthony will help you with the cake, won't you?"

Though the child had been staring at her for hours, her attention made him shy and he buried his face in his uncle's chest. "Who is she?" he asked.

"I told you. She's my friend, Bernie."

"But Bernie's a man's name." Anthony peeked at Bernie, then hid his face again.

"Not this time," Mark laughed. "It's short for Bernadette."

Anthony turned to look at Bernie consideringly. "Is she your girlfriend?"

"No."

Anthony frowned up at Mark. "How come? She's pretty."

"Well, maybe you'd like her for your girlfriend."

Anthony turned to Bernie again. She put out her hands and he reached for her. Mark transferred him to her lap.

"Don't you have a boyfriend?" Anthony asked in concern.

Bernie hugged him. "I do now."

Suddenly finding the cheerful warmth of his family closing in on him and needing to escape, Mark quietly pushed his chair back—just in time for Cece to take the place in his lap Anthony had vacated. He kissed her cheek and tried to put her on her feet. "I have to go outside for a minute, sweetie," he said.

She wrapped her arms around his neck and her legs around his waist. "I can come with you."

After a moment of indecision, he sat down again, Cece carefully cuddled in his arm.

Becky came by with the baby resting on her shoulder and the coffeepot in her free hand. She looked down at her daughter in Mark's arms and refilled his cup. "You okay?" she asked quietly.

"Sure," he replied with a quick smile. Bernie saw him glance at the baby, then away. "Only problem with this house is, it's full of lap-sitters. Once you fold your knees, it's impossible to get up again.''

Becky gave him a look filled with sympathy and sweetness, leaned down to kiss the top of his head, and moved on. Mark closed his eyes and drew a steadying breath.

After dinner the men and boys retired to a badminton game in the backyard, while the girls fussed over Paul and the women cleaned up. Bernie fought the insidious warmth.

"Keep your head," she told herself. "You're vulnerable now because you're lonely. This family has everything you want—the very things you left the convent to find; children you could fuss over without worrying that next week you could be transferred away from them. And it has a man you could fall in..." She stopped herself. Mark was her employer and nothing more.

A love of people and an instinct to reach out to them drew her to Mark, but she was too unsure of her own path at the moment to offer a helping hand to anyone. She'd once thought her own life could never be diverted from the path she'd set, but she'd been wrong. She wasn't the same person she'd once been, and she still couldn't decide whether or not that was something she should have been able to control. And though she was excited about her new life, she wondered if she'd ever resolve the guilt it had brought with it.

The men came in at dusk, and the family settled in the living room. As Bernie carried a bowl of popcorn to the children gathered around the television with Father John, she passed an alcove in the living room where Tony, Cecelia and Mark argued.

"Mom, if he has to go..." Tony was saying.

"He can stay a little while longer," Cecelia insisted. "It's still early. And he hasn't even looked at the baby. Marco, it isn't healthy to..."

Mark listened to his mother patiently, but he looked desperate.

Bernie delivered the popcorn, and resisting Anthony's coaxing to sit with him, pulled off the apron Cecelia had lent her. She returned to the alcove with a look of feigned surprise. "There you are." She smiled at the group, then focused her attention on Mark. "If you're going to have Waterworks's film developed in time for their appointment tomorrow morning, we should probably go."

For one awful moment, she thought he was going to undermine her ploy to help him leave the party gracefully. Then she saw the look of quiet gratitude in his eyes before he turned to Tony with a long-suffering shake of his head. "One week in my employ and she's already telling me what to do."

Cecelia gave him one of her maternal slaps to the chest that looked as though it could pulverize ribs. "That's because you need someone to get you on the right track. All right, you can go," she said magnanimously, reaching up for his hug. "But you watch it, Marco. She's going to report to me, so don't think you're getting away with anything." She drew back and asked gently, "Don't you want to say goodbye to Paolo?"

"No I don't, Mom," Mark replied patiently, though Bernie felt his arm tense under her hand.

"Paul's asleep, Mom," Tony said, shaking his head at Cecelia and pushing her toward the door. "Give Mark a break, okay?" He looked over his shoulder to shout. "Hey, everybody! Mark and Bernie are leaving!"

The family massed at the front door. Bernie was hugged and passed from person to person until she finally reached Mark. They went out to his van in a flurry of waves and shouts of goodbye.

"Mark!" Father John pushed his way through the family to close Mark's door and lean into the open window.

"I'm glad you came," he said quietly. "When are you coming back to church?"

"Next baptism, I guess," Mark replied. He didn't mumble or stammer, Bernie noted. He was comfortable with what appeared to be an alienation from God. Or he thought he was.

Father John nodded. "I'm free for dinner on Thursday nights if you ever feel the need to treat me. I conduct inquiry classes on Mondays, Bible study on Tuesdays, sessions on dealing with grief on Wednesdays, and am available at the ring of the telephone any time of the day or night." He slapped the open window and took a step back. "Don't forget that. If he forgets, Bernie, remind him. Good night."

The rumble of the car's engine seemed like a whisper after the noisy afternoon and the priest's subtle-as-a-sledge prodding.

"I knew that was going to happen if I showed up at the church," Mark grumbled.

"That's what God pays him for," Bernie said, defending Father John. "He was just doing his job."

Mark was silent most of the way home. Within a few blocks of Bernie's apartment, he stopped at a traffic light and glanced at her. "Thank you," he said.

She laughed lightly. "Don't thank me. I haven't eaten so well since my summers at the motherhouse."

He glanced at her again. His eyes were dark, his manner distant. "I meant for coming up with a good excuse to get me out of there." The light changed and he accelerated.

"You love your family," she observed, "but you find it hard to be with them."

"Yes," he said.

She turned to study his profile. He was all tension now. "Have we known each other long enough for you to talk about it?"

"No," he said quietly, but without hesitation.

She nodded, able to understand. She'd often seen pain so deep that it smothered trust. The way back was a long one.

As Mark pulled into the parking lot of her apartment building, Bernie felt a sense of sadness. While she could look at his dark withdrawal clinically, she couldn't accept the possibility that he could never learn to trust again. Despite her doubts about herself, she would still try her best to help him.

She smiled cheerfully. "Want to come in for a cup of coffee?"

"No." It was another decision made without hesitation. "Thanks anyway," he added belatedly. "See you in the morning."

"Right. Good night.

He stayed in the lot until she unlocked her door and turned to wave at him. He tapped the horn, then drove off into the night. Bernie watched him go, feeling curiously sad.

Chapter Five

A man and a woman in a paddleboat. A sea gull. The narrow channel of the Neccanicum River. Two young boys with expressions of glee, paddling for all they were worth. His photographs weren't very inspired, Mark decided, but he thought Waterworks Boat Rentals would consider them passable.

He slipped the magnifier to the next shot on the contact sheet and studied the image—a man and a woman embracing in a small boat aimlessly adrift and a flock of mallards.

Groaning at the sudden onset of a formidable headache, he turned off the light. He stood quietly in the dark and downed the last of the bourbon in his glass. It was too much for one swallow, but he wanted oblivion tonight. The liquor bit its way down his throat and into his empty stomach. He could feel the comforting buzz beginning in his head.

He should make his way upstairs to bed, he thought, before it was too late. But he suspected it already was. When everyone had been eating this afternoon, he'd been concentrating his efforts on holding himself together. He'd known seeing Paul would be hard on him. Even now his empty arms ached with parental memory. But he'd been dealing with the pain for a year. The skill was honed to an art.

Still he hadn't expected the loving warmth of his family to fill him with this gut-wrenching jealousy. He'd been prepared to feel the loss, but not the longing. They were couples, families, tight little units in the encompassing Costello identity. He was alone.

Anger rose in him, as fresh and livid as it had been the day he'd lost everything. The darkness closed in on him, but he made no move to leave the room. Inside and out, he'd become part of the unrelieved blackness. It was familiar and comfortable.

The image of Bernie's face materialized in his mind's eye—delicate, smiling, caring. He hadn't been alone. He made himself face that honestly. She'd stayed by his side all afternoon, and she'd made an excuse to leave when it all become more than he could bear. She represented everything he'd been taught to revere, but also everything he'd come to mistrust and resent. Well, that would make it easier.

Easier. He needed more bourbon. Despite the growing fuzziness in his brain, he went unerringly to the door that connected the darkroom to the back studio where he'd left the bottle. One of the small spotlights he'd left on near the love seat almost blinded him. He put a hand over his eyes and reached to the top of the trunk for the bottle. He took a long swig and fell onto the love seat.

Hiring Bernie had been a mistake. Not professionally; she was good at her job. Personally she was going to be a problem. The family liked her. So did Father John. That was bad. They were determined to bring him back, and he was just as determined to stay where he was—lost. Lost to God and lost to man, just as everything he treasured had been lost to him.

He took another pull on the bottle and noticed that the bright light that blinded him had been joined by friends on either side. Everything else in the room was beginning to blur around the edges. The larger pieces were undulating. He leaned sideways to rest his head against the arm of the love seat. He should do something with the bottle, but he didn't seem to be holding it anymore. Or if he was, he couldn't feel it. He tried to curl his legs up on the cushions but couldn't coordinate the movement. He wrapped his arms around himself to still the ache in them and closed his eyes.

"BA, BA-BA-BA, baba ba ba ba!" Bernie sang to the tune on her new Walkman as she turned off Holladay Drive onto the Promenade. Rain beat against her umbrella, and the ocean spread out to her right growled and snarled in what the morning news's meteorologist said was the first serious storm of the season.

Bernie was enjoying every moment of it. She was glad Mark hadn't picked her up for work this morning. Los Angeles had been so sunny. She loved the belligerent Northwest weather. And her new sneakers were so comfortable! She did a little step to the music in her earphones. Life was good.

Her Sunday afternoon spent with the Costellos had been invigorating. A little scary, but invigorating. She knew they were all hoping something would develop between her and Mark—a relationship that would ease the demons that drove him.

But families had a tendency to be overprotective. She thought she'd come to know Mark well enough in the short week they'd worked together to feel certain that he'd be fine. He was intelligent, talented and basically warmhearted. Whatever had hurt him would eventually recede and he'd build a new life as deftly as he was building a new business. Besides, she had herself to worry about.

Satisfied with her conclusions, Bernie turned up the walk to Good Impressions. On the porch she shook out her umbrella, and leaving it open, propped it in a corner. Then she tried to open the door. It was locked.

For a moment she stared at it in surprise. She looked at her watch. Five minutes to nine. She'd been earlier than this several days last week and the office had already been open. She pushed the doorbell and waited. From inside came the sounds of rapid clicking, then something crashing into the door. Through the Victorian lace curtain over the window in the door appeared two dalmatian heads, their expressions love-crazed.

"Hi, guys," Bernie called, tapping her fingers on the glass. "Where's your dad?" She waited several minutes while the dogs grew more desperate to reach her and there continued to be no sign of Mark.

Bernie walked around the house and tried the back door. It, too, was locked. She then remembered that Mark had a 9:30 appointment this morning. If he'd forgotten it and gone out for something, someone had to be on hand to greet the client.

Just beyond the back-porch railing was a window into the darkroom. She recalled that Mark sometimes left it open to air out the strong smell of chemicals. If she was lucky, it wasn't locked. She leaned precariously over the railing and pushed on the window. It rose easily. Now all she had to do was get from the railing to the open window, then through it, without killing herself.

She smiled up at the clouds. "I'm not carrying health insurance yet. Please guide my steps."

Using a plant shelf for balance, Bernie climbed onto the railing, extended her arm to the open window, then leaned her upper body sideways and into the opening. As she dangled there precariously, getting wet as she slipped downward, dangerously close to the garbage can, she wondered if there was some law of physics that applied here of which she was unaware. Like the bottom of a woman is heavier than the top—a fact to which she'd paid little attention as a nun.

Pushing against the siding with her toes, she pulled upward with a heroic grunt—and made no progress. Then suddenly something had a firm grip on one of her arms, another bold hand on the backside of her new linen pants, and she was hauled, shrieking, into the black hole of the darkroom.

MARK KNEW THERE WAS SOMETHING familiar about the scent and the sound of the intruder, but he couldn't focus on it under the pounding of a hangover. He felt a breath against his bare chest, and wondered vaguely what someone no taller than his shoulder was doing in the dangerous business of breaking and entering. He grabbed a fistful of shirt front and froze. It took him a moment to assimilate what he held. His right hand seemed to be molded over a breast. A beaded nipple grazed his palm, sending shock waves up his arm. He drew back with a start, and empty metal trays clattered to the floor behind him. He put one hand to his head in a vain attempt to keep it from shattering and reached the other over his head for the light pull.

The bare red bulb highlighted a familiar flower-like face made eerily unfamiliar by the crimson light and the glint of anger that had been foreign to it until this moment.

"Bernie!" Mark said in surprise.

She gave him a dark glance while brushing off the sleeves of a hip-length sweater. "You were expecting maybe a serial killer?"

He folded his arms, frowning down at her. "I thought you were a thief. What's wrong with the front door, anyway?"

"It's locked." She enunciated carefully, as though to a child.

He stared at her a moment, apparently trying to absorb what she'd said. Then he ran a hand over his face and sighed. "Of course. I just got up. I'm sorry."

Finally, over the shock of her precipitous yank into the room, Bernie noticed Mark's appearance. He was shirtless and in bare feet, was still unshaven, and she suspected that the red in his eyes had nothing to do with the darkroom light. He reeked of alcohol.

Her mental absolution of his problems as she walked to work this morning ran through her mind like a bad recording. This did not look like he'd be fine. Not at all.

She headed for the square of light coming from the open door of the back studio. There were pillows on the floor and a bottle on its side. A standing spot lay against the love seat. She righted it, careful not to look at Mark, who stood in the doorway. Despite all her resolutions, she wanted desperately to shout at him. She reminded herself that it wasn't her business. She'd promised not to interfere in his personal life.

Beyond the studio door, the dogs could be heard whining and scratching. She went toward it and Mark shouted, "Don't! Ah!"

She turned around and found him holding both hands over his head. He sank onto the love seat.

"You're drunk," she accused quietly, scooping up pillows and tossing them beside him. "I'll have to report this to your mother, you know."

"I am not drunk," he said in a gravelly voice, still holding his head. "That was last night. This morning I'm hung over." He leveled glaring eyes on her, just in case she wasn't kidding. "And don't threaten me with telling my mother. I'm sure she knows I came home and got drunk."

She picked up the nearly empty bottle and looked at him in surprise. "Why?"

He shrugged and it seemed to hurt. "I don't know. Anyway, don't look so stricken." He got to his feet with effort.

"I'm a dissolute at heart, Sister Sunshine. If you can't handle it, you should seek employment elsewhere."

She put the bottle in the wastebasket, then picked up the basket to throw its contents in the trash. She paused to roll her eyes at him. "Big, bad Mark Costello," she said quietly. "For the past few years I've dealt with pushers, pimps and the dregs of mankind, whose aspirations weren't even that high. You don't horrify me. In fact, as a lost cause, you're unimpressive."

She started to leave the room with the wastebasket and he caught her arm. He spun her around, glaring, and opened his mouth to tell her what he thought of her opinion. Then he realized that she'd just told him he wasn't the reprobate he'd claimed to be. How could he chew her out for that? He looked down at the carefully blank expression in her soft hazel eyes, and saw the censure deep in them. Despite her claim, she was disappointed in him. It irritated him that her opinion mattered.

He dropped her arm. "This is my studio," he shouted angrily. "Ah." He put a hand to his head, waited a moment, then went on more quietly. "I don't feel like listening to your impressions of my character."

"Fine," she said. "But I hope you feel like a shower, because you could use one. And Mr. Phillips from the First Coastal Bank is due in . . ." She clutched the wastebasket to her to check her watch. "Twelve minutes."

"Dear God," Mark said feelingly.

"You might want to look elsewhere for help," she said airily. "You've written Him off, remember? I'll try to get the brewery smell out of the studio while you shower and change."

With a descriptive curse and a groan, Mark hurried through the kitchen to the stairs. Bernie made strong coffee, then searched under the kitchen sink for an air freshener. She had the studio set to rights by the time Jonathan

Phillips arrived. He was a small bespectacled man in his fifties, with a high voice and a manner that suggested continuously jangled nerves. Mark was on hand to greet him, scrubbed and shaved in clean jeans and a soft blue woolen shirt. The anger had left him and he looked touchingly sad, despite his cheerful manner toward the client.

Bernie felt instant remorse for her unsympathetic response to what had obviously been a difficult night for him.

The office door opened some time later and Angie and Becky walked in carrying between them two vintage school desks, the seat of one connected to the front of the other. Bernie hurried forward to help.

"What's happening?" she asked.

Angie pointed her chin toward the porch. "Could you get George and the box, please? Mark begged some things from us for a kids' store layout. Do you know where he wants this?"

Bernie pointed to the front studio, then stepped onto the porch to retrieve a box filled with balls, toy soldiers, a cowboy hat, four eighteen-inch-high Teenage Mutant Ninja Turtles and a plastic light saber. George appeared to be a stuffed gorilla almost as tall as she was. Delighted with him, Bernie carried him inside.

The front studio door opened as she passed and she turned her head with a smile for Mr. Phillips, who was apparently ready to leave.

MARK WAS A LITTLE SURPRISED to come face to face with a four-foot gorilla. But the ugly, very real face was vaguely familiar. It lived in Anthony's room, as he recalled.

Mr. Phillips, however, had no such knowledge of the beast. When he found its large, square teeth and angry eyes five inches from his face, he tossed the notes he'd taken and the brochure Mark had given him in the air, and flattened himself against the wall with a terrified, high-pitched, "Aaaaggghhh!"

Bernie's head peered around the gorilla, her confused expression proving she was innocent of any deliberate attempt to frighten a client to death.

"Mr. Phillips," Mark said, taking his arm. "Are you okay?"

The man was ashen and shaking too violently to respond. Fighting a choking need to laugh, Mark snapped at Bernie. "Get some water!"

Bernie stared at him for a moment, assimilating what had happened. She looked at the fierce expression on the gorilla in her arms, then at the small man flattened against the wall, shaking. Mark saw the amusement rise in her eyes and the quick hand she raised to her mouth to hold the laughter back. She dropped the gorilla in her desk chair and ran into the kitchen.

Becky helped him guide Phillips into the outer office, Angie fanning him with a child's Golden Book as they walked. Neither woman spoke, and Mark guessed from their expressions that it was because they couldn't. They were holding back laughter out of deference to his client.

Bernie solicitously held the water glass while Phillips drank. "It's a toy, Mr. Phillips," she said, her voice suspiciously fractured. "I'm so sorry I frightened you."

Phillips nodded. After a moment he regained his color and his decorum. He adjusted his tie and straightened his jacket. Mark gathered up the things he'd dropped and put them in a folder.

Phillips smiled weakly at Bernie. "Quite all right. We have auditors at the bank this week, and I'm afraid I'm a little..." he cleared his throat "...high-strung." He shook Mark's hand. "It's certainly been exciting doing business with you, Costello. I'll bring this information back to the board and be in touch."

Mark walked him to the door, watched until he was safely down the stairs, then stepped back inside the office. He closed the door and leaned against it, booming laughter erupting from his chest. Becky and Angie leaned on one another in hysterics. Bernie, standing in the middle of the office, now had both hands over her mouth. She lowered them to try to explain.

"I didn't..." she began, having serious difficulty talking. "I mean, I was helping Becky carry...and...I did hear the door open...but I didn't think..." She bit laughter back as Mark closed in on her.

"Do you think," she asked, her lips trembling, "he'll go to another photographer?"

"Even if he does, it was worth it," he said, enfolding her in his arms as the memory of Phillips's scream removed any serious sting from the possible loss of his account.

Bernie held on to him and let the laughter come. "Do you suppose," leaning heavily against him, "that his mother was frightened by... by a Tarzan movie?"

Mark was laughing too hard to answer. His head was killing him, but nothing had been this funny in more than a year. "Maybe," he suggested finally, "the gorilla resembles one of the auditors."

As Bernie broke into new peals of laughter, she clung to Mark. It was a moment before she became aware of the muscled arms and chest enfolding her, the scent of aftershave in her nostrils, the strong heartbeat right there against her breast. Awareness rippled through her.

Lost in the beautiful joke, Mark hadn't realized he was holding Bernie Emerson until he felt her soft cheek against his. The touch of her silky skin brought the past back in a flash, and with it all the pain he'd felt the previous night and almost forgotten in the silly episode with the gorilla.

He drew away, laughter suffocated into silence.

Bernie looked into his eyes and saw the morning's misery there. She understood it and sympathized with it. But it was harder to deal with the strong urge she felt to pull him back into her arms. Part of the urge was emotional, because she knew he needed comfort, and the day would have to come when he'd have to resist the pull of his pain and go forward. But the other part was purely physical, and for a woman conditioned to ignore that part of her existence for so long, its power was formidable. Her body felt warm every place his had touched her. It seemed to strain toward him of its own accord. And the security of his embrace defined every insecurity she'd known as a child and carried with her to adulthood—her mother's death, her father's long absences, the many moves from place to place, the difficult adjustment to life in the cruel heart of an angry city and the ugly things people did to each other there.

Mark and Bernie looked at each other, a foot of space between them. For a moment, the need to draw back into each other's arms was almost overwhelming. Then Mark squared his shoulders and indicated the gorilla seated officiously behind her desk. "Maybe you'd better put him away," he said. "I don't think our insurance covers gorilla-induced coronaries."

"Sure." She turned away from him, pleased to have something to do. "He hates everything you love," she told herself. "What are you doing?"

Mark had disappeared into the studio, where Becky and Angie could be heard talking and laughing. Bernie picked up the gorilla and smiled into his fierce expression. "You don't scare me, you know," she said. "He does, but you don't. I guess because need is so much more frightening in someone than blood lust. Anyway..." She sighed and carried George into the other studio. "I think you're cute."

BERNIE FROWNED AT THE standing water in her kitchen sink, and put another Dorito in her mouth. She clutched the bag to her bosom with both arms, as though it represented the security sadly lacking in her life at this moment. The apartment manager and his wife were out for the evening.

She could wash dishes in a pan in the bathtub, but that wasn't the point. She should know how to handle this sort of thing. This was just one more insignificant but clear reminder that she was hip-deep in a new life she knew very little about. She'd seen clogged plumbing before, but there'd always been a handyman to call, or someone in the community of sisters who knew what to do. She didn't. Just as she didn't know what to do about this afternoon, when Mark had held her in a moment of shared laughter. It had been on her mind ever since, suggesting possibilities she'd never had the freedom to entertain before.

The doorbell rang. She ran eagerly to answer it, hoping it was the apartment manager responding to the message she'd left on his answering machine. It wasn't. It was Mark. She swallowed, hoping her recent thoughts didn't show on her face.

"Hi." Standing under the weak outside balcony light, he took in her grubby sweater and sweatpants, water-stained from her struggle with the drain. His smiled turned to a frown. "What's the matter?"

"The kitchen sink's plugged up," she answered, looking at him in surprise. "What are you doing here? Did I forget to do something?"

"No." He shifted his weight, pushing his hands in his pockets. "I need children for the Kids' Kingdom shoot and I was hoping you could put me onto some, since you work with them at the after-school program. I want to get on it right away and I forgot to mention it. Want me to look at it?"

"Look at what?"

He shifted his weight again and said patiently, "The sink."

"Oh." She stepped aside and let him in. The small, close room seemed to shrink further. She led him into the narrow corridor kitchen. "I have a call in to the landlord, but he's out for a while. It'll be all right until tomorrow. I wasn't really anxious to do dishes anyway."

Mark handed her his leather jacket. Stretching his arm out in the confined space to roll up the sleeves of a plaid shirt, he struck her shoulder. "Sorry," he said. "Do you have a plunger?"

"No." She leaned down to look over his shoulder as he rested his weight on one knee and turned two knobs under the sink. He rose suddenly, bumping into her. He apologized again and steadied her.

"A wrench?" he asked.

"No."

"How about a snake?"

She rolled her eyes. "Rattler or garden variety?"

"Is that a no?"

"I come from a convent, remember? Not a hardware store." With a grin, she offered him the bag she held. "Dorito?"

He drew a long-suffering sigh and dipped his hand in the bag. "I suppose this was dinner, along with some exotic flavor of yogurt?"

She shook her head. "Actually I went to the extravagance of warming soup, and now I can't wash the dishes."

He feigned sympathy. "Life on the outside is filled with struggle. I might have a wrench in the van. Be back in a minute."

While he was gone, Bernie took the opportunity to dash into her minuscule bedroom and comb her hair. Changing her clothes would be too obvious a gesture, so she simply straightened them and slipped on an inexpensive pair of canvas shoes. She was filling a saucepan with water when he returned with a short-handled tool.

She leaned around him to watch as he made some adjustments to it. When he stepped back to move under the sink, he collided with her a third time. He set the wrench down, put his hands at her waist and lifted her onto the counter, out of his way. "This kitchen isn't big enough for both of us."

The small move completely stole her breath. "You're in a bad way, Bern," she told herself.

Mark concentrated on the trap under the sink. In twenty minutes he'd removed it, drained the standing water into a plastic basin, then pulled out a messy clog onto an old newspaper with the tip of his pocket knife. He replaced the pipe, ran the water for several minutes to check for leaks, and declared the immediate plumbing crisis over.

"The flow's still kind of weird," he said. "You should ask your landlord to have a plumber look at it."

Bernie shook her head in wonder and leapt off the counter to inspect his handiwork. That placed them close enough to bump arms, and she shooed him into the living room. "Bathroom's just off that little corridor," she said, pointing, "if you want to wash your hands. Can I pay you off in cocoa and cheesecake, or are you going to demand sixty bucks an hour?"

"You bake?" he asked in surprise.

She laughed. "Of course not. But you can find almost anything you want in the world in the frozen-food department of the grocery store. Life in the outside world has its compensations."

He grinned and went to wash his hands.

With the small cheesecake decimated, Bernie tucked her legs under her and studied Mark in the opposite corner of the sofa. "What kind of kids are you looking for?"

"Genuine kids," he replied, putting his cup on the coffee table. "I could get models from Portland, but the manager of the store thinks he'd prefer kids that don't have a professional look. I'd need a bunch, a mix of boys and girls, obviously. I was thinking we could even work after school during the period they're in your child-care program, so their whole routine isn't upset. And maybe a Saturday or two."

Bernie mentally ran through the faces she'd come to love so much since she'd begun volunteering at the school, and knew she could provide Mark with his models. "When do you need them?"

"I'd like to take test shots as soon as we can get parental permission and round them up."

"You'll want to come with me, won't you," she suggested, "to pick them out?"

"I'll leave it to you," he said shortly.

There it was again. His withdrawal from children. She guessed putting a camera between him and them would make the situation workable for him. But he was reluctant to have to deal with them face-to-face. She didn't understand why he felt that way, she just knew it wasn't healthy.

"You'll have to come," she said. "I wouldn't know what to look for."

He shrugged. "Personality."

She laughed softly. "Have you ever met a child without it? I'll call Sister Ann in the morning and tell her to expect us about four."

Mark looked her in the eye. Her purpose in insisting he accompany her to the school was transparent. He had no doubt she'd know what to look for in a child's face. The simple truth was she was on to him. She didn't know the details, but she'd grasped the essence of his withdrawal.

"Good." Mark shifted and sat forward, angry with her for making him admit to himself he'd become somewhat of a coward. She might prevent him from keeping his distance from the children, but she couldn't stop him from keeping *her* at arm's length. "I came, also, to apologize for this afternoon," he said.

"Now, he's coming to it," she thought. She had wondered why he hadn't waited until morning to ask her about the children. Hurt and disappointed by his apology, she pretended to misunderstand. "I imagine you're entitled to drink too much if you want to. It doesn't solve anything, but it is your business."

His eyes caught hers and held. "You know that's not what I'm talking about."

She looked back at him innocently for a moment, then relented. "Yes," she said.

He stood and paced the small room, looking very confined in it. "It was wrong of me to take advantage of your..."

"My laughter?" she suggested when he hesitated. "That hardly requires an apology."

"Still," he insisted, "I'm sorry. I mean, you're..."

She was going to hit him in a minute. "I was a nun," she said, getting to her feet, "but I'm not anymore. And that doesn't mean I've never laughed with anyone, or that no one has ever put an arm around me."

With a sigh, he reached down to pull her to her feet. He held her arms and looked at her grimly. "I know that," he said, his eyes dark and earnest. "I'm just trying to warn you away from me."

Bernie felt strong emotion in his hands and worked at remaining cool. "Is it necessary to warn away simple affection?"

He studied her with debilitating concentration, as though he saw her not as she was, but in another time, perhaps, another place. "Bernie, a photographer learns to see the potential in a shot."

When she looked at him and waited, apparently missing the point, he sighed again, obviously having difficulty expressing himself. "We begin to see things before they happen. The skill," he said, "doesn't stop with photography."

A ghostly ripple of feeling too complex for identification moved up her spine.

"You're the first bright spot in my life in a long time," he said. "But I'm not ready to come out of the dark. And you're starting over."

She thought of the pain she often saw in him, and wished she understood it. Her heart ached for him. "I can take care of myself," she reminded gently. "Remember the alley?"

He closed his eyes to summon patience. "I'm talking about things that can't be handled with a kick to the gut."

She smiled. "Karate's as much a skill of the mind as of the body."

Mark shook his head over her stubbornness. He went to the front door as she opened it for him. "Sister Mary Sunshine," he taunted quietly.

"No," she said. "Just Bernie Emerson, private citizen. That's what you keep forgetting."

"No," he corrected, stepping onto the gallery. "I don't seem to be forgetting it. That's the problem. Good night."

Chapter Six

Our Lady of Victory School's playground was occupied by ten children, rather than its usual one hundred and thirty-seven, but in Bernie's estimation the activity didn't appear to have diminished in proportion to the number of children. Swings swung, children raced down the slide, the merry-go-round spun crazily and little bodies swung on the monkey bars in heart-stopping acrobatics. Without having to wait in line for a turn on the playground equipment, the children in the after-school program seemed to fill the space, like water seeking its own level.

She caught Mark's hand and pulled him away from the van and toward the merry-go-round.

At first glance Mark thought a tall child pumped the merry-go-round in ever faster circles, earning delighted squeals from the two little boys holding on for dear life. As he and Bernie drew closer, he noticed the black garb, the black stocking and the sensible black shoe that pushed the ground away and might have gained the air if the piece of equipment hadn't been bolted down. A nun.

"Sister Ann!" Bernie shouted.

A pink-cheeked face no older than Bernie's looked up with a broad smile. Mark thought wryly that when he'd been in grade school, the sisters had been kind but stern and had never joined in games. His eighth-grade teacher had umped a few ball games with a competence that had startled him and his classmates. But he'd always thought declaring players out or safe had been pretty much in keeping with her line of work anyway. She'd never gotten right in and played the game with them like this one did.

Sister Ann waved, then lifted her propelling foot onto the stand until the spinning circle slowed and finally stopped. The squeals of the two riders turned to "Aw!"'s of disappointment. She leapt off, dutifully got the merry-go-round spinning again, then came to join Mark and Bernie.

"Whew!" she exclaimed, a hand over the silver dove on a leather cord around her neck. "I keep hoping I'll wear the children out, but all they want is more and faster. Hi, Bernie. Welcome to Our Lady's, Mr. Costello."

"Thank you for letting me come, Sister." He shook hands with the small woman whose smile grew even wider as she linked arms with Bernie.

"Friends of Bernie's have got to be good people," she said.

"Annie and I were postulants together, but we'd kind of lost touch in the meantime," Bernie explained, waving as a child on the swings called to her. "I was so shocked to come to mass the first Sunday after I arrived in Seaside and find Sister Ann had been transferred here last year."

"We were always in trouble together," Sister Ann laughed. "It took us a while to get a grip on the dignity and decorum required of us." She sighed and tilted her black-veiled head toward the merry-go-round. "As you can see, I lost my grip on it the moment I made my final vows. So what's this about pictures?"

As Bernie, surrounded by children, was drawn toward the monkey bars, Mark followed Sister Ann to the now vacated swings and explained the Kids' Kingdom job. "I'll contact the parents, of course, before we go any further, but there'll be money in it for the kids—and a donation to the school, if you'll let me do some outdoor shots on the playground.''

"I see." Sister Ann sat on a swing and absently pumped with her legs until the swing began to move.

Type A-personality, Mark guessed. Probably never sat still. While she considered, he sat in the swing beside her. It had been a long day in the darkroom and his feet hurt.

"Bernie's a licensed care provider," Sister Ann said, her veil flying out behind her as she sailed up and past him. "So there'd be no problem letting the children go with her to the studio."

"I'm insured," Mark said. "Not that I'd ask them to do anything dangerous, but I've got all the proper protection in place."

Sister Ann lowered her feet and dragged them until the swing stopped. She turned to smile at him. "It sounds like a great idea to me. And I'm sure the kids will love the attention. I'll get the parents' names and phone numbers for you when you decide which children you'd like to use."

Mark returned her smile. Holding back would be like trying to resist the rays of the sun. "I'm glad you approve. I'd appreciate your help, Sister."

Mark felt a small pat on his back. He looked over his shoulder to come face-to-face with a grubby little boy wearing a deep-billed baseball hat, the bill pushed back and at a slight angle. One front tooth was missing and the other was a new jagged little stump. Between his side teeth was a wad of purple chewing gum the size of a golf ball. Mark guessed his age at about six.

"Want a push?" the boy asked. His eyes were wide and blue and solemn.

"No, thanks, I..." Mark began to decline, but Sister Ann interrupted quickly, "Mr. Costello, this is Buster Flynn. Buster, this is Mr. Costello. He's a friend of Bernie's."

Buster absorbed the introduction without reaction or comment. He asked again, "You want a push?"

"I..." Mark began to refuse the offer a second time but something in Sister Ann's face held the words back. She didn't do anything as obvious as nod, but her dark eyes said clearly, "Yes. Please say yes."

"Ah...sure," Mark replied.

Another sister appeared in the school's main doorway and shouted for Sister Ann. "Telephone!" she called.

"Coming!" Sister Ann shouted back. "Excuse me, Mr. Costello. Buster, be careful." She ran for the door, skirts flying. She stopped to exchange a quick word with Bernie, asking her to keep an eye on the children, Mark guessed, then disappeared inside the building.

Mark heard a loud grunt behind him, then felt himself propelled about a foot forward. He swung back the same small distance then felt two small hands against his back and heard a louder grunt. He swung forward several feet and back. The same procedure was repeated until his legs were clear of the ground and he could help Buster by pumping.

"I'm sure this looks cool, Costello," he said to himself, noticing that Bernie had looked up from the cluster of kids at the monkey bars and was watching all six-foot-plus of him sailing through the air on the narrow strip of canvas. He felt like a fool, but the kid was so earnest—and Sister Ann had silently but specifically asked for his cooperation. "I knew I shouldn't have come. I should have stayed at the studio and made Bernie come on her own. I just want to photograph these kids, I don't want to *know* them."

Now Bernie and the other nine children on the playground were coming toward them. Mark put his feet down, trying not to think about what the action was doing to his ninety-dollar Dexters. He was going to take one look at each face and then he was out of here.

BERNIE COULD NOT BELIEVE what she saw. It wasn't the very tall man on the very small swing working the air with self-conscious awkwardness that made her mouth open. It was Buster Flynn pushing him. Buster Flynn who never talked to anyone, who had stoutly resisted her every attempt to get close to him, who sometimes went into the utility closet just inside the school's back door and cried.

She couldn't help but wonder how Mark had accomplished that when he hadn't wanted to come at all; when he wanted nothing to do with children, except those in his own family and only then because he felt he had to.

Laurie Flynn, Buster's eight-year-old sister, suddenly appeared beside her. "Who's Buster playing with?" she asked.

Bernie watched Mark catch her eye, raise his eyes to heaven in supplication, then lower his feet to stop the swing. A smile rose from deep inside her. "That's my friend, Mark," she replied, putting an arm around Laurie's thin shoulders. "Come on. I'll introduce you."

She didn't realize Mark had attracted the rest of the children's attention until she approached him with Laurie and found him looking a little nervously beyond her. She turned to find eight children clustered behind her, watching the stranger with interest. She introduced them, pulling each child forward so that Mark could have a good look. She explained to them what he was doing.

Laurie, blond and thin, whose mother had been fighting financial destitution since the death of her husband ten months earlier, told Mark gravely, "Models get three hundred dollars an hour."

Mark saw Bernie bite her lip and held back his own amusement with difficulty. He wasn't sure it was fair to laugh at someone so well informed anyway.

Buster, leaning an elbow on Mark's shoulder, made a disgusted sound. "She doesn't do anything unless you pay her. I have to give her a nickel to pour my cereal."

Mark frowned at him. "Why don't you pour it yourself?"

Buster shrugged, accepting his frailties. "I get it all over. She doesn't."

"Ah." Mark turned his attention to Laurie. "You have to be pretty big stuff to make that much. Actually I was thinking of twenty dollars an hour and all the ice cream you can eat."

"Wow!" "Radical!" "Cool!" The children exclaimed excitedly. A tall redheaded boy in the back said, "Make it Gummi Worms and you've got a deal."

Mark winced. "Gummy worms?"

"They're sort of like Jujubes," Bernie explained, "but softer." When Mark still looked vague, she said, "I'll introduce you to the delights of Gummies later. Okay, kids. Line up and let Mark have one more good look at you."

As the children dutifully fell into formation, Bernie moved from one to the other, pointing out the outstanding feature in each child. Then she came to stand beside him.

"What do you think?" she asked softly.

Mark's eyes went over face after face and he wondered if he'd somehow magically landed in the mother lode of all beautiful, expressive children. They all looked so hopeful. He had expected to have to bribe children to sit for him. He hated the thought of disappointing any of them.

He sighed. "From a practical standpoint, the notion of using all of them is out."

She looked up at him, her hazel eyes catching the waning sun. "Why?" she asked.

For a moment, his mind didn't register the question. There was gold in her eyes, he noticed. It seemed to reach out to him, to draw him in. He felt like a man standing on the edge of a cliff, seduced by the thrill of a free-fall.

"Mark?" she said, frowning.

"Because," he replied calmly, calling himself back, "using ten kids means calling ten parents, for one thing."

She shook her head. "There are ten kids, but only four families involved." She pointed into the group. "Laurie and Buster are brother and sister, the three redheads are brothers, those two..." two little dark-eyed, dark-haired girls on the end "...are twins. The Lums..." three beautiful Oriental faces, one female, two male, looked at Mark "...are in the same family."

Mark looked the children over one more time, then turned to Bernie with a sigh. "You swear on a stack of Bibles you will not take a sick day during this shoot and leave me alone with all those kids?"

She smiled and squeezed his arm. "It only takes one Bible, but you don't need it. You can take my word."

He ran a hand over his face and surrendered to the inevitable. "Okay." Taking a last look over the group, Mark noticed that one of the kids was missing. He spotted Buster sitting alone on the highest point of the monkey bars.

"Here you are, Mr. Costello." Sister Ann joined them, distracting him with a slip of paper. "While I was in the office, I got you the names and phone numbers of all the parents involved."

"Good," Bernie said, "because he's decided to use all of them."

A communal roar rose from the children, but Mark's gaze was drawn toward the quiet boy on the monkey bars.

"What's Buster story, Sister?" Mark asked as the children dispersed to return to the serious business of play.

"Grief," Sister Ann replied. "His father worked for a road crew and died in an accident ten months ago. His mother's doing the best she can, but she works full time and takes all the overtime she can get to make ends meet. So Buster and Laurie end up here until she gets home from work and sometimes spend the evening with Bernie when their mother is really late. He misses his father terribly.'' She looked up at Mark, her eyes reflecting surprise. ''You're the first person he's talked to of his own accord in months. He even keeps his distance from the rest of the kids.'' She smiled and touched his arm. ''Thank you for letting him push you.''

Mark's eyes went to the monkey bars again. Buster wasn't there. ''It's a crummy world,'' he thought. He considered what he'd been through, and couldn't perceive of a merciful God allowing a child to suffer that way.

Hands in his pockets he walked toward the van, Bernie wandering along beside him. ''This promises to be fun,'' she predicted with a laugh. ''I know you're horrified now at the prospect of having ten kids around, but you'll like it.''

When he gave her a doubtful glance as he opened the van door for her she challenged, ''Want to make a small wager?''

He frowned at her. ''Doesn't the church frown on gambling?''

She blinked at him. ''The church that popularized bingo in the western world? Anyway, gambling large amounts of money you can't afford to lose is one thing. Small amounts that make life interesting is something else.''

He folded his arms, wondering if she'd ever stop surprising him. ''Like what?''

''If I win, you owe me a portrait of Sister Ann and the kids. If you win, what do you want?'' She grinned. ''Remember, please, the paltry salary you pay me and the rising price of frozen yogurt.''

''Ah...let's see...'' He tried to think of something absurd or something outrageous, but couldn't. ''Nothing comes immediately to mind. Can we just leave my winnings open-ended?''

When she looked skeptical, he added, "If I promise to bear in mind your penurious employer and your culinary extravagances?"

She considered a moment, then offered her hand. "Deal. But it's a good thing for you I'm conditioned to take things on faith."

"You coming back?"

Mark and Bernie turned at the small voice to see Buster standing behind them, leaning against the side of the van.

Bernie touched his face. "Of course I'll be back. You know I come every—"

Buster interrupted her with a grubby finger pointed at Mark. "I mean him."

Mark experienced a jolt of surprise and concern. He didn't need a child putting a move on him. He was determined to keep his distance from everyone. When he'd rejoined the human race and come home, he'd known it was the only way he'd make it.

"You're coming to see me," Mark replied, trying to pick his words carefully. He wanted to be sure Buster knew all the other kids were part of the project, too. "We're going to work together, if it's okay with your mom. Sister Ann will tell you all about it."

The boy's eyes widened. "We're...going to work together?"

Mark nodded. "Yes. You and all the other kids."

"Bernie!" Sister Ann arrived at the van at a run. "I forgot to tell you," she said breathlessly, excitedly, "that all our old cohorts are coming to Seaside for a retreat in a couple of weeks."

Bernie grabbed her arms. "You're kidding! Where?"

"Right here. Mr. O'Connor on the parish council owns the Waterfront Motel across the street, and he's reserved forty rooms at a very low rate. All the sessions will be held right here in the school. Our old Mistress of Novices is coming and Sister Agatha, the motherhouse cook, and Sister Marcella . . .''

"Oh, Annie!" Bernie gave Sister Ann a ferocious hug, then gave one to Buster for good measure. She turned on Mark, her face beaming. "I suppose if I hug you," she said, "you'll feel called upon to apologize for it later."

Mark saw Sister Ann look quickly from him to Bernie, then back again. He smiled a little sheepishly at the nun. "Don't ever tell her anything you don't want broadcast on a cable network." He turned back to Bernie. "The thought is sufficient, thank you."

As Sister Ann skipped back toward the playground, trying to lure a reluctant Buster to join her in the playful step, Mark closed Bernie's door, then climbed into the driver's side of the van.

"I've missed them so much!" Bernie enthused, her hands crossed over her chest, her eyes closed as she considered the approaching visit. "I can't belive they're coming *here!*"

She carried on all the way back to the office, and Mark listened patiently but without comment.

"I probably feel like you did," she said as he unlocked the office, "when you came home to Seaside after all those years."

He had been anxious to see his family, Mark remembered, but he'd dreaded it also. He'd known he'd be subjected to his mother's less than subtle efforts to bring him back to church and the human race.

"My family," he said dryly, "is a little like coming home to the Dalton Gang." He pushed the door open, stepped aside, then followed her in. "Since the children are still at school, it's safe to assume their parents aren't home yet. Would you mind putting in a little overtime and calling them after dinner?"

"Of course not," she replied, pulling off her jacket. "I'll take the list home with me." She went toward the phone, intending to let the answering service know they'd returned. Mark intercepted her.

"I thought I'd ply you with my mother's ambrosial spaghetti. My freezer is full of her sauce. Then you can make the calls from here and I'll be on hand if the parents have any questions."

Bernie was happy to agree. Dinner with someone sitting across the table was very appealing. "Okay. I won't even ask for time and a half."

He led the way to the stairs and beckoned her to follow, pausing at the back door to let Dot and Dash in. They circled his legs, then Bernie's, then trotted on ahead, tails beating the walls of the narrow corridor.

Mark's living quarters over the studio were unfurnished, though a new sofa and chair sat in the middle of the living room. There was a bedroom off it, with a mattress on the floor, covers in a tangle across it. Another room held a desk and a kitchen chair. Unpacked boxes were everywhere.

"Forgive the mess," he said. "I've concentrated on getting the studio ready and ignored this part. Have a seat while I feed the dogs."

While the dogs ate as though they hadn't been fed in weeks, Mark retrieved a freezer carton of his mother's marinara sauce and hoped that he had noodles. He rummaged in the cupboard and finally located an unopened white-paper-wrapped bundle of his mother's homemade pasta. He was in luck. Or was he? He peered into the living room where Bernie stood with her back to him, studying a collage Angie had made as a housewarming present of some of his better known photographs.

A memory of Kathy rose sharply to grind his gut in a clawed hand. She used to study his work with that same gesture—head tilted to the side in concentration. Mark had to take a deep breath to maintain a grip on himself.

"You're playing with me, aren't you?" he asked under his breath of the Power that was supposed to guide all trusting lives but had abandoned his. "Kids, warm beautiful woman. Well, I'm not falling for it. Once was enough. Your efforts are wasted on me."

"Can I help with anything?" Bernie asked, startling him out of his very private conversation.

He looked up from putting a pan of water on to boil to find her standing in the doorway. She folded her arms and smiled at him. "Set the table? Make a salad?"

He pointed to the refrigerator to her right. "Salad greens in the crisper. I'll get you a cutting board and colander."

Bernie stacked lettuce, scallions, radishes and tomatoes in her arms, then dropped them on the counter. She went to look over his shoulder, distracted by the bowl of sauce near the microwave. "Meatballs!" she exclaimed.

He glanced down at her while measuring a portion of pasta in the circle of his thumb and forefinger. "Does that surprise you with spaghetti?"

"Mmm." She murmured in apparent anticipation. "No. It's just that I've never had homemade noodles."

Mark held the long noodles up for her inspection. "Observe," he said, dropping them with an expert flourish into the boiling water. "Homemade and unbroken."

She groaned. "I can hardly wait."

He laughed and pushed her back to her task. "How do you feel about garlic toast?"

"Strongly," she replied, pulling the lettuce out of its plastic bag. "I love it."

Mark sliced Italian bread and made garlic butter while Bernie tore and sliced and chopped. "Are you going to need time off," he asked, "to go to this retreat thing your friends are coming for?"

"No." She grinned up at him. "Didn't I promise not to leave you alone with the children?"

"We don't know their parents will agree yet?"

"I think they will. Anyway, retreats are usually conducted on a weekend, and I'm not sure they'll let me participate. I'm not one of them anymore. I just thought I'd be able to visit them while they're here."

Mark looked up at the wistful sound in her voice. "Maybe when you see them, you'll *want* to be one of them again."

She sighed and shrugged. "I don't know. Sometimes I miss the camaraderie and the sense of belonging and commitment so much, I wonder. But I think it's just cowardice. Once I find those things in life on the outside, I think I'll be fine."

Her words, Mark thought as she continued making salad, were more convincing than her tone.

"I'LL GET TO THOSE CALLS right away," she said, pushing back from the table.

"Don't you want ice cream first?" Mark asked, carrying the salad bowl and Parmesan shaker into the kitchen.

She followed him with their plates. "What flavor?"

"Goo Goo Cluster," he replied.

She put the plates down on the counter and blinked at him. "Say that again."

"Goo—" he enunciated slowly, deliberately "—Goo Cluster."

She grinned. "I heard you. I just wondered if I could get you to repeat it. You really went to the grocery store and personally bought a flavor of ice cream called Goo Goo Cluster?"

He was losing control of an answering grin. "Tony and Becky brought it the day I moved in. You want some or not?"

"Depends," she said doubtfully. "What's contained in a cluster of Goo Goos? Are we talking animal or vegetable?"

He wielded the scoop he held threateningly. "How'd you like a dimple?" he asked.

She backed away from him, laughing, and came up against the counter. One moment he leaned over her with a teasingly menacing expression, the next, a subtle change took place in his eyes as they focused on her mouth. He reached behind her to put the scoop down. She couldn't move, paralyzed by the depth of his sudden concentration.

Bernie felt his hand slip under her hair with a gentle touch that caused a ripple of sensation along her scalp. He applied the smallest amount of pressure, forcing her head into a tilt. Breath left her in a rush when his head came down, hovered for a moment as his eyes went over her face, apparently as puzzled by something in himself as by whatever he looked for in her.

Bernie had known when she left the convent that this day would come. A man would kiss her, and she'd begin to understand the mysteries of men and love that most other women knew. She had expected to be nervous, had even been afraid she might embarrass herself with her complete naïveté.

Instead she waited eagerly for the first touch of his lips. She *was* nervous, but not afraid. Her pulse quickened, and the rest of her body seemed poised on the brink—waiting. Then his fingers cupped the shape of her head and his mouth closed over hers. His lips were warm, tasted of oregano and tomato, and were as tender as her adolescent dreams had imagined a man's lips would be. They moved on hers, encouraging her movement in response. She followed his lead, her hands rising to his neck in search of the support she suddenly seemed to need.

Mark couldn't believe what he was doing. The thought was clear and conscious, but not as strong as his need to hold Bernie even closer, to encourage her gently to respond. He was both delighted and concerned that she seemed to need very little encouragement.

He hadn't wanted a woman in more than a year. He'd had several, but he hadn't really wanted them. There'd been no sweetness in the pairing, no meeting of souls as well as bodies. He'd known it was because he'd been sure he no longer had a soul. Or if he had, it had grown so shriveled and black it could no longer make contact—not with God, not with another human being.

The tip of Bernie's tongue touched his lips with an artless hesitancy that turned his spine to powder. Feeling squeezed his lungs, stealing his breath. He deepened the kiss for a moment, then memory burst into his awareness and he stiffened, pushing her away from him.

For a moment they looked into each other's eyes, hers wide and startled, his dark with anguish. Then he dropped his hands, said something about getting the list of parents' names and left the room.

Bernie stood in the middle of the empty kitchen, resigned to the feeling of lonely isolation that froze her where she stood. For a moment, Mark's kiss had suggested hopeful possibilities and she'd responded instinctively, trying to show him she was also willing to explore their potential. But apparently she hadn't impressed him. Worse than that, she'd upset him. Or something else had; that dark something that lived under the surface of his witty, smiling competence.

She drew a deep breath and tried to steady herself. In her work as a nun she'd been ignored and occasionally even threatened. But physical rejection was something new…and it was harder to take, she thought, than she could have anticipated. Civilian life was not as easy as it looked.

Behaving as though the kiss and his sudden abandonment of it had never happened, Mark handed Bernie the list, poured her another cup of coffee, and led her to the living-room telephone. "Kids' Kingdom could prove to be a regular, lucrative account if we do this job well," he told her with all apparent cheerfulness. "Use your charm to get them to agree."

"Right." Ensconced in a corner of the sofa, Bernie tried not to think about how completely her charm had just failed her and tapped out the first number.

Mark stood in a corner of the kitchen, ostensibly brewing espresso, while the sound of Bernie's sweet voice filtered in from the living room. He shut his eyes tightly and gripped the edge of the counter. "Kathy," he whispered desperately. "Christian!"

He couldn't let this happen. He'd lived through the last year with their faces emblazoned in his mind to support the fury, the hate, the resentment that were all that kept him functioning. He'd crumple without them.

Their faces formed in his mind's eye—pink-cheeked, blue-eyed faces filled with laughter and love for him. He focused on them, but before he could get a clear picture the images disappeared. He chased it into his mind, but it refused to stop for him. He stared at the emptiness in a kind of panic.

Chapter Seven

"I deserve a bonus for this." Bernie leaned a shoulder against the molding in the kitchen doorway, her expression carefully serene.

Mark looked up from the espresso maker with an expectant smile. "They agreed?"

"Every one of them."

"You're a genius."

"Yes, I know." She grinned blandly, then straightened, as though the pose of casual neutrality was suddenly too much. "I'd better go."

Mark knew he'd hurt her, felt her polite withdrawal. He hated himself. "How about a cup of espresso first?" he asked.

"No, thank you." She turned away to get her coat and purse, barring further argument.

He drove her home in moody silence. He pulled into a parking space in the lot, letting the motor idle as she gathered up her things and pushed the door open.

"Thanks for dinner," she said. She glanced at him quickly as she prepared to step out, her sad hazel eyes stabbing him.

His self-preservation instincts notwithstanding, he couldn't let her go like that. In a short time she'd become the best friend he had. He caught her arm. "Bernie, I'm sorry," he said.

She sighed and shook her head, a hint of grim humor in her gaze. "Don't be. I'm not experienced in these things. I..."

"It has nothing to do with you," he insisted gently.

She made a small sound of confusion. "You kissed me, then pushed me away," she said. "How can it have nothing to do with me?"

Mark turned the motor off, then pulled her back into her seat. "Close the door," he said.

She did and they were immersed in sudden silence. She turned in her seat to face him, but folded her arms in a defensive attitude.

"I enjoyed kissing you," he said, taking her completely by surprise. It had certainly seemed that way to her, but then she was new at this. She'd also counseled enough women to know that in matters of attraction, things weren't always what they seemed.

"I enjoyed being kissed," she admitted quietly. "Didn't you want me to?"

He lifted a shoulder. "It wasn't as though I analyzed the whole thing. It just happened." He gave her a fractional smile. "But it'd help a whole hell of a lot if one of us hadn't liked it."

"Why?"

He sighed and leaned his head back on the rest. He closed his eyes and Bernie watched his profile tense as he grimaced. "Because my wife and baby died last year and I'm not over it. I've spent a year determined not to get over it, because the pain was all that let me know I was alive." He opened his eyes and expelled a ragged breath. "I'm not a healthy specimen for a sweet young woman fresh out of the convent to get involved with."

She put her hand over his on the seat between them. Despite the caution he'd just given her, he locked his thumb over her fingers and held.

"Can you tell me what happened?" she asked.

He withdrew his hand and swallowed painfully. "I don't think so," he said. His voice was strained, almost a whisper.

She put a hand on his shoulder. "Try. Go as far as you can."

After a moment, when he still said nothing, she prodded. "Did you have a son or a daughter?"

He stared ahead, his eyes unfocused. "A son," he said, putting both hands side by side on the bottom of the steering wheel, his knuckles white. "His name was Christian."

He stopped, a faint smile on his lips telling Bernie he was lost in his memories.

"He was perfect. Beautiful, bright, happy. Kathy always said that..." He stopped and swallowed. Bernie heard his indrawn breath that held back a sob. "That God had distilled the best of both of us and put it in Christian. Then she'd laugh and say she'd bet He had trouble finding much in me to give him except my appetite and my temper."

He closed his eyes against the image he saw and his hands tightened further on the steering wheel. Bernie inched closer, closing her right hand around his upper arm. Tears shone in his eyes in the shadowy interior of the van.

"The three of us were sitting on the front lawn on a warm Sunday afternoon when the phone rang in the house," he said. His voice and his composure were on the point of breaking. "Chris was eighteen-months-old, and in a playpen. Kathy and I were lying on a blanket beside him. We joked about which one of us should get up to get the phone. Finally I went. When I came back..." Bernie heard his painful intake of breath again. "There was a car where the playpen had been. My wife and son were dead."

"Oh, Mark." Bernie leaned her forehead against his arm, her own pain diminishing in the presence of the staggering depth of his. "I'm so sorry."

Tears streamed from his eyes and he wiped them away with an angry swipe. "Everybody was. It didn't help. I wanted to kill." He turned to her, the will to murder fresh in his eyes. "I would have killed that drunk if my neighbor hadn't pulled me off him." He shook his head, his eyes and his voice desperate. "He didn't even know what he'd done! He was humming some stupid song, and Kathy and Christian were dead under his car." He slapped the flat of his hand against the steering wheel so hard that the column supporting it trembled.

Bernie brushed her own tears away, groping desperately for words of comfort. "Ugly, unexplainable things happen," she said gently, knowing as she spoke them how inadequate the words were. "You can't let that end your life, too."

"Why not?" he demanded in a voice grown chillingly quiet. "We did everything in good Christian fashion. We fell in love, got married in the church with our families and friends looking on. We had a beautiful..." his voice broke and he hesitated before going on "...a beautiful child. Took care of him like the special gift he was." He closed his eyes, seeming suddenly torn between tears and anger. His voice darkened but remained steady. "It was all swept away in a heartbeat."

"Mark..." she pleaded.

He looked at her, his expression calm, open, as though he awaited an answer. "When your beautiful family is sitting safely on your own front lawn, and they're killed by some drunk who's probably never seen the inside of a church and who's ruined his own life and now yours, and he's hauled away unhurt..." He paused to let the enormity of that set in. "Tell me what's left to believe in. Tell me."

Bernie sighed and lowered her eyes, cursing her sorry lack of words. "I don't have an answer for you," she admitted. "Except that we can't always understand His wisdom."

"Yeah. I've heard that one. I don't buy into it anymore."

"Have you talked to Father John?"

He shook his head. "He sells the same thing you do, Bernie," he said with quiet rancor.

"You did nothing to earn that kind of pain," Bernie said reasonably, "but if you want to think of life in terms of fair play, what have you done to deserve the wonderful family you have, your beautiful gift with a camera that serves and enlightens all of us, your healthy body, your good looks, your..."

He turned on her angrily. "My family was killed on my own front lawn!"

"Do you want to know how many women I came across whose husbands had died or left them with children who fell victim to the greed and ignorance of the ghetto and died one by one because the cycle is so tight and so eternal..."

Mark put a hand up to silence her. "Look, Sister Sunshine, you're going to have me feeling sorry for them as well as myself."

"Please don't call me that," she scolded.

"In your reformer mode," he said, "the name seems so appropriate."

"I'm not trying to reform you," she denied. "In the first place, I don't think you're as horrid as you'd like everyone to believe, and in the second place, I was just trying to remind you of what we always forget—how much good there is in our lives that was simply given to us. And how many other people, just as deserving, have nothing.

"And in the third place, if you want to be accepted for what you are—a man in pain who, at the moment, isn't able to climb out of it—please accept me for what I am—a woman in search of a new life. Don't tease me because I was a nun. And don't scorn me because of what I know to be true."

His feelings hurt, Mark asked coolly, "If you have so much faith, why aren't you still in the convent?"

Bernie closed her eyes and accepted that the question was valid. "I explained that," she replied, "and I suppose I can't be disappointed that you didn't understand, because I'm not always so sure I understand myself. I went because I had a strong faith, a fairly good working relationship with God, and because I was so lonely and scared I didn't know what else to do." She looked him in the eye. "I know what you're thinking now."

"What?" he challenged.

"That I used the convent as long as I needed it," she replied defensively, "and now that they've helped me grow, I've abandoned them to follow my own pursuits."

He shook his head. "Just goes to show you you're not as smart as you think you are. I wasn't thinking that at all."

"Really." Unconvinced, she asked, "What were you thinking?"

He sighed and turned toward her, his expression softening. "That I was a jerk to ask the question. It's none of my business, and also I think I know you well enough to know you'd never make a selfish decision."

She subsided, suddenly very tired. "Don't be so sure. It's just what I've been thinking. I left because I changed, I guess. I found myself wanting things for *me*." She rubbed absently at a throbbing temple. "I've never had my own family, Mark. I envy yours so much. My father spent so much time away, my mother died when I was young, then my father died and I gave up my friends to join the convent. Suddenly I was pushing thirty and wanting a husband, a baby, so badly I couldn't say my prayers or concentrate at mass for thinking about it."

Mark touched her shoulder, his grief different from her longing but close enough that he thought he understood how she felt.

"There's nothing selfish," he said, "in wanting to share your life."

She shook her head, not sure about that. "I had promised it to God."

"Maybe He gave it back to you," he suggested gently. "Maybe the fact that a family was on your mind all the time was Him telling you He wanted you to have that."

Bernie looked at him, wide eyes filled with surprise. She found that a comforting thought and was startled he'd conceived it.

"I thought you no longer believed in God," she challenged with a smile.

He returned it. "I don't believe He looks my way, but I'm sure He'd take care of you. In fact, I'm sure He has wonderful things in store for you, so stop torturing yourself. Relax."

Bernie studied him a moment, then nodded. "Thank you."

"Anytime."

She opened her door and stepped out, then leaned back inside. "Good night," she said.

He sketched her a wave. "See you in the morning. Go on. I'll wait until you're inside."

As Bernie waved from the gallery, then went into her apartment, Mark started the van and looked up at the sky with a threatening glare. "You'd better take care of her."

BERNIE HAD AN UNCONTROLLABLE urge to try the slide. In the school playground, set amid oak trees lending perfect fall color to the scene, Mark had young female models sitting on playground swings and the boys climbing up the swings' structure to show off sturdy canvas pants. He'd thought the familiar surroundings rather than the confinement of the studio would make the first Kids' Kingdom shoot easier.

Bernie had expected them to be rambunctious and to show off their playground expertise, but instead they were touchingly eager to please.

Mark's behavior was similarly unpredictable. Since their discussion in his car the previous week, he'd been very much the man she'd come to know, except for the most subtle inclination to keep his distance from her.

While she was grateful for that, she found herself living with a very real disappointment. She tried to tell herself practically that relationships were dangerous and she was vulnerable, and any development of theirs, however cautious and careful, would only result in more confusion for both of them—something neither needed.

But the well of feelings beginning to rise inside her paid little attention to her brain. That was a definite downside to being attracted to a man, she noted with clinical insight—the feelings he generated in a woman could make her forget what she knew to be true, and worse, to disregard it even if she did remember it. She was developing empathy for all the women who'd come through her office in Los Angeles, the victims of big hearts and poor judgment. Without the harbor of convent walls, it was a little more difficult to protect herself from what she suspected might be bad for her.

With everyone occupied, Bernie shrugged off her heavy thoughts and climbed the narrow perpendicular ladder. At the top she took a moment to tuck her red-and-gray plaid skirt around her knees. She looked around, enjoying her high vantage point, then let herself slide, putting tomorrow and all its concerns behind her. The air was crisp, full of the tang of wood smoke and the salty bite of the ocean, and she gulped it as she sailed down, dropping her feet into the soft sand at the bottom.

Laughing to herself, she ran around the back of the slide, climbed the ladder and perched on top again, oblivious to everything but the bright blue of the sky, the perfectly scalloped clouds and the fragrance of the Northwest that she'd been able to remember even in the middle of hot and smoggy Los Angeles. She started down with the wind, then let out a scream when she saw Mark, his camera poised, standing precisely where she would land in about two seconds.

He stepped aside at the last instant and caught her by the waist in the crook of his arm. Breathless, she held on to him and laughed into his eyes.

"Are you crazy?" she demanded. "My feet are lethal weapons."

His gaze was lazy. "Your smile's pretty deadly, too. You're supposed to be helping me with the children, not acting like one."

Bernie absorbed the compliment and ignored the mild reproach. "I'm afraid that's an awful truth about me—a decided lack of decorum at inappropriate times."

The children formed a line to climb the slide's ladder and began streaming down.

"Whoa!" Mark pulled Bernie out of the way as Laurie landed, spewing sand. "We've got a couple more shots to do and one of the first things you have to learn as models is respect for the clothes. Anything we stain or damage, we buy. Everybody to the merry-go-round."

The children groaned and grimaced and climbed down, except for Buster who'd already been perched at the top and took advantage of the fact. Arms out, he headed deliberately for Mark, still standing at the bottom. Mark didn't budge. Buster collided with him, forced to wrap his arms around Mark's middle to avoid being knocked backward.

He looked up at him uncertainly. "Hi," he said with wide-eyed innocence.

Bernie was on to Buster. He'd done that for the body contact, to feel the solidity and security that had once filled and stabilized his little life and was now missing. She wondered if Mark, in his careful distance from children, would notice or understand.

"What'd I just tell everybody?" Mark asked quietly, fixing Buster with a stern look.

The light went out of the boy's eyes and Bernie's heart fell. Mark was going to scold him.

"We gotta suspect the clothes," Buster replied, self-consciously tugging at the sleeve of his colorful jacket.

"*Re*spect," Mark corrected, gently disengaging the boy's fingers and readjusting the jacket sleeve. "They don't belong to us. We're just borrowing them for the pictures. Okay?"

"Okay."

Mark took several steps toward the other children gathered at the merry-go-round. When he stopped halfway to say something to Bernie, he noticed Buster, looking crestfallen, shuffling after him. Bernie didn't look pleased either, he noted.

"What?" he wanted to shout. "I know what the kid's doing, but I don't have what he needs. I'm going to see him three or four times, then I'll be out of his life forever. What good could a little attention from me possibly do him?" Nothing, in the long run, he knew. But today—maybe something small, something that would help him get through.

He put his hand out to Buster who took it instantly, his face transformed. Christian had reacted that way to him from the time he'd been three weeks old. God. How could anything be right that made him remember that?

He looked down at Buster, saw that his smile had widened, and wondered how anything could be wrong that made a child light up like that. Without looking back at Bernie, he led the child to the merry-go-round.

He took shot after shot of the children in various positions, then turned to Bernie on a sudden inspiration. "Do you think Sister Ann would pose for us?"

The children squealed at the idea and Bernie laughed. "Really?"

"Really. Nobody moves this thing like she does. Go ask her."

Bernie returned at a run, towing Sister Ann. Mark, touched by the sight of the woman committed to God hand in hand with the woman trying to find herself but still inextricably linked to the life she'd left behind, raised his camera and committed them to celluloid.

Sister Ann gave the merry-go-round shot the spark of energy it needed. The children, reacting to her, came to life in a way they never would for a stranger behind the camera.

The sky was darkening by the time they'd finished. Sister Ann and the children clustered around Mark and Bernie at the door of the van, wanting to know when they'd be needed next and when they could come to the studio.

"I'll need you the day after tomorrow," Mark told them. "Bernie will pick you up in the van."

They cheered and waved the van off. In the rearview mirror, Mark watched the little crowd follow Sister Ann toward the gymnasium, bouncing with enthusiasm. He couldn't fight the smile that came to his lips. He couldn't remember ever having such enthusiastic models. That had been far less painful than he'd expected.

Feeling Bernie's eyes on him, he glanced at her in the passenger seat to find her grinning at him.

"What?" he asked.

"You look happy," she said, a certain satisfaction in her tone.

He shrugged. "I am. The shoot's over."

"And you didn't enjoy it?"

He considered that. "It was better than the month I spent in Beirut."

She punched his arm and he laughed. "Okay, okay. They're cute kids."

She sobered slightly. "Buster really likes you."

He sighed, laughter gone. "I know. I don't think that's a good thing."

She shifted toward him. "Why not?"

He pulled up to a stoplight and absently watched the cross traffic while he tried to reply. "I guess because he needs someone to replace the father he misses. All I am is somebody he could get attached to for a couple of days, then never see again."

There was silence for a moment, then Bernie asked, "Then why did you take his hand?"

"Because he seemed to need it," he replied defensively, turning to face her.

She was smiling. Her expression always gave him a feeling that despite her worldly innocence and his considerable experience, she knew things he'd never understand. "That's the only reason you ever need for anything. He needed your help and you gave it. The Good Samaritan didn't have to hang around forever to provide the world with a lesson it would remember for two thousand years. He saw a need and filled it and moved on."

He sighed and accelerated as the light turned to green. "A sort of hit-and-run ministry?" he asked.

"That's what a lot of life is all about," she said.

Mark dropped the subject. It was getting a little too heavy for him to handle. Living on the surface of emotion didn't accommodate thoughts of such profundity, or discussions of the Good Samaritan.

"You remembered we're going to Hal and Angie's for dinner tonight?" he asked with a stab of perverted pleasure. They'd argued about the invitation for a week, and this was his opportunity to bully *her* for a change.

Bernie put a hand over her eyes. "I'd forgotten." She dropped it suddenly and said reasonably, "Mark, I really have no business there."

"You were invited."

"But it's a family thing. They just asked me because they think..." She made a pointing gesture from him to herself. "Because...they want..."

"Their brother to get some action." He cast her a dry glance.

She rolled her eyes. "Nicely put, Costello."

"They invited you because they like you."

"If I come, they'll get the wrong impression."

"That you like them?"

She sighed impatiently. "That there is something going on..." She made that gesture again.

Mark turned onto the narrow side street off the Prom where he parked the van. "So you'd stay away from helping plan my mother's birthday party because you..."

"Because it'll save you embarrassment."

He turned the motor off and laughed. "You're talking to the only photographer to get a four-page layout on the Adirondack Natural Air Camp."

When she looked back at him, obviously confused, he explained, "Nudists. I wasn't embarrassed."

Bernie put both hands over her eyes. "You're being difficult."

"And you're being selfish," he returned quietly. "What happened to 'find a need and fill it'? Afraid you might be asked for more than you're willing to give?"

Bernie dropped her hands and looked at him. The question had nothing to do with planning Cecelia's birthday party. She and Mark were always dancing around each other, attracted but repelled like particles that couldn't touch. But he was pushing her today, and she didn't understand what that meant. She only knew she wanted to go with him.

"So I'll come," she said.

"Good." He reached across her to open her door. "I'd hate to have to report you to the Pope."

CECELIA'S PRESENCE in the front office, both dogs asleep at her feet, stopped Mark and Bernie in their tracks.

She looked from one to the other, her expression half severe, half hopeful. "Where have you been?"

The dogs ran to Mark and he stroked them absently. "Taking pictures. Something wrong?"

"No," Cecelia replied, getting to her feet. Mark moved forward to take her arm and kiss her cheek. "I wondered if you and Bernie wanted to come to dinner."

"I have plans," Bernie said quickly at the same moment Mark said, "We've got a date."

Cecelia frowned and looked from one to the other.

Bernie smiled nervously. "I have plans—with him," she said, indicating Mark with a sideways point. "We're going together. To a movie." She came to an abrupt halt, knowing how unconvincing she sounded.

Cecelia looked them over once more, her expression definitely suspicious. "Mark hates to go to the movies."

"He's doing it for me," Bernie said.

Cecelia folded both hands over the front of her coat, her black purse hanging from one wrist. "You know, if I was the suspicious type," she said, "I'd think all my children were avoiding me." There was just the right note of forlorn self-pity in her voice.

"You mean Bernie and I weren't your first choice to invite to dinner?" Mark asked with a brutal grin.

Cecelia gave him a look that told him he was hopeless. "I wanted to have all of you over. You know how I cook."

He nodded. "If Jesus had had you, he wouldn't have needed the loaves and fishes." He put an arm around her and walked her to the door. "Can we come tomorrow?"

Cecelia planted herself in the doorway, refusing to move any further. "What are you up to, Marco?"

"Seduction, Mom," Mark replied simply.

She looked from one to the other. Her sudden smile was bright and blinding. She turned her head to wink at Bernie. "Then I'll see you both tomorrow. Don't do anything you won't be able to tell me about."

Mark closed the door behind her, then leaned against it, exhaling a breath. "That was close," he said, loping across the office to drop his equipment near the darkroom door. He grinned at Bernie as she took her place behind her desk. "You don't lie well, Emerson. Not at all."

She shrugged off the criticism. "That was considered a plus in my profession. Do you think we hurt your mother's feelings?"

"She thrives on that," he said with a grin. "It's something she can use against me later." At Bernie's reproachful expression, he laughed and sat on the edge of her desk. "She looked willing to forgive me anything because I told her we had a hot date."

"Mmm," she said, leaning back in her chair to give him a challenging look. "Seduction, I think you said.

The laughter in him quieted subtly, as he returned her look. "I suppose that's not included in your plans for the future."

She shrugged a shoulder and reminded gently, "You're the one who keeps pushing me away."

He acknowledged the rebuke with a faint smile. "I've lost my emotional equilibrium. Have patience."

She opened her mouth, closed it, then tried again. "Under the right circumstances, seduction might fulfill my dreams."

Mark studied her face, all innocence and wisdom, and wondered if he could ever be the man this singular woman would need. There'd been a time when he'd been up to it, confident, caring, hopeful. But he'd metamorphosed into something else when he lost his family, and he wasn't sure there was anything left of the man he'd been.

Yet, looking into Bernie's eyes, he felt drawn to explore the possibility. That was frightening, in itself. He hadn't cared in so long, but he was starting to care now. Things were beginning to matter. The darkness was dissipating just a little.

The telephone rang, jarring both of them. Mark picked it up.

Bernie had both hands joined together in her lap for steadiness. Seduction, she thought. Mark. The two words came together in her mind with a rightness she couldn't deny. The prospect excited and terrified her.

Mark cradled the receiver and she made herself look at him calmly.

"That was Angie," he said. "She wants us to stop at the market and pick up a half gallon of Goo Goo Cluster."

Bernie grinned. "I'll wait in the car."

Chapter Eight

Hal, sitting on the floor, his back leaning against the sofa, passed a tray of sausage-and-pepperoni pizza to Mark. "What about one of those tennis bracelets?" he suggested.

Tony sprinkled red pepper on a slice of taco pizza on his paper plate. He looked up at Hal as though he'd grown purple antlers. "When was the last time you saw Mom play tennis?"

When the room erupted in laughter, he looked from one to the other of his companions in blank confusion. Becky, sitting beside him near the fire, backhanded him in the chest. "You don't wear it to play tennis, my Genovese genius. They just call it that."

"Why?"

"I don't know. It's just a row of little diamonds. They look very elegant."

Tony rolled his eyes, then pointed to Angie and Mark. "You guys can share the cost of the diamonds. Becky and I'll buy the clasp." He reached over to hit his brother-in-law on the head with an empty tray. "Diamonds? Get serious."

Becky took the tray away and gave her husband a stern look. "What about a microwave?" she asked the group. "She still doesn't have one."

"Because she doesn't want one." Angie, sitting between Hal's legs, grimaced. "If something doesn't take eight hours to cook, she doesn't think it's edible."

"Something to wear?" Mark asked. He was stretched out on the carpet, supported on an elbow. Bernie sat beside him, her legs tucked under her. He picked at the olives she'd pulled off her slice of pizza.

Becky shook her head. "She'll only save it in a bottom drawer and give it to Angie or me three years from now."

Angie, leaning back against Hal, said thoughtfully, "It's got to be something special. She's always doing for all of us. I wish we could think of something brilliant."

Bernie, though made to feel more than welcome, had sat back quietly most of the evening, thinking this was a family summit and something in which she really had no say. But a thought had begun to form as she watched and listened to their antics.

"What about a plane ticket to visit her sister Theresa in New York?" she suggested into the sudden quiet.

For a moment she thought they were ignoring her. Then Angie sat up and turned to Hal, her mouth open. Tony and Becky looked at each other.

"That's it!" Angie shouted.

"Perfect!" Tony confirmed.

"She talks about her all the time," Bernie went on, spurred by their enthusiasm. "And how much fun they had when your aunt came here to visit. I'm sure we could get a good price on the ticket if we check around."

Angie began to make notes on a steno pad. "Okay, Bernie, that's your assignment. You check on the tickets." She pointed her pen at Tony. "You call Aunt Theresa and tell her what we have in mind."

Tony turned to his wife.

"Don't look at me," Becky said. "She asked you to do it."

He winced. "You're better at handling her."

"Nobody handles her." She turned to Bernie to explain. "Imagine Mom with twice the energy, twice the capacity to interfere..."

"Twice the mouth," Tony added.

Bernie laughed. "That's hard to picture."

Tony sighed. "Well, it's alive in New York. Okay, I'll call Aunt Theresa. What else?"

Angie tapped the pen against her chin. "We'll have to get her from the airport to Queens."

"Hire a car," Mark said.

Angie nodded and scribbled. "Good idea. You handle that."

"Right." He smiled up at Bernie. "Remind me," he said.

She nodded dutifully. "Don't forget to arrange for a car to—"

"I mean," Mark interrupted with a playful swat on her arm, "to remind me later."

Bernie smiled down at him, caught in the laughing warmth in his eyes. She wondered for one swift, sharp moment what it would be like to truly be a part of this family. She felt at home among them, experiencing almost the same sense of belonging she'd experienced in the convent in her early days. Except that men gave the atmosphere a dimension her community of sisters had never had. And not simply in a sexual way.

The Sisters of Peace had been a tightly knit group, with all the personalities and problems one found in ordinary everyday life. But everywhere she'd served, in East Los Angeles, particularly, they'd banded together to support one another against those who scorned their beliefs and those who considered them in the way. They'd all experienced a healthy fear of their environment.

In the Costello family, the women were just as close, just as supportive of one another, though the problems they faced were considerably different. But between them and whatever threatened them was a fortification of men so strong and steady, she envied Cecelia, Angie and Becky the sense of security they must feel. It touched her only occasionally when she was in their company, but it was a feeling she hadn't known since her father died.

Mark shook her arm gently. "What's the matter?" he asked. He'd sat up and was looking at her in concern.

She shook the thought off. Thou shalt not covet thy neighbor's goods. Security didn't necessarily qualify as goods, but the concept was close enough.

"Nothing," she replied brightly. "Why?"

He frowned. "I'm not sure. I just didn't like the look in your eye."

"It's astigmatism."

"It looked like sadness."

She shook her head. "In this house? You misread it."

Mark studied her with concentration, trying to decide whether or not she told him the truth. The silence of the room suddenly penetrated his awareness and he looked up just in time to see his brother and sister exchange a speculative look. Hal and Becky stared at them with unabashed interest.

"Will you kiss her, for God's sake," Tony encouraged, "so we can get on with the plans?"

Bernie expected Mark to deny that that was on his mind, or to put him off with some witticism. Instead, he closed a hand over the nape of her neck, drew her gently forward and kissed her—quickly, lightly, but with an unfinished quality that suggested completion at another time. Her inexperience was probably reading something into the kiss that wasn't there, she thought. She felt reasonably sure all he'd want to do later was grump at her for putting him in that position in the first place.

Tony's eyes widened in disapproval as he looked at Hal, then at Mark. "That's it? World traveler, bon vivant, man of the world, and that's it?"

Mark grinned at them, then at Bernie, who was valiantly fighting a blush. "In front of an audience, yes."

"How much privacy can you expect in the middle of a pizza-strewn living room?" Tony asked.

"And this is my house," Hal pointed out. "Where would you like me to go so that you two can play kissy-face?"

Mark glanced at him. "Serbia would be nice."

Angie scribbled and said seriously, "See about a ticket to Serbia, too, would you, Bernie?"

Hal cuffed her gently on the side of her head. "As though you could live without me. Have you checked on the kids lately? They're awfully quiet."

Everyone stopped to listen. The loud silence sent Angie and Becky to investigate.

Tony got to his feet. "We need more wine. Where'd you put it, Hal?"

"In the dishwasher," Hal replied.

Tony started toward the kitchen, then turned to look at him as his answer registered.

Hal shook his head pityingly. "Well, it was a stupid question. Try the refrigerator."

Tony drew a forebearing sigh and went off mumbling.

Hal folded his hands behind his head, leaned back and closed his eyes. "I'm not getting up, you two, but I promise not to look."

"Will you let up?" Mark said. "You'd be wise not to annoy Bernie. She's a black belt, you know."

Hal's eyes widened. "You're kidding."

Mark laughed lightly. "I'm not. Go ahead, Bernie. Dump him on his head or something."

Hal held his glass up as Tony returned with the wine. Tony ignored him, filling Bernie's, then Mark's.

"Don't be boorish," she scolded. "We're guests in his home."

Tony, who'd apparently overheard, finally filled Hal's glass. "How do you know she didn't just tell you that to make you behave like a gentleman?"

Mark toasted her with his glass. "Because I watched her wipe out three hoods who attacked us last week."

Hal gasped, and Tony sat on the ottoman opposite Mark. "What?" he demanded, frowning.

Mark quickly repeated the scenario.

Hal grinned at Bernie. "You handled three beefy punks?"

Bernie shook her head modestly. "Two and a half. Mark had stunned the third one."

Hal and Tony made the most of it, hooting and laughing, until Mark interrupted them quietly with, "Look. You might remember who among us knows that you two went to a gun show when you were supposed to be shopping for Mom."

Hal put a finger to his lips and glanced toward the stairs to make sure that remark hadn't been overheard.

Tony looked defensive. "Mom might have liked a Charlesville musket."

Mark rolled his eyes at the absurdity of the suggestion. "Yeah. Right."

"Hal!" Angie's shriek had genuine distress in it. Everyone got to their feet, and Hal went to the foot of the stairs to catch his wife by the arms as she ran toward him. "Now, you have to promise me you'll stay calm," she said breathlessly.

Hal stiffened. "What happened?"

"Promise?"

"Is one of the kids hurt?" He tried to go past her but she pulled him back.

"No, they're fine," she said quickly. "But . . . the toilet's flooded."

"What? How...? He started up the stairs and water came down to meet him.

As he stood, stunned, Tony left the room at a run, shouting, "I'll turn the water off!"

"You know how Cameron loves to play basketball, but the bigger kids won't let him?" Angie followed Hal up the stairs. "Well, he thought the toilet would make a good basket and started slam dunking the contents of his toy box."

"Why didn't Anthony and Janie stop him?"

They'd reached the top of the stairs, and Angie's anxious voice was barely audible. "They were taking bets on what would sink and what would float."

As water began to puddle at the bottom of the stairs, Mark and Bernie, laughing hysterically, hurried to roll up the oriental rug.

"THIS ISN'T THE WAY HOME," Bernie pointed out an hour later as Mark turned the van toward the beach instead of toward her apartment. A thick mist billowed around them and foghorns cried mournfully off the coast. She peered through the windshield, no longer sure. "Is it?"

"We're headed for the beach," he said, pulling up at a stop, looking both ways, then moving cautiously on.

Bernie knew he always kept a camera in the car, and she'd been riding with him on several occasions when he'd stopped to take a spur-of-the-moment photograph. "Can you get pictures in the fog and the darkness?" she asked.

He glanced at her with an expression she couldn't interpret. "I'm not going to take pictures," he replied. He pulled into a public parking lot on the north end of the Promenade, a distance from the studio and downtown Seaside.

With a flash of sudden and new sexual instinct, Bernie knew what he had in mind. She remembered the brief kiss at Hal and Angie's house and the expression he'd worn then—as though the experience were something he wanted to explore in private.

She could admit to herself that she wanted the same thing. It occurred to her that it was odd, considering how much she wanted to see her fellow sisters again, how much she missed her life with them.

But the growing attraction between her and Mark seemed to exist and grow apart from her ambivalence about how she would spend the rest of her life. She was beginning to feel as though she were two women—one who might feel forever bound by her old contract with God, and one who wanted to run headlong at what the world had to offer.

Bernie didn't ask any questions. Mark opened her door and helped her out. Then he led her across the Prom to the stone wall that ran the length of it, separating it from the beach. The old street lantern cast a weird angle of light over Mark as he leapt onto the stone wall and looked down at her. Tiny droplets of fog swirled and tumbled around him and Bernie felt for a moment as though she were caught in some unexplainable, metaphysical experience.

Then he reached a hand down for her and hauled her up beside him and she was grounded in reality again. His touch was firm, solid, warm.

Mark leapt off the wall four feet down into the sand, then turned and raised his hands for her. She leaned down to him, feeling his fingers brace her waist as her hands grasped his shoulders.

Mark held her there for a moment, arched into him like a diver suspended in midair. He understood the danger in what he was about to do, and tried to think of it in terms of his work. When he'd taken risks as a photojournalist, he'd always balanced the danger to himself against the results. He would glimpse the truth. He would illuminate only a minute corner of life, but sufficient candlepower could be seen for miles. He would learn something. That had always seemed reason enough for risk.

Though he'd virtually kidnapped her on this little side-trip to the beach, he could see in her eyes that she wasn't alarmed. He swung her to the sand, took her hand, and walked toward the sound of the water.

Bernie could feel the damp sand through her Avias. Fog bit her cheeks, beaded on her eyelashes and got into her lungs—cold and vaguely metallic-tasting.

Mark stopped them somewhere near the water; she could hear it rush on the shore like a gust of wind, then recede with a quiet sound that reminded her of low laughter. She could see nothing beyond the two of them but billows of fog and the eerie light it gave to the darkness. It was as though they were trapped in a pocket of timelessness in a place built of imagination and dreams.

Mark framed her face in his hands and tilted her head up. She looked into his grave, dark eyes and felt shaken to the very core of who she thought she was. Bernadette Josepha Emerson, military brat, Sister of Peace, woman.

The memories of her childhood, good and bad, were always with her, and her years as a nun had shaped the person she'd become. But it wasn't until that moment, snared by the eyes of a man who desired her yet seemed almost to fear her, that she understood for the first time the real power of her womanhood. A perfect male specimen eight inches taller than she was and who outweighed her by sixty pounds shook slightly as he touched her. She felt startled and somehow changed.

She put her hands to his chest and felt warmth, muscle, and a rapid heartbeat. His arms wrapped around her and she moved hers to circle his waist. The thickness of his sweater through his open jacket and her wool coat were all that was between them, and even that seemed to disappear when he leaned down and locked her in his arms.

Breath left Bernie in a soft little moan. The muscular pressure against her breasts was something new and the firm pressure of his hand between her shoulder blades intensified the pleasure it provided. Sensation stirred in her nipples, blossomed in her chest, channeled down into her lower body yet, in anatomical paradox, caused its greatest disturbance in her head. She felt disoriented, dizzy, as though she'd truly slipped into another dimension.

Mark's fingers wove up into her hair from the nape of her neck. As Bernie leaned back into his touch his mouth came down without warning or hesitancy. Any point of reckoning she'd been able to hold on to in this mystery world fled, and she clung to him, giving herself over to him and all his touch promised.

Mark felt the subtle release of tension in her body and knew she'd committed herself to his care. But he didn't want to be the gentle swain this time, like the day he'd kissed her in his kitchen. He'd brought her here to examine once and for all just what he felt—what it was that made her so impossible to resist.

He touched her tongue with his, teasingly at first, then determined to know if she would be as passionate in his arms as she was about life. And if she was, if he could deal with it.

She responded instantly, not skillfully but eagerly, and something melted inside him. He deepened the kiss out of a need to show her what it could hold, rather than any personal search for pleasure.

When he felt her gasp for air, he pulled the collar of her coat aside and planted kisses up her throat to her ear. He traced her cheekbones, her eyelashes, the line of concentration on her forehead.

Bernie was afraid she might fly apart. Was every kiss like this? her fevered mind wondered. Did every man and woman react to each other with such cosmic excitement?

She was trembling from head to toe, and something that had never been a part of her character suddenly invaded with alarming force—greed. She wanted more. It was the first clear thought she'd had in minutes. *I want to keep kissing him, for him to keep kissing me until we're lying in each other's arms and I finally know the secrets that have made and toppled men and empires. I want to know every hidden atom of his body, every thought in his head, every wish in his heart. I want to make love with Mark.*

It was a moment before she realized they stood apart, each dragging in thick, damp air.

With the wisdom of hindsight, Mark waited for her reaction, thinking for the first time he might have approached this differently. Any woman might take exception to the fact that she'd been sidetracked onto a foggy beach late at night and kissed without direct consent. Particularly a woman whom he'd kissed before—and pushed away. He wondered if she'd understand.

Bernie smiled. Mark stared at her, then with a small groan pulled her back into his arms. "You are a miracle," he said.

She looked up at him, her eyes brimming with wonder and that little sparkle of greed. "I kiss that well? I thought I'd need more practice."

"I mean," he scolded gently, "that you never react the way I think you're going to. I thought you might be upset, yet you turn out to be Sister Seductress."

She made a sound of distress, and he immediately regretted his choice of words.

"I mean—" he tried to explain.

"I know what you meant," she interrupted quietly. "When we disagree, or when I confuse you, you call me Sister. Sister Sunshine, Sister Seductress." She looked him in the eye. "I think you do that because it makes it easier for you to make me a nun again—at least in your mind. That puts me out of reach and you out of danger. That's just another way of pushing me—''

"I'm sorry," he said quickly. Having her read his mind so precisely scared the hell out of him. He decided to tell her what he'd learned and see if he could scare some sense into her.

He pulled her down on the sand until they sat knee to knee. A foghorn blared, then the night fell still except for the rush and retreat of the waves.

"You're falling in love with me," he said, putting the truth in front of her with stark clarity.

She'd never been one to deny the truth. She looked back at him and replied, "I know. And you're falling in love with me."

"Yes," he acknowledged. "Have you got a Solomon-like decision about what we do here?" He added wryly, "Should we pray over it?"

"Don't be sarcastic," she scolded.

"I'm not." He raised both hands in denial. "But we've got a problem."

"Love is never a problem."

"When you want it and someone can't give it, it is."

She frowned. "The someone being you or me?"

Mark took a handful of sand and let it drift through his fingers. He looked up at her, his eyes bright with sudden impatience. "You're a spiritual woman, and I'm a man who'll never see the inside of a church again except for family baptisms and weddings. You're an optimist and I'm a cynic. You love children and I swore I'd never contribute to the conception of another baby. I can't even bear to hold my new nephew. And . . ." He gave her a look that was curiously, tenderly reproachful, and put a hand to the side of her face, running his thumb gently over her cheekbone. "Frankly, Bernie, every time you get near the kids, or the church, or Sister Ann, or you talk about your friends from the motherhouse coming to visit, you get all misty-eyed and wistful, and you make me wonder how committed you are to this life on the outside.'' He dropped his hand but not his eyes. ''What reasonable man would let himself fall in love with a woman who could be back behind convent walls after the retreat?''

Bernie opened her mouth to deny that was possible, but couldn't lie. What if she couldn't find the caring and commitment she needed to live happily in the world? She'd wondered more than once since she'd come out if returning to the Sisters of Peace and abandoning all thought of husband and children wouldn't be better than waiting for the magic elements that configured her dreams.

Sometimes she even wondered if the convent had made her too much of a nun to ever fit into the world, and her brief sojourn into the outside had made her so much of a secular being that she'd never be happy again as a nun.

Bernie looked at Mark and wondered what life would have been like had she met him when she'd been in high school—before life had made them two people who'd find it difficult to be happy together.

Then she remembered something she had a tendency to forget. She wasn't in control here, and neither was Mark.

''I guess,'' she replied, ''the same kind of man who'd attract a woman who'd risk her affections on a man who might never let her in.''

It was a complicated concept but one he had no trouble following. He was even able to find a little comfort in the fact she was also taking a risk. ''So what do we do?'' he asked.

''I have an answer,'' she said, getting to her feet and brushing off the seat of her coat. She grinned at him. ''But you're going to hate it.''

''What?'' he asked warily, springing up beside her.

She took hold of the sides of his jacket and pulled him down until they were nose to nose. "Have a little faith," she replied, then released him and marched off toward the car.

"Hey!" he called.

She turned defensively, silently daring him to deny that faith would work.

"You're going to need a lot of faith," he said with a trace of a grin, "if you're planning to walk on water." He jerked a thumb behind him. "Car's that way."

She let her shoulders slump in an affected attitude of dejection. Mark laughed, hooked an arm around her shoulders and led her across the sand.

BERNIE GASPED WHEN she saw Buster. "What happened to your hair?" she asked.

Buster, too young to be concerned that the thick blond hair that usually fell to his eyebrows was reduced to an irregular stubble of varying lengths, none of them longer than three quarters of an inch, smiled and took a seat behind her in the van.

"Laurie was practicin'," he explained as the culprit sat beside him and the rest of the children piled in.

Bernie didn't have to ask what the little girl had been practicing; she'd long ago confided to Bernie her desire to be a hairdresser when she grew up. Bernie looked at Laurie and gasped again. Apparently not pleased with her efforts on Buster, Laurie had tried to perfect her style on herself. It hadn't worked. Bernie wondered what Mark would say when she arrived with two of the Kids' Kingdom models coiffed like bufflehead ducks.

"Ah..." he began hesitantly, holding Buster by the shoulders as he studied his innovative cut. The rest of the children dispersed in the studio, checking things out with a firm directive from Bernie not to touch anything.

Take 4 Free
SENSATIONS

plus

2 Free Gifts with no obligation

Silhouette Sensations are modern stories of love and intrigue, beautifully written to combine sensuality and sensitivity.

To introduce to you this exciting series we'll send you 4 Sensations, a cuddly teddy bear plus a special mystery gift absolutely FREE when you complete and return this card.

We're so sure that you'll fall in love with Sensations that we'll also reserve a subscription to our Reader Service for you; which means you could enjoy...

- *4 brand new Sensations sent direct to you each month (before they're available in the shops).*

- *Free postage and packing - we pay all the extras.*

- *Free monthly NEWSLETTER - packed with horoscopes, author news, competitions and much more.*

- *Special Offers - selected exclusively for our subscribers.*

There's no commitment - you may cancel or suspend your subscription at any time. Simply complete and return this card today to receive your free introductory gifts.

SEE OVERLEAF FOR DETAILS

Reader Service
FREEPOST
P.O. Box 236
Croydon
CR9 9EL

FREE BOOKS AND GIFTS CLAIM

YES! Please send me, without obligation, 4 free Silhouette Sensation romances, together with my free teddy and mystery gift.

Please also reserve a Reader Service subscription for me. If I decide to subscribe, I will receive 4 Sensations each month for just £6.60 postage and packing free. If I decide not to subscribe I shall write to you within 10 days. The free books and gifts are mine to keep in anycase. I understand that I may cancel or suspend my subscription at any time simply by writing to you. I am over 18 years of age.

12S1SS

Ms/Mrs/Miss/Mr _____

Address _____

_____ Postcode _____

Signature _____

Offer expires 31st January 1992. The right is reserved to refuse an application and change the terms of this offer. Readers overseas and in Eire please send for details. Southern Africa write to Book Service International Ltd, P.O. Box 41654, Craighall, Transvaal 2024. You may be mailed with offers from other reputable companies as a result of this application. If you would prefer not to share in this opportunity, please tick box ☐

"I'm going to have a beauty shop when I grow up," Laurie announced defensively, when he looked at her hair with the same careful expression with which he'd studied Buster. She folded her arms and added with a sigh. "I know I need more practice. Can we still model?" When Mark hesitated, she added, "My mother could use the money."

Bernie's heart melted with affection for Laurie. Admitting one's needs as well as one's failures gave even a small child stature. But Mark had different considerations here. She waited for his answer.

Bernie had worked with him long enough now to know that his frown simply meant concentration. Laurie didn't. Her bottom lip began to quiver.

"We could bring up her hair..." he said, taking a handful of the wavy blond length and piling it up until the curls on the end covered her forehead. He looked at Bernie for approval. "What do you think?"

Bernie smiled at him warmly. "I think you're brilliant."

He walked Laurie to a small mirror at the back of the room. She peered in at herself then giggled. "I look pretty!" she said in surprise. To Mark she added solemnly, "When I have my shop, you can work for me."

"Thank you," he replied gravely. Then he turned to Buster, pressed to find a different solution. "What do you want to be when you grow up, Buster?" he asked, rummaging through the stack of clothes to be used in the day's shoot.

"A horse," Buster replied with all seriousness.

As Mark's eyes flew to Bernie's, bright with amusement, Laurie expelled a sigh of disgust. "He always says that. You're a boy, dummy. You can't grow up to be a horse. You have to start as a horse."

Buster folded his arms pugnaciously. "I can be whatever I want. And I want to be a horse."

Mark pulled a brightly striped painter's hat out of the pile and pulled it low on Buster's head.

"I want to be a beer horse," Buster said, extending his arms as Mark fitted the hat to hide his hair. "A big one."

"A Clydesdale," Mark said, stepping back.

"Yeah."

Bernie moved beside Mark and slipped her arm into his. "Perfect," she praised. "Crisis averted. You'd have made a great nun."

He grinned and pinched her chin. "Round up the others, will you, and turn the phone over to the answering service. I think I'm going to need you."

She laughed softly. "I don't want to alarm you, but I think you're going to need the National Guard."

Mark worked with the children over an hour, grouping them in the classroom setting he'd created around the school desks Becky had brought. The children teased, mugged, played tricks on one another, but the moment Mark stepped behind the camera, they seemed to sense the importance of the job.

Finally he lined them up arm in arm for a straight shot of their designer T-shirts.

"Okay, everyone," he said, loping back behind the camera. "Big smiles. Like you're all great buddies and you're having the best time in the world."

When their smiles were a little stiff, Mark bellowed, "Bigger smiles! Bigger!"

Behind him, Bernie began to mug. She made faces at the children, did a silly two-step, crossed her eyes and turned her mouth sideways. The children laughed. Prompted by their responses, she went to greater lengths. Involved in a particularly complicated miming of Mark at work, she looked up to find him watching her, his elbow leaning on the camera.

She smiled guiltily and the children roared. Fortunately their uninhibited laughter was just the look he wanted and he disappeared under the focusing cloth again to take shot after shot.

Sister Ann met the van as Bernie delivered the children. "How're they doing?" she asked, then made a horrible face. "What did Mark say about Madame Laurie's haircuts?"

"They're doing beautifully." Bernie leaned out the driver's side window to laugh with her friend. "Mark put a hat on Buster and you probably noticed we remodeled Laurie's hair."

"Good. I'm glad it wasn't a problem. You like the job?"

"I love it."

"You like the boss?"

Bernie looked into Sister Ann's neutral expression and suggested in a mild scold, "Matters of romance are out of your realm, aren't they?"

Sister Ann raised an eyebrow. "As a participant, not as an interested observer. Father John was telling me about him."

"Really. What did he tell you?"

"That he's a fine man burdened by grief. That he hopes something…" She cleared her throat. "Or *someone* brings him back to the Church."

"I don't do that anymore, remember?"

"You'll always do that. It's the way you are. People are drawn to your warmth and your caring and that gives you a certain responsibility whether you're under a veil or not."

Bernie sighed and stared at the gravel drive. "It's complicated."

Sister Ann reached up to pat her arm leaning on the open window. "You'll figure it out. Incidentally, I've got two messages for you."

Bernie grinned at her. "From God, right?"

Sister Ann laughed lightly. "From Mrs. Flynn and Mother Catherine. Mrs. Flynn has to go to some kind of training seminar to get the promotion she's wanted so much.

But it means leaving the kids for three days. She wants to know if you'll watch them from Thursday night through Sunday. She'll pick them up after school on Monday.''

Bernie frowned. "I'll have to see if Mark will adjust my schedule."

Sister Ann nodded. "Let me know as soon as you can. The seminar is three weekends away."

"Right. What about Mother Catherine?"

Sister Ann patted her arm again, smiling. "She wants you to join us for the retreat."

Bernie's smile started from deep inside. A weekend with her old friends, two days of prayer, contemplation and self-examination. She thought about Mark's kiss and all the warnings that had followed it. She could use some time to think.

Chapter Nine

"Bernie's a beautiful girl," Cecelia said.

"I know, Mom." Mark replied distractedly, glancing at his watch as he waited for the red light to change. He was ten minutes too early. If he and his mother arrived at Tony's now, they might not be ready. The surprise party was timed to the minute, and Becky was a stickler for precision. Even Bernie had left the office early to lend a helping hand. He had the airline ticket to New York in his pocket, and an envelope with spending money, including a large clump of change the grandchildren had contributed. Aunt Theresa was eagerly awaiting her sister's arrival.

"Are you dating her yet, or are you going to let some banker or doctor get her first?" Cecelia rested both hands on the clasp of the purse in her lap and looked at him with resigned disapproval.

Mark felt his temper stir. He always swore she wouldn't do this to him, yet she always managed to, and usually before they'd been together five minutes. At least, he consoled himself, today it had taken ten minutes and he liked to think it was because he'd exerted willpower in honor of the occasion. "You shouldn't be so judgmental. As it happens, we are sort of . . . seeing each other."

The light turned green and he moved on, making a sudden turn onto a side street. The driver behind him honked his annoyance at the last-minute signal.

Cecelia turned to him as he pulled into a parking spot. "Seeing?" she asked, obviously intrigued as well as concerned. "Seeing what?" She looked around. "What are we doing here? Becky's expecting us for dinner. We'll be late and you know how hard she..."

"We're not due until six," he replied patiently, "and I have to pick up my cleaning." He made a pretense of rummaging through his wallet for a cleaning receipt.

She glanced at her watch, and apparently deciding Becky could wait for them a few moments longer, repeated, "Seeing what?"

"Ah." He made a sound of disgust and closed his wallet. "Can't find it." Then he smiled at her, trying hard to convey innocence. "You know. Dating."

A gray eyebrow rose higher than the top of her wire-rimmed glasses. "Get out of here," she said in disbelief.

He opened his door. "I am, as a matter of fact. I'm going to get my cleaning."

She caught his arm and pulled him back. Her eyes were serious now, and touchingly hopeful. "Dating? Really?"

He never really forgot how much she loved him, how much she loved all her children, but he'd lived with the knowledge so long he often took it for granted. He leaned toward her to kiss her cheek. "Really. Be right back."

He explained his delaying tactic to Joe Mason, who'd done the Costello family dry cleaning for thirty years. Joe was happy to discuss football scores for ten minutes.

"Tell her your cleaning wasn't ready," he said as Mark left the shop. "She'll enjoy giving me a bad time about it when she comes to pick up her winter coat."

"It wasn't ready?" Cecelia said of Mark's explanation as he drove away. "It took him thirty minutes to tell you it wasn't ready?"

Mark took the side streets to Tony's. "It was only ten, and we talked about football for a few minutes."

"Huh," she said, fussing with the scarf in the throat of her suit jacket. "No wonder your cleaning wasn't ready, if he spends all his time discussing football with his customers. How do I look?"

"Beautiful."

"You didn't even look at me."

"Mom, I'm driving. And I looked at you when I picked you up. You looked beautiful then. I'm sure you still do."

"Next week I'm going to be seventy."

"I know." He had trouble holding back a smile. The party was planned a week earlier than her birthday to surprise her and so that she could spend her actual birthday with her sister. Mark knew she was concerned that no one had mentioned the usual potluck at Angie's, held every year to honor her day.

When he made no mention of party plans, she uttered a long-suffering sigh. "So, Bernie likes you?"

He glanced at her with a grin. "Mom, who wouldn't like me?"

She gave that remark the roll of her eyes it deserved.

"Are you serious about her?"

"We're good friends at the moment." That wasn't precisely true, but telling her too much could be deadly.

"Ha!" Cecelia flung out a despairing hand. "Men and women cannot be friends. It doesn't work."

"That's old-world thinking, Mom," Mark said. He turned down Tony's street.

"You need more than friendship, Marco," she said gravely. "And so does she. Both of you need to turn the corner and start again. If you can't give each other that, then you shouldn't waste your time.''

Mark pulled into Tony's driveway behind his truck. The other cars were parked a block over to insure surprise. He turned to his mother and smiled gently. "Mom, Bernie isn't even sure she made the right decision coming out of the convent."

She reached up and patted his cheek, a decidedly devilish glint in her eye. "Then it's up to you," she said, "to show her what life with a good man has to offer her."

BERNIE WAS ON HER KNEES behind the sofa with Janie and Cece. Other family members were hidden throughout the living room and muffled giggles erupted from dark corners. The doorbell rang and there was a loud rustle as everyone crouched lower.

"Everybody ready?" Becky whispered.

A loud, unanimous "Yes!" was whispered back. The door opened.

Janie began to giggle again, but Bernie put her hand over the child's mouth to stifle the sound.

"Becky, sweetheart. I'm sorry we're almost late. I made Marco pick me up early so we'd be on time, but he had to stop and pick up his cleaning." Cecelia's voice grew louder as Becky drew her to the middle of the room, according to plan. "It wasn't even ready. Of course, he didn't have his ticket. And Joe kept him almost half an hour talking about footb—"

"Surprise!"

The shout reverberated in the air, as adults sprang out of the shadows and children vaulted over furniture to greet Cecelia. Her eyes wide, she backed into Mark, uncertain for a moment what was happening. He laughed and wrapped both arms around her, kissing her cheek. "Happy Birthday, Mom."

She was passed from Mark to Tony and Becky, then to Hal and Angie, while the children jumped up and down to claim her attention.

Bernie watched with a tightness in her chest. What a lady, she thought longingly. What a family. How wonderful it must be to know that a little part of you existed in all those faces filled with love and happiness.

Cecelia passed Bernie, as Angie led her toward the table to see the cake the children had decorated for her. Bernie hugged her tightly. "Happy Birthday, Cecelia. I hope you have many, many more."

Cecelia fluttered a hand over her heart. "Another surprise like this and I might not live to see another one."

As Angie led Cecelia away, Bernie went to Tony and Becky's bedroom to retrieve the presents that had been hidden away. She stacked packages in her arms and turned to the door—to find Mark blocking it. She stopped, every sensory receptor in her body suddenly attuned to him. This had been happening to her every time he approached her since the kiss on the beach and she wasn't sure what to do about it. She'd been so sure she could deal with their developing relationship if she could just consider each step. But a part of her seemed to want to leap ahead without thought or caution.

He wore a burgundy lattice knit sweater over gray slacks, and exuded a more relaxed air than she ever remembered seeing in him. His smile came slowly, teasingly, as he approached her.

"Absconding with those?" he asked.

She looked around as though checking for witnesses, then whispered, "Pretend you haven't seen me," and tried to move past him.

He moved into her path. "But I have seen you."

"I can probably count on your discretion."

"Think again."

"All right," she sighed exaggeratedly. "What's your price?"

He reached under the boxes to grasp her elbows and pull her closer. Then he removed the deep box on the top of the stack and leaned down to kiss her. He did it slowly, deeply, lingeringly, until Bernie almost forgot where she was. Then he replaced the top box, took the stack from her and turned to the door.

While she remained fixed to the spot, still dazed, he turned back, looking slightly dazed himself. "Where am I going with these?" he asked.

"Carpet in front of the fireplace," she replied.

Dinner was chaotic. Bernie helped Becky and Angie in the kitchen, cut the children's food, held the baby so Becky could eat, then occupied Cameron so Angie could eat. She refilled serving bowls, poured milk and kept the coffee brewing.

Mark finally caught her hand, pulled her to a stop and with a deft yank landed her in the empty chair beside him.

"I . . ." she began to protest.

He leaned toward her to say quietly, "You are no longer dedicated to a life of service. At least, not at the moment. Eat something before it's all gone."

For a moment Bernie glared at him, half affronted, half flattered that he cared that she hadn't eaten. He returned her glare with one of mock severity and she dissolved into laughter.

"Not good," Tony cautioned from across the table. "If you can't scare her now, how do you hope to control her when you . . . later?" He hesitated just long enough for everyone to know he'd almost asked how Mark hoped to control her when they got married.

There was an instant's tension, but when Mark pretended not to notice it passed. He turned to Tony with a laugh. "The way you control Becky, you mean?"

Tony caught Becky around the waist as she passed him holding a pair of tongs she'd used to transfer ears of corn from the empty bowl in her other hand to the one on the table. He looked up at her. "You do everything I tell you, don't you, Beck?"

She kissed the top of his head. "Of course I do, darling."

"See?" While Tony looked back at his brother smugly, Becky pinched his earlobe with the tongs.

He bellowed, releasing her, and she walked away with a grin of satisfaction while everyone laughed.

"Well, personally I'm shocked," Hal said from the other end of the table.

Angie, separated from him by two high chairs, asked seriously, "Because he thought he controlled Becky?"

"No," he replied, "because she isn't afraid of him. That face is enough to frighten the devil."

The teasing went on until it was time for Cecelia to open her presents. The family crowded into the living room and Tony moved a chair near the fire and stationed the children at her feet to hand up the brightly wrapped packages.

Bernie and Mark shared a smallish sofa with Hal and Angie. Mark propped his arm along the back of the cushions to make more room, pulling Bernie closer to him as Angie protested the tight quarters.

Bernie could feel his warm torso against the back of her arm, his taut thigh against hers. It took all the self-control she possessed to resist the urge to turn into his shoulder and plead to be held.

"Comfortable?" Mark asked.

Bernie gave him a quick glance to assure him she was, but it was just long enough for him to read the truth. She felt the same thing he did—awareness, excitement, the bud of desire. He had to concentrate to make himself relax.

Cecelia opened gift after gift. There were handmade things from the children—a light pull, a pot holder, a colorful drawing, the indistinguishable subject of which was tactfully passed over by Cecelia as she expressed appreciation of its artistic mastery.

Small things had been purchased for her also. Even Aunt Theresa had sent a gift to contribute to the charade.

Cecelia sat surrounded by her booty, her eyes damp, her cheeks flushed. "God has blessed me with the best children in the world," she said, her voice trembling.

"He wouldn't dare do otherwise," Hal leaned around the women to whisper to Mark. "He knows what He'd be up against when she reaches the pearly gates."

Angie swatted him into silence.

"There's more, Grandma," Janie said importantly, kneeling down beside her.

"Janie..." Becky warned.

With a sigh of indignation, Janie put a hand to her hip and turned to her mother. "I wasn't going to tell her about the ticket," she said.

Becky groaned, Tony dropped his head into his hands and everyone else laughed as Janie put both hands over her mouth, realizing what she'd done.

Cecelia frowned. "Ticket?"

"We're sending you to a rock concert, Mom," Hal said. "Guns and Roses. You'll love it."

Mark handed Bernie the envelope that contained the ticket and the cash gift. "It was your idea, you give it to her."

"No." She tried to resist, drawing her hands against her chest. "It's from all of you."

"Come on, Bernie," Angie prompted.

"Do it, Bernie," Tony encouraged. "You thought of it."

There was general applause and Bernie finally took the envelope from Mark with a glance that promised a reckoning later. She knelt in the midst of the children and handed over the envelope.

The crowded room fell silent as Cecelia opened it. Mark felt his throat tighten. He cleared it to ease the sudden, un-expected rush of emotion and was dismayed to find that it didn't work.

At the height of his own personal Gethsemane, he'd screamed, he'd sworn, he'd threatened and rebuked, but he'd never cried. In the long year since, every emotion but pain had been buried so deep inside him he had no memory of ever having felt anything but loss.

Until now. Until this young woman with the short hair and the wide eyes and the big ideas had crept inside him. And there was something about seeing her there, on her knees near his mother, that brought feeling flooding back. She embodied everything he'd thought he would never be again—new, hopeful, loving.

Those things were beginning to unfurl inside him. He could feel the cautious stretch, the wary turn in the direc-tion of the future. He wasn't sure how safe this was for either of them, but there seemed to be no turning back now. His mind and his heart were filled with her.

Cecelia frowned over the strange, computer-generated ticket. "I don't understand," she said.

"It's an airplane ticket to New York," Bernie explained when the rest of the family simply stared at her with broad grins. "Everyone chipped in to send you to your sister Theresa for your birthday. She's expecting you."

She stared another ten seconds, then her face crumpled and she dissolved into tears. Bernie leaned over to wrap her arms around her.

Everyone gathered around her to tell her about the car that would pick her up at the airport, the reservations for two to see *The Phantom of the Opera*, the plans Theresa had made for her visit.

"Tell me one thing," Cecelia finally said, drying her eyes.

"What, Mom?" Tony asked.

"The ticket." She looked from one son to the other. "Is it just one way?"

BECKY AND ANGIE distributed cake and coffee, but Bernie was prevented from helping. Cecelia demanded her company. She ordered Tony to pull up another chair near her and she small-talked while the children sat at the table with their cake and the men clustered around the television to catch the end of a football game.

Bernie knew Cecelia was up to something and waited.

"Mark tells me you're seeing each other," she said finally.

"Sort of," Bernie replied. Seeing Cecelia didn't approve of her answer, she tried to embroider it. "We've gone a few places..."

"Dinner and the beach."

"Yes."

"Doesn't sound very serious to me."

"It might not be, Cecelia," Bernie said gently. It wasn't fair to let her assume what she hoped would come to pass between them was a possibility. Then again, she hated to upset her at her birthday party. "We're very interested in each other, but...well...he's still not over his wife and son and we can't make him get over it faster than he's willing to do it."

Cecelia considered that a moment, then dropped her fork on her plate and dabbed at her lips with a paper napkin. "I don't think that's true," she said. "I think we all like to stay where it's comfortable, and pain can be comfortable. Being happy, being alive is hard. I think, if you care for my son, you'll help him see what he's missing by sitting back."

"I'm not God, Cecelia, I'm..."

"You're not God," Cecelia repeated with a nod. "You're woman, second only to God in power, mercy and kindness. Being a woman is also hard. We put all our emotions and our openness out there and sometimes those we love the most step all over them—but that's who we are. The world exists because of us—because we can do that again and again and never give up."

"Cecelia..."

She held a hand imperiously for silence, then lowered it onto Bernie's arm. "When a man is hurt, what does he do? He kills his opponent, or if he can't, he curls up and hates himself because he couldn't stop what happened. If God had made only man, the world would have stopped turning long ago and not because of sex. They'd have figured out test-tube babies, or that artificial stuff or whatever."

Bernie resisted the impulse to mention that even test-tube babies required a woman's contribution. She simply listened.

"It would have stopped turning because men don't understand that love lives on. That it's there in pain and sorrow and the deepest, deepest heartache. They'd just look for other solutions. I don't think Mark knows that the same love he gave to Kathy and Christian is still alive in him. Because he found himself with no one to give it to, he wanted to kill it—and because he wanted to, he thinks he did. You can show him he didn't."

"Cecelia..."

Cecelia pointed her fork at her. "I'll trust you to do that while I'm hitting the hot spots in New York."

"YOUR MOTHER LOVED her party." Bernie dawdled up the steps to her apartment, Mark following behind her.

"Thanks to you," he said.

"It was more than the ticket. It was the fact that you went to the trouble to surprise her, that you tricked her with that silly story about your cleaning, that the children contributed their allowances and that they decorated the cake.'' She stopped on the top step, then turned around to sit down. She didn't want to let him go yet. She didn't want to let the evening go.

Mark sat beside her and put an arm around her shoulders. She worried him when she got that look in her eye—as though she saw something in her mind she was sure she couldn't have. It made him feel responsible, somehow.

''I'm glad you had a good time,'' he said softly. Then he leaned forward to kiss her. He'd wanted to do that all evening, since the first taste of her in Tony's bedroom.

She leaned into him, slipped a hand around the back of his neck, held him a moment longer when he would have drawn away. The suggestion his mother had made about showing her what life with a man could be like flashed in his mind. He sometimes thought she might not need much persuasion. Then she'd get that wistful look in her eye, and he didn't know what she wanted.

He pulled her close and she settled easily into his shoulder.

''I'm taking Mom to the airport next Monday,'' he said. ''The retreat will be over by then, won't it?''

She nodded against him. ''They're going back Sunday afternoon.''

''You want to come with me? We can do some shopping in Portland after we see her off.'' He added to gauge her reaction, ''That is if your friends don't take you back with them.''

She punched him lightly in the ribs, smiling. ''I can't reenter the convent until Mrs. Flynn has her seminar weekend. You promised me that Friday off, remember?''

''That's right.'' He grinned. ''You are getting to be a lot of trouble.''

"Who's going to watch the studio if I go to Portland with you?"

"We don't have anything scheduled, and the service will take the calls."

She smiled, kissed his cheek, and got to her feet. "Then I'd love to come with you."

Mark followed her along the gallery to her door. "Mr. Phillips from the bank is coming in the morning," he said, taking her key from her and opening her door. "Lose the gorilla, okay?"

She laughed, remembering the hilarity of the moment Mark referred to, and the instant discomfort that had followed his taking her into his arms. There was no discomfort in it now, she thought. For her, there was only security, pleasure—and the suggestion of all kinds of things she couldn't even imagine.

She wasn't sure what Mark found in it, except that, like her, he seemed always to want more.

Mark noted the faintly puzzled look in her eye, coupled with that sweet weakness for him he was just beginning to identify. He kissed her one last time, then loped down the stairs to his car while he could still make himself do it.

Chapter Ten

They looked like an army. A wry smile quirked Bernie's lips as she stood just inside the back door of the church and looked at the rows and rows of black-habited Sisters of Peace. They had all the discipline of an army, the same purpose and dedication and self-sacrifice, but their target was prayer and peace. They had goals much of the world couldn't understand, much less relate to, but they were banded together in pursuit of them all the same.

But this weekend, gathered at our Lady of Victory for the mass that would begin the retreat, their goal was something they seldom had time to indulge in—contemplation and self-examination. A little like the soldier's R and R.

Though her friends from the motherhouse were here somewhere, it was almost impossible for Bernie to identify them from the back. She crept forward cautiously, looking for an empty corner in a pew she could slip into with a minimum of fuss. She felt self-conscious in her blue skirt and jacket. In the pre-mass silence, heads turned, wondering, she was sure, who the civilian was and what she was doing in their midst.

Then a face turned in her direction several pews ahead and Bernie spotted Mother Catherine who had been her Mistress of Novices. She raised a hand to beckon Bernie, whispered something to the sister on her left and everyone in the pew squeezed together to make room for one more. Bernie genuflected, blessed herself and slipped in.

Father John appeared, preceded by acolytes, and everyone stood as the ancient ritual of the mass began.

Bernie had come hoping to maintain a certain detachment from the proceedings. She'd wanted to observe and analyze and decide just what it was about the convent that sometimes made her wonder why she'd left. She wanted to know once and for all if her decision to leave had been a mistake.

She wouldn't think of Mark, she'd promised herself. She would think only of herself and what God and life asked of her.

God, however, didn't allow detachment—at least not in her. She'd forgotten the power of prayer said in common, the sweetness of two hundred soprano voices raised in praise, the atmosphere of invincibility generated by a shared faith. It brought back clearly all the fever of her first years in the convent. She was no longer that idealist, she knew, but there was so much of the nun left in her. She needed desperately to know if it was enough to call her back.

Breakfast in the school cafeteria followed mass, and there was finally time for hugs and questions and catching up.

"This cinnamon roll is dry," Sister Marcella said to Bernie who sat beside her. She banged her fork on it and achieved a little thud. She was cook at the motherhouse. "Don't you think it's dry? Wait until it's our turn to host retreat and you'll see what good cinnamon rolls are."

Sister Ann squeezed in between Mother Catherine and Sister Agatha, who put out the order's monthly newsletter. "Hi! Remember me, Mother Catherine?"

Mother Catherine, a small woman with calm dark eyes, gave her a grinning glance. "Who could forget you, Ann? You were reprimanded more than anyone in the history of the order. How are you?"

Missing or ignoring the gentle slight, Ann smiled up and down the table. "Did Bernie tell you about her young man?"

Mother Catherine looked up with a smile. "No, she didn't." There was an expectant pause.

Bernie didn't fill it. She didn't want to think about Mark at this moment. It would confuse her. She was enjoying the camaraderie of her old friends and she didn't want to complicate it with other things. She wanted to ride the crest of their friendship and pretend this weekend would provide the answers to all her questions.

"He's a photographer," Sister Ann supplied. "He's using my children in a layout for..." She went on to tell the whole story of the Kids' Kingdom campaign and the Flynn children and Laurie's haircuts. Then she supplied his name.

Sister Agatha dropped her spoon. "*The* Mark Costello?"

Sister Ann looked confused. "Well...I don't know." She turned to Bernie. "*The* Mark ... ?"

Bernie nodded.

"What's he doing in Seaside?" Sister Marcella wanted to know.

Sister Agatha explained about his wife and son. "It was in all the papers at the time. Poor man. It wasn't that long ago either."

"A little over a year," Bernie said, her bubble burst. Her mind was now filled with him. She smiled. "It was a hard time for him, but he's coming around."

"Thanks to you?" Mother Catherine asked.

Bernie shrugged, looking away from her perceptive gaze. "I think it was just time."

She felt Mother Catherine study her a moment longer. Then the Mistress of Novices said, "Speaking of time, we've got ten minutes until the first session. Eat up. They won't feed us again until one o'clock."

Sister Agatha banged her cinnamon roll. "Maybe we're lucky."

Bernie and the Sisters of Peace gathered in the school auditorium for a morning of lectures on spiritual and practical solutions to the problems shared by those in public service.

Lunch was noodle casserole and salad that Sister Marcella judged unimaginative but passable. Everyone stared at the dessert.

"What is it?" Sister Ann asked, studying the little mound in her glass cup suspiciously.

"Purple," Bernie replied, unable to make herself put her spoon in it. It was stiff and definitely uninviting.

"Grape something," Mother Catherine guessed, bravely picking up her spoon.

Sister Agatha took a cautious bite, rolled it on her tongue, then nodded. "Prune whip," she announced.

The afternoon session dealt with the temporal and spiritual benefits of self-sacrifice.

"They set us up for this with the prune whip," Sister Ann whispered to Bernie.

"CAN YOU TWO COME and sit with us for a while?" After dinner, Mother Catherine pointed toward the motel. "We've got a large room and a great television." She winced. "We can relive your days among us to pay for our sins."

"A sort of slumber party," Sister Ann laughed. "I'd love it, but I'll have to ask my Superior. Bernie?"

Bernie nodded. "Count me in. Tell Sister Superior I'll walk you back afterward. But I have to get something first."

The question was unanimous. "What?"

"Never mind. It's a surprise. Be right back."

She sprinted the two blocks to Safeway, was delighted to find the frozen yogurt flavor of the day was pecan praline, and filled a half-gallon container. She bought a package of paper cups and a box of plastic spoons and raced back to the motel.

The sisters were laughing over one of Ann's early transgressions when Bernie returned.

"Honestly," Ann said. She'd removed her veil and a shock of strawberry blond hair curled around her face. "You remember what Sister Clement was like. She was always stopping postulants in the hall and giving them trick quizzes to see how they'd react."

Bernie laughed with the others as she spooned frozen yogurt into paper cups. Sister Clement had been noted for her sour disposition and her dislike of the giggling, inexperienced young nuns.

"But she was always invoking Saint Clement," Sister Marcella reminded her.

"But I didn't know that," Sister Ann explained, looking around the room for support. "I'd only been in the convent three days. Bernie was with me—she remembers. I didn't know my veil was askew. When she stopped me in the hall on my way to vespers and exclaimed, 'Saint Clement!' I thought she was testing me, so I gave her the only logical answer."

"You said, 'Pray for us,'" Bernie laughed, handing her a cup. "Because I laughed, both of us had to stay an hour after vespers saying Hail Marys."

While everyone laughed, Bernie distributed cups and sat on the edge of the bed next to Sister Ann. The other sisters sat around the room in an unstylish collection of bathrobes.

"This is one of the things I like best about life on the outside," Bernie said, sampling the contents of her cup. "Frozen yogurt. Isn't it great?"

Even Sister Marcella agreed that it was. "What else do you like?" she wanted to know.

Bernie thought a moment. "Going to lunch in the middle of a busy day and ordering whatever you want."

There was a communal groan of jealousy.

"Walking on the beach," she went on as the list began to accumulate in her mind. "Buying clothes." She rolled her eyes and added in an aside, "High heels are awful, though. Purgatory can't be worse. Watching television until midnight if I want to," she went on with a distracted smile. "Walking to work in my new sneakers, getting to know a wonderful, wonderful family without being held slightly apart because I'm a cleric."

There was a moment's silence while her friends contemplated the wonders of her new life with her.

"This Mr. Costello's family?" Mother Catherine asked.

"Yes," Bernie replied. She told them about Cecelia and the birthday party, and quoted some of her more memorable remarks.

Mother Catherine smiled. "She sounds like a woman we could use. So all the old mother-in-law jokes aren't true? She really likes you and you like her?"

"It's hardly come to that," Bernie denied quickly. "I just think they're all very special." She sighed and turned to Sister Ann, suddenly feeling the strain of eluding the Mistress of Novices' gaze. *She knows I'm confused,* Bernie thought. *I know she was disappointed in me when I left.*

"We should go, Annie," she said. "We all have to get some sleep. We have to be up early."

Sister Ann hugged Mother Catherine. "It's so good to see all of you again. Meet you tomorrow at mass."

The visiting sisters huddled behind the door and waved them off as Bernie and Sister Ann turned at the street.

"How're you going to get home?" Sister Ann asked as Bernie walked her through the chilly darkness across the playground and toward the convent.

"I'm going to run," Bernie said with a grin.

Sister Ann looked horrified. "It's half a mile. You can't go all that way on foot in the dark."

"'Be not afraid,'" Bernie quoted, "'I go before you always. Come, fol...'"

Sister Ann rolled her eyes at her. "Don't give me that," she whispered as they approached the convent. "If Sister Camille is up, she'll drive you home."

"She will not," Bernie whispered back. "I'm going right now. See you in the morning."

"Bernie!"

"Bye!" Bernie hurried across the playground toward the street.

The sudden honk of a horn startled her into stillness. The Good Impressions van pulled up in front of her.

"Mark!" she said in surprise as he pushed the passenger door open. "What are you doing here?"

"I called the convent to find out what time this do would be over tonight. Sister Camille told me you'd promised to walk Sister Ann back and that you didn't expect to be more than an hour. I suspected you wouldn't have a way home."

She smiled at him across the dark expanse of the van and buckled her seat belt. "And you just sat here and waited?"

He drove down the quiet street. "It wasn't a problem. How's it going? Do you feel refreshed and renewed?"

Bernie studied his profile, trying to determine if there'd been a sarcastic quality in his voice. "Are you being snide?" she asked.

He glanced at her with a frown, apparently offended that she'd asked. "No. That's why people go on retreats, isn't it? For renewal and refreshment?" And to put aside the things and the people who usually clutter and confuse their lives, in the hope of gaining a new perspective. Only he hadn't wanted to be forgotten, so he'd come to make sure she had a ride home.

"Somewhat," she replied carefully. "Mass was beautiful, the sessions were enlightening and we had some great laughs talking over old times." She related the story of Sister Ann's confrontation with Sister Clement.

Mark laughed.

"I ran to the market to get frozen yogurt so they could all try it."

"What did they think?"

"That it was much better than the prune whip we had for dessert at lunch."

"Yuk."

"That was the general consensus."

Mark took a manila envelope from the dashboard and handed it to her. "First proofs of the Kids' Kingdom thing. Tell me what you think." Without taking his eyes from the road, he reached up to turn on the overhead light.

Bernie pulled the proof sheet out and tilted it until she had a clear view. They were wonderful, particularly the one with Sister Ann propelling the merry-go-round. The children were wild with laughter, faces expressing various stages of delight and excitement. Except for Buster.

Bernie ran her eyes over the proof sheet a second time and saw that in almost every frame, Buster was watching Mark. His expression was touching, a little haunting, and probably something that should hang in a gallery or a museum.

"These are wonderful," she said as he pulled into her apartment parking lot. She stared at one print in particular that featured just Laurie and Buster, arms around each other. Laurie mugged for the camera, looking brash and confident. Buster simply stared at the camera, or probably at Mark, his eyes filled with a beautiful innocence that had clearly been hurt.

As the motor died, Bernie turned to Mark in amazement. She'd been aware of his professional status, of course, but she hadn't expected to find that his insightful style could lend a quality of magic to a sales layout. "How did you find that in Buster's face?"

He raised a shoulder. "It was there."

"I didn't see that in him when we were face-to-face."

He smiled and leaned back against the headrest. "That's photography's special gift to the world. Our eyes do reflect all we are and know and feel, but we're usually so animated that expressions come and go without notice. The camera catches that fraction of a moment. And everything the subject felt in that instant is distilled on a small space of film and recorded forever. Or as long as the film will last."

She smiled. "Then you have to see like the camera does, otherwise how would you know what to photograph?"

He shrugged again. "You learn to know where the potential lies and trust the camera to do its work. A child's face is pretty certain ground."

He'd told her that before, she remembered, about knowing where the potential lay. But at the time, he'd been talking about the two of them.

"So we're still on for Monday?" he asked as casually as he could. He could tell he hadn't fooled her. She gave him that faint little smile that told him she'd read his mind.

"Did you think I'd go back to the convent?" she asked.

He didn't look away. "It's a possibility, isn't it?"

"Would it upset you if I did?"

"So far," he said, leaning an elbow on the steering wheel, "we've exchanged four questions and no answers."

She glanced at him. "That's the problem with us, isn't it? All questions and no answers. Well, I do have one answer for you." She put the envelope on the dash, unbuckled her seat belt and turned to face him. "I'm still confused about what I want, but I whiled away a whole session this afternoon thinking about you and wondering what you were doing."

That was music to his ears. "I thought about you," he said quietly. "I even printed you an eight-by-ten of Sister Ann and the kids on the merry-go-round."

"You owed me that," she teased. "I won the bet. You are enjoying the kids."

He smiled. "I get to send them home to somebody else."

She laughed. "You're hopeless." She reached for her door handle. "Good night, Mark. Thanks for the lift."

He caught her arm and stopped her before she could step out of the van. "I suppose," he asked carefully, "that a good-night kiss would interfere with your spiritual continuity or something?"

She hesitated, then released the door handle.

"Maybe," she suggested softly, "it would help me balance my options."

Mark shaped her head in his hand, leaned forward and drew her toward him. He kissed her tenderly, out of respect for her small journey of self-exploration and to show himself there was still a gentleman inside him.

But he longed for more. He thought about her day and night now. He was beginning to burn with wanting her.

With a sigh he freed her and leaned back. "Want me to pick you up tomorrow?"

Shaken by his tenderness, Bernie had to clear her throat before she could find her voice. "No, thanks. They all leave on the bus tomorrow afternoon and I want to see them off."

"Okay." He reached across her to open her door. "Come on. I'll walk you up."

At her door, Mark took her key and opened it, then leaned his shoulder against the door frame. His dark eyes held hers. "It would upset me if you joined up again," he admitted. "You've become very important to me. More than important."

Essential, Bernie thought. *I need to be essential to you.*

She touched his cheek. "You're important to me, Mark."

He opened his mouth as though there was more he wanted to say, then he changed his mind, turned his lips into the palm of her hand and kissed it. "Take care, Bernie. I'll pick you up Monday morning."

Bernie watched him walk away. He hadn't promised anything, or even offered anything, but she'd seen the need in his eyes and it drew her like a rope tied around her waist. And she felt little doubt that it was the woman in her reacting, and not the soul-saving sister.

When he drove off with a tap of his horn, Bernie went inside, kicked off her shoes and turned on the kettle. She thought wryly of all the women she'd counseled at the clinic.

She remembered what Cecelia had said. "You're woman, second only to God in power, mercy and kindness. We put all our emotions out there... but that's who we are. The world exists because we can do that again and again and never give up."

She felt the power now, tonight, more than she'd ever felt it before. She just wasn't sure what had fueled it—the retreat with the Sisters of Peace or the need in Mark Costello's eyes.

MOTHER CATHERINE hooked her arm in Bernie's after Sunday-morning mass and led her away from the cafeteria where all the other sisters were headed and into the quiet neighborhood around the church.

"But we'll miss the prune whip," Bernie protested laughingly.

Mother Catherine slanted her a grin. "You always were astute." She started to walk around the block, smiling at the cozy-looking beach homes. In front of one, a fat yellow cat and a small black-and-white dog lay curled together on the porch. She laughed. "Now there's a fine example of the Christian principle at work."

"If only people were so willing to share their space," Bernie said.

Mother Catherine pulled her along. A breeze blew from the ocean, smelling of salt and morning. "Which brings us to the reason I've chosen to starve you this morning."

Bernie had known the Mistress of Novices had something on her mind. The fear that she was that something appeared to be confirmed.

"Sister Jeanine from the clinic in East Los Angeles stopped by on her way to visit her father in Klamath Falls," Mother Catherine said. "She says they miss you, but they're doing well. So you can stop worrying about them."

Bernie looked at her in surprise. "I wasn't worried."

Mother Catherine nodded. "Then why do you look at all of us as though you expect to be scolded for something?"

Bernie laughed. "Do I? I'm sorry."

"You're not thinking about coming back, are you?"

Bernie was stopped in her tracks by the point-blank question.

She laughed again. "That doesn't sound like you'd want me."

"I don't." Mother Catherine pulled her along, waving at a little girl on a porch step rocking a doll in a blanket. She waved shyly back. "Not if you're brought back by misplaced feelings of guilt."

Bernie sighed and looked up at the sky. "I guess I'd just like to be sure I'm doing the right thing. I'm having a little trouble adjusting, and that makes me wonder if I was wrong to leave."

Mother Catherine was silent a moment. "I thought you'd fallen in love with Mr. Costello?"

"I think I have," Bernie admitted. "But I'm not sure he'll ever be able to fall in love with me." She smiled thinly. "Life was so much easier when the convent gave me assignments."

"Maybe he's your assignment. Father John was telling me about him. A good man with a heavy burden, lost in the dark." She squeezed Bernie's arm. "Ever think of yourself as an Eveready flashlight?"

Bernie laughed, disengaging her arm and putting it around the small sister's shoulders. "I miss you."

"And I miss you," Mother Catherine said, her tone suddenly brisk. "You were the best novice I ever had. You attacked everything you did with such dedication and such love. But you had a problem that I think you still have. You spent so much time in a military atmosphere, you think you have to have orders to do anything. You don't. Do what you feel."

"But you have to know which course to take. I guess I'll always feel guilty that I left the convent in search of what *I* wanted."

"How do you know that what *you* want isn't what God wants for you?"

"That's what Mark said," Bernie remembered aloud.

Mother Catherine stopped her on the corner of a quiet intersection, her eyes earnest. "It isn't selfish to want to live in the world, Bernie. It isn't selfish to want to love a man and have babies. That's a vocation, too. Let yourself find it and be happy with it."

"Mother," Bernie said, her throat tightening, "I think I could have all that with Mark, but he's never told me how he feels, except to say that I'm important to him."

"You have to make him see just how important you are," Mother Catherine said, as though it should be the easiest thing in the world. "And you have to be fully dedicated to him to do that. You can't have one foot in the Convent."

"I've been praying about it."

Mother Catherine started across the street, pulling her along. "Sometimes you have to stop praying and just listen."

Bernie smiled down at her. "How did you get to be so wise?"

Mother Catherine smiled heavenward. "I like to think it was divine infusion of the Holy Spirit, but actually it comes from a lifetime of making mistakes and learning to fix them."

BERNIE AND SISTER ANN watched the yellow bus and the hands waving out the window until it turned the corner and disappeared. Where five minutes ago there had been hugs and laughter and promises to write, there was now a ringing silence. The retreat was over. Bernie's indecision was over. She loved Mark Costello, and as Mother Catherine candidly pointed out as Bernie carried her suitcase to the bus, "While loving God and loving a man are not mutually exclusive, it cannot be done from a convent."

"Want to have dinner with us?" Sister Ann asked.

Bernie drew a deep breath of the crisp early evening air and shook her head. "Thanks, but I've got things to do at home. I'll see you Tuesday."

Sister Ann looked into her eyes. "You okay?"

Bernie raised an eyebrow. "Of course. Why do you ask?"

"I don't know. You look...different."

"That's because I have a new identity."

Sister Ann's eyes widened. "Really? What?"

Bernie laughed softly and hugged her. "Bernadette Emerson. Flashlight. Bye."

Chapter Eleven

"My freezer is full and everything is marked." Cecelia turned awkwardly under her shoulder harness to look at Bernie seated behind Mark in his van. "I want you to help yourself. I know Marco gets too busy to cook and he eats that junk you get in disposable boxes."

Mark groaned without taking his eyes from the creative maneuvers of the other cars jockeying for position in the parking area at Portland International Airport.

"And he won't eat a vegetable," Cecelia confided, ignoring him, "unless you cover it with cheese sauce or put it in dill dip. He probably has stuff in his arteries you could use to seal windows."

"Mom." The car now safely parked, Mark leaned his elbows on the steering wheel and put both hands to his head. The nearly two-hour ride, with Cecelia giving last-minute instructions, had been a very long one for him. "For God's sake..."

"For God's sake," she said matter-of-factly, "I should have made you eat vegetables when you were a baby."

Bernie clenched her teeth together to hold back the laugh. She'd enjoyed the ride enormously.

"And Bernie has to know about you," Cecelia went on, fussing with her seat belt. "If she's going to take care of you while I'm gone."

Mark drew a weary breath and leaned over to release her belt. "It's not her job to take care of me, Mom."

Cecelia rolled her eyes at Bernie, inclining her head at Mark. "To think that I gave birth to such a rock-headed man. We all take care of one another, Marco," she said to him. "That's the way the world works. You used to know that."

Mark ran a hand over his face and replied firmly, "Mom, if you miss your plane, I'm putting you on whatever plane's going far away from here. I don't care if it's a cargo flight to South America."

Cecelia demanded of Bernie, "Do you hear how he talks to me? The woman who carried him for nine months and suffered the agonies of—"

"Mom," Mark reminded firmly, leaning across to push her door open.

She folded her arms and remained seated. "I'm not going anywhere until you promise you're going to eat right and listen to Bernie."

Withholding the promise, Mark leapt out of the van, took her bags out of the back and put them down near the passenger door. When he reached for Cecelia's arm, she slapped his away.

"I promise!" he shouted, frustration and amusement equally loud in his voice.

"And you're going to stay at my place and water my plants and make sure nobody breaks in and steals your grandmother's china."

"I already promised that."

Cecelia smiled and allowed herself to be lifted out of the van to the pavement.

Mark carried her two large bags, and Bernie slung her tote bag over one shoulder and took her arm. Cecelia gave her a broad wink and whispered, "The rest is up to you."

Bernie laughed and squeezed her arm, and hurried her along to keep up with Mark.

When her flight was called, she started to cry and pulled Bernie into a fierce hug. "If I don't come back, remember what I told you."

"Why would you not come back?" Mark asked, pulling her out of Bernie's arms and into his. "After nine days with you, Aunt Theresa will probably put a stamp on your forehead and stuff you in a mailbox."

When Cecelia continued to cry, Mark sobered and hugged her tighter. "You're going to have a wonderful time, Mom. We'll all be fine while you're gone." When she looked up at him in distress, he added quickly, "Not as fine as we'd be if you were here, but we'll get by. And when you come home, I'll throw a party and you can show us your pictures over and over again." He started to lead her toward the gate. Bernie followed. "I'll eat, I promise. We'll empty your freezer."

Mark handed her ticket to the attendant standing at the mouth of the long tubular walkway. The steward returned him the passenger copy, and Bernie smiled when he folded it and with artless tenderness put it in Cecelia's purse.

Cecelia smiled up at him. "If you can make yourself do it, you should say a prayer so your mother doesn't fall out of the sky like a diseased sea gull."

Mark nodded and hugged her again. "I'll do it."

"Me, too," Bernie promised.

"Mrs. Costello?" A tall, dark-haired stewardess bearing a startling resemblance to Cher in conservative clothing gave Cecelia a dazzling smile.

"This is her," Mark said, pointing to his mother. "She's a little nervous. Would you . . . ?"

"I'll take care of her, don't you worry." Putting an arm around Cecelia's shoulders, she led her toward the plane, telling her in detail about the lunch menu. Cecelia turned once to wave, already distracted. Arm in arm, Mark and Bernie watched her round the corner and disappear.

Mark put a hand to his chest and gasped. "Double bourbon, quick. I feel myself slipping."

Bernie yanked on his arm as he turned in the direction of the bar and pulled him toward the window beyond which Cecelia's plane was visible. "Then slip on over here," she said, "and while we're watching her take off, say that prayer you promised. Then you can have the bourbon."

When he opened his mouth to speak, she arched an eyebrow and reminded, "You promised to listen to me, remember?"

"That seemed safe enough," he said. "I can listen to you, and then ignore whatever you say."

She uttered a little laugh and looked out the window. "But I can make your body useless in a second, don't forget."

Mark grabbed her arms and turned her toward him. "Then I'll learn to work with my feet," he said, trying to look tough.

She didn't seem impressed. In fact, she gave him the most dazzling smile. He felt himself go weak. He had to have her, he thought desperately. He had to bind her to him somehow.

"I'll just keep breaking body parts," she said softly, "until I find something that's important enough to you that you'll keep your promise to your mother."

"Ooh," he said, his voice low and deep. "Seductive talk, Sister Flyweight." Her eyes darkened and he corrected himself immediately. "I'm sorry. I mean, 'Seductive talk, Bernadette.' Want to discuss body parts over lunch?"

"WHAT IS THAT?" Bernie pointed to a large disk-like apparatus on a stand. A handle protruded from the middle of it and lay along the radius of the disk. "It looks like something you'd find in a ship's engine room."

Mark looked up from his inspection of adjustable stands. "A dimmer," he replied, "for special-effects lighting." He came up to her to look over her shoulder. "Goes from full intensity to blackout. Want one?" he teased.

She grinned up at him and wandered farther down the aisle. Photographic supply shops were as filled with foreign objects, she thought, as hardware stores.

Bernie slipped down to her knees to inspect an array of carrying cases in all sizes, from very small to large enough to hold the body of a man. "Why don't they put wheels on these?" she asked. "And show a little consideration for the photographer's assistant who acts as freight mule."

Mark knelt beside her. "Are you angling for a raise?"

She kissed him lightly and got to her feet, reaching down to offer him a hand up. "No," she said. "Are we finished here?"

He indicated the bag tucked under his arm. "We're finished." He got to his feet, letting himself wonder about her curious distance for a moment. She wasn't angry or moody, just a little remote. He decided to let it ride for a while and see how the afternoon developed. There was something he wanted to discuss with her. "Why? Is there something you want to shop for?" he asked.

She nodded, smiling. "Makeup. When I started job hunting, I bought some foundation and a lipstick, but there's more to it than that."

He led her toward the door, frowning down at her. "Just don't get carried away."

"Angie and Becky wear a lot of stuff, and they always look wonderful. It's all in knowing how to do it. Let's go."

On the sidewalk, he resisted her tug toward a large department store up the street. "I'll meet you later," he said.

She continued to pull on him. "Oh, come on. How will I know if I find the right things or not, if you aren't there to tell me how they look to a man?"

"I have never been in a cosmetic department," he said, as though that somehow exalted him.

Bernie rolled her eyes. "Afraid of female hormone poisoning? I spent an hour with you in a hardware store before we went to the photo shop, and you don't see me growing a beard or breaking out in testosterone, do you?"

After gaping at her for a minute, he allowed himself to be led down the street. "Sometimes, Bernadette," he said, shaking his head. "You say the damndest things."

Seated beside her on a pink stool at the cosmetics bar, Mark watched the transformation of Bernie Emerson take place. When she'd trustingly placed herself in the hands of a beautiful young woman who appeared to Mark to be overly gilded, he sighed and prepared to endure the process and then criticize.

It wasn't long before he forgot his discomfort at being in a stronghold of femininity and began to enjoy Bernie's reactions. There seemed to be a dozen steps to follow, so many that he lost track. But the cosmetologist explained each step as she performed it.

"A little like sizing a wall before you paper it," Bernie said with a little laugh as the woman worked over her.

"Or a canvas," the cosmetologist replied, looking at her critically before selecting a pot of flesh-colored cream from a rack beside her. "We're not redecorating you, we're turning you into a work of art."

Mark smiled, thinking that somewhere along the line in Bernie's interesting past that had already been done. He watched, warmth spreading in his middle as she worked her mobile little face in response to the woman's instructions. She was angelically still while the woman applied something she called a contour color. Mark could only see Bernie's profile, but he watched the procedure with skepticism. The color was muddy and he worried about it.

Bernie closed her eyes, then widened them while the woman applied stuff from a little pot of color, something else with a minute brush, then something on her lashes. Bernie parted her lips and tilted her head back as the woman painted them. That pose required Mark to swallow and get a grip on the counter.

The woman continued to fuss with her for several moments, then stepped back to admire her "canvas." She took a comb and began to work on Bernie's hair, fluffing it until her short do laced against her cheek in a soft wave.

Bernie stared at herself in a mirror the woman handed her. She looked closer, then held the mirror away, turning her head this way and that. Then she turned to Mark. "What do you think?" she asked.

He couldn't speak. He'd thought her pretty before. She had an inherent sweetness that showed, and natural good looks he'd been sure didn't need the enhancement of cosmetics. But now she was beautiful. A soft green on her eyelids and the artfully subtle darkening around her eyes seemed to make them leap at him, caress him, overpower him. Her cheeks were softened with an apricot pink and her lips shone very faintly with a darker shade of the same color. They looked moist and soft and agonizingly inviting as she parted them, waiting for an answer. She frowned suddenly and looked back at the mirror. "You don't like it."

"I do," he said quickly. When she turned back to him, he shook his head, still stunned. "You take my breath away."

Bernie smiled at the cosmetologist. "Got any oxygen back there?" Then laughing at her own joke, she asked the price of the entire beauty program. The woman told her.

Mark caught her before she fell backward off the stool. "Wrap it up," Mark said, then put Bernie on her feet, steadying her. He passed the woman a credit card.

"Mark, I haven't spent that much for clothes!" she whispered urgently. "And I can't afford . . ."

"It's a gift from me."

"No," she said softly, firmly. "You've already . . ."

"Bernie . . ."

"Mark . . ."

He looked down at her grimly. "Do you want to spend another hour in the hardware store?"

She smiled faintly. "I'd rather have my fingernails ripped out."

"Then shut up."

BERNIE LOOKED AROUND in wonder at the interior of the restaurant, which had been styled after an English manor house. Genuine dark wood paneling covered the walls, and oak tables and chairs graced a room warmed by the fire in an enormous stone fireplace. Over the mantel were antique rifles, and harness brasses decorated the walls. White lace tablecloths and elegant crystal softened the atmosphere of old-world country comfort.

Bernie looked away from the fire to find a young man at a table occupied by four businessmen, staring at her. The message in his eyes did not require experience to read. She lowered her eyes quickly, feeling color brim in her cheeks.

Noting her embarrassment, Mark looked over his shoulder to see what had caused it, and noticed the Wall Street type across the room staring at Bernie. Mark gave him a look that had once made an East German border guard hesitate in shooting him long enough for his journalist companion to deck the guard with a tape recorder. The young man held his eyes for one stubborn moment, then looked down at his plate of pasta.

Mark turned back to Bernie, the primitive territorial burning in his chest startling him. "Pretty girls learn early that flirting can get them in trouble," he said, sipping at a glass of chardonnay.

Detecting the subtle note of censure, Bernie replied lightly. "He's not very big. One chop and he'd be out for an hour."

"Flirting can get you in trouble," Mark enunciated quietly, "with the man who brought you."

She raised an eyebrow, curiously pleased and a little excited by his attitude. "I wasn't flirting," she said, then flipped an exaggeratedly casual hand at her hair. "I can't help it if I've shed my cocoon, burst into bloom, turned from an ugly duckling into..."

"A goony bird?" he teased.

She sighed. "I thought you liked my new look?"

"I do like it," he said, fighting off a growing feeling of ill temper. "Just be careful how you use it. The world is full of men who wouldn't be sensitive to your innocence as I am."

She sighed as though she found him tiresome. A little possessiveness was exciting, but too much when he made no promises was irritating. "I'm celibate, I'm not innocent. I've seen too much to be innocent. And who made you my keeper?"

"We're all responsible for one another, remember? Cecelia Costello, 1990."

"She meant people should care about one another, not criticize."

"You're new to the outside world, Emerson. I'm just trying to tell you how it is."

Not certain how the day had turned from fun to filled with friction, Bernie directed her attention to the cobb salad the waitress brought and ignored Mark until she was finished. She picked up her purse. "Permission to go to the ladies' room?" she asked.

With a sigh of impatience, he pushed away a half-eaten ham and Swiss on rye. The waitress bearing a calorically opulent dessert tray prevented his reply.

"That one, please." Bernie pointed to a wedge of chocolate cake with a cluster of macadamia nuts on top if it, then went off in search of the rest room.

When she returned, the dessert and a fresh cup of coffee waited at her place. Mark, sipping coffee, had apparently chosen to abstain.

Bernie savored the first bite noisily. "Mmm. You should have ordered some, Mark. You seem to be suffering from a sugar low this afternoon." She looked up at him, her expression softening a little. "Do you want to tell me what's wrong, or are we going to drive a hundred miles home snarling at each other?"

"Do you want to move in with me?" he asked abruptly.

Bernie put her fork down and stared at him. She was stunned, though she thought she understood what drove him. Falling in love again was frightening, but living together and promising nothing was safer than taking vows before God. He wanted to pin her down without committing to anything.

Yes, she thought. *I would love to be with you all the time. I'd love to have every meal with you, to learn all my body's mysteries with you, to fall asleep with you and wake up with you—and have babies with you.*

"No," she said quietly. "Did you think I would?"

He had no idea what made him ask that. He knew her better than that. Unless it was that he couldn't promise her forever because he didn't think they had it, yet he didn't want to lose her to someone else. Still, he'd asked and he was now required to defend his position.

He almost smiled. "No. I think you want to, but I knew you wouldn't."

Bernie had to think about that a minute before deciding he was right. "This is your idea of sensitivity to my innocence?" she asked. She was becoming annoyed. Not outraged at his suggestion but simply, deeply annoyed that he hadn't gone about it differently.

Leaning back in his chair, he regarded her with vague frustration, and tossed her words back at her. "I thought you were celibate, not innocent."

"I'm leaving, is what I am." She wrapped her cake in her napkin and stood. "If you want a ride to Seaside, you'd better pay the bill and hustle."

He didn't budge. "I have the keys," he said.

She shouldered her purse and looked down at him dryly. "You want to know how many dilapidated convent junkers I've hot-wired in my time?"

When Mark wandered out to the parking lot with deliberately lazy steps, the van was still parked where he had left it, but Bernie was sitting behind the wheel. He got in the passenger seat and handed her the key. "You know how to get onto the freeway?" he asked. When she turned to glare at him, he raised both hands and said, "I know. Don't tell me. You were probably the Sisters of Peace entry at Le Mans."

She didn't bother to reply, but peeled out of the parking lot with a screech of tires and a small whirlwind of litter. She found the freeway after going the wrong way on a one-way street and turning around through a gas station. As she joined the thick fast-moving traffic, Mark thought his mother would have been pleased; he was praying.

He said nothing while she maneuvered through the Portland traffic, except to direct her into the appropriate lane at the interchange. Once she settled down, she drove with considerable skill and a calmly defensive technique that spoke of refined freeway-fighting experience.

When they were finally off the freeway and on the straight stretch of road that would take them over the Coast Range and home, Mark made a point of relaxing in his seat. "Many couples live together today without benefit of marriage," he said. "If you want to fit in, you shouldn't betray such shock."

Bernie knew what he was doing, but she was down to a simmer now and better able to cope. "It wasn't shock," she replied calmly. "It was annoyance."

"Why?"

She gave him a quick, mild glance. "No woman wants half a proposal, Mark. Even a lonely ex-nun."

He gasped, clearly affronted, and turned to look at her. "It wasn't a proposal at all," he said. "It was an offer to share space, to combine . . ."

When he hesitated, she asked lightly, "Bodies?"

That sound again. "Will you stop finishing my sentences?"

"If you'd learn to finish them yourself."

"To combine emotional resources," he said, his voice a trace louder, "so that we can finally find ourselves in a world in which neither one of us really fits."

She rolled her eyes and smiled at the road. "You sound like a yuppie with a Ph.D. in motivational sex."

Mark leaned his head against the rest with a groan and put a hand over his eyes. "I give up. Forget it." He felt the car slow down and turn. When he opened his eyes again, he found that they were in the parking lot of a Dairy Queen. She unbuckled her belt and turned to him, her eyes calm. He could have throttled her for that.

"I resent," she said quietly, "that you made a physical offer, when what you feel for me is so much more than that."

He tossed his belt aside and turned to challenge her. "How do you know my intentions were simply physical?"

She didn't bat an eye. "Do couples live together in separate beds?"

"We have a good time together," he said, struggling not to get angry. "We talk about everything, we laugh. We enjoy a lot of the same things. We're good for each other."

"We do all those things now," she pointed out reasonably. "We spend ten hours together at the office."

He looked into her eyes. Silence fell. "I want more," he admitted quietly.

Bernie felt herself melting inside, but that wouldn't be good for either of them. "Of what?" she asked.

"Of you," he said.

It was getting harder to hold on. "You want to know me, the person, better. Or you want to . . . ?"

"Yes, I want to make love to you." He said it swiftly, flatly, honestly. "I'm sure even a celibate woman can find that easy enough to understand. What you might not realize is that men and women find out a lot about each other that isn't physical while making love."

He was beginning to disarm her. But this was how it worked, she knew. She'd counseled enough women in her time.

"Did you live with Kathy?" she asked gently.

He was momentarily taken aback by the question. She'd been a model, and he'd been on assignment in Paris. Then, after knowing her two days during which they'd talked nonstop, he'd been sent to Moscow. They'd connected again in Paris for one brief afternoon in a sidewalk café. He'd been sent away again, consumed with thoughts of her. He remembered clearly that every thought had involved permanence. "No," he said quietly.

Mark saw Bernie's eyes darken and the softness of her face stiffen. "Then I'm less to you than Kathy was."

Anger, frustration, irritation with her, with himself, danced over him with cleated shoes. "What the hell kind of a question is that?"

She leaned back against the door, looking more vulnerable than he'd ever seen her. "A painful one, I know. But I had to ask it. I don't want to be someone you settle for until you get over Kathy and Christian. I want to be someone you're committed to and with whom you're prepared to start over."

Mark felt as though she had exposed his soul and poked it with a pointed stick. The need to retaliate was overwhelming. "You mean you expected me to propose marriage." He knew that would embarrass her, suggest she was too naive for the workings of today's world.

She looked him in the eye, her gaze filled with understanding and a trace of disappointment. "I didn't expect you to propose anything. I know you're not ready."

"Really?" He didn't understand why her compassion deepened his anger, but it did. So he went with it. "It's not a matter of being 'ready,' as though I'm on some road to recovery. I don't ever want again what I had with Kathy and Christian. That part of me was stripped away." He held her quiet, patient gaze so that she would know how serious he was. "What's left is a man who'd be grateful for a good day's work, and a female friend he could take to bed. Life doesn't let you keep anything else."

Bernie shook her head, asking softly, "Do you think that would prevent you from grieving for me if I died?"

"It would prevent me from being torn apart," he replied calmly. "From falling into a pit so dark and horrible there's no way out. I don't think I deserved that."

"You had a wife and child who, though you lost them horribly and suffered great pain, probably gave you more happiness in your short time together than many people see in a lifetime." He was looking away from her now. He was either lost for a rebuttal or he had tuned her out, she wasn't sure which.

Bernie sighed, seeing everything between them that had lit her lonely life begin to dim. "Mark, if you can't see that every contact between you and people who are kind to you and care for you is a wonderful gift from the hand of God, Himself, you'll have to hire someone for your bed. No woman, even one who isn't looking for permanence, will come to a man that distanced from the nature of things."

He didn't understand what she was saying, and he didn't want to. He said simply, "I think I've earned the right to live my life my way."

"I'm sure you have." She nodded sadly. "But what I want is very different. There's no way we could live it together."

He was convinced she was being naive and sanctimonious, yet he felt destroyed by her rejection. He shrugged and smiled to cover the hurt. "Then that answers my question. If you'd done that in the first place, we'd have saved fifteen minutes of argument."

Bernie recognized the pain in his eyes. It echoed precisely what throbbed in her chest. "I'm learning all the time," she said, then opened her door. "You can drive the rest of the way. The sun's in my eyes."

That was as good an excuse as any, Bernie thought, to keep them closed the rest of the way home. They did ache and burn, but it had more to do with the emotion she held back than with the lowering sun.

Mark drove the beautiful, treacherous road with a lack of concentration he'd find frightening later when he thought about it. His mind was too full of Bernie to admit anything else for consideration. How dare she ask him about Kathy? How dare she fling her lofty ideals at him when he'd once done everything right—and been kicked in the teeth anyway? How dare she make him feel small about offering to share his physical life with her? His stance made perfect sense to him; he just didn't understand why he wasn't more satisfied with it. Why he didn't feel righteous, rather than pitiful. Why a glance at her still and remote profile made him feel as though he'd just struck an angel with a club.

It was dusk when Mark dropped Bernie off at her apartment. She thanked him politely for lunch and for the large bag of skin-care products and makeup, and told him with forced cheer that she'd see him in the morning.

He was still angry, but he couldn't part company with her like this. The warmth of their friendship and the hesitant spark of their comfortable romance had been more important to him than he'd realized. The last hour and a half, with her sitting silently beside him, completely removed from him emotionally, had first annoyed him, then worried him, and now made him feel as though he'd lost something vital to his person.

"Get some rest," he said gruffly. "Next week's going to be rough. We've got two days of processing, one more day with the kids, and a meeting on Friday with Mr. Phillips from First Coastal Bank."

She nodded, unsatisfyingly docile. "I'll be ready. See you."

Mark watched her walk safely into her apartment, then drove toward the studio. He'd only been honest with her, he told himself. So things hadn't come out the way he'd have preferred. That was a chance you took when you reached out to someone—even with only half a proposal. He'd live.

He parked the van on the side street near the studio and sat for a moment, letting himself hurt. The pain was vague—like an emptiness. And he had to acknowledge that he knew precisely what was missing.

He'd been honest with Bernie, he thought wryly as he got out of the van and locked it. But he had to wonder if he was being honest with himself.

Chapter Twelve

"Guess who held me in his arms?" Cecelia demanded, shouting over the perfect cross-country telephone connection.

Mark, sprawled in the wicker love seat in the studio, swung his legs up to rest them on the arm and let his head fall back on the pillows at the other end. He had to scoot forward until his knees hung over to have enough room. "I give up," he replied. "Who?"

"King Kong!" she said with a girlish laugh. "Do you believe it? They have a man dressed like him at the top of the Empire State Building."

"You bringing him home to meet the family?"

"We already have one oversized bad-tempered monkey. We don't need another one."

"Nice words, Mom. Tony thinks you love him. How's Aunt Theresa?"

"The same. Grumpy, opinionated, cheats at canasta. But I'm having a wonderful time. She went next door to return the chairs she borrowed. She's had friends over to meet me every night this week."

Mark smiled, thinking she sounded happy. "I'm glad you're having fun."

There was a long silence. "You and Bernie engaged yet?" Cecelia asked.

Mark closed his eyes but kept his voice light. "Don't I have any peace, even when you're three thousand miles away?"

"You won't have peace," she said, "when I'm in my grave. How is she?"

"You want to talk to her?"

"Yes, but first I want to know how *you* think she is."

"She's beautiful," he said sincerely. To himself, he added, *And cheerful and helpful and increasingly desirable, and she treats me like a friend. I'm going quietly mad, but she's beautiful.*

"So, what more do you want in a woman?" Cecelia asked. She made a sound of impatience. "Put her on, please."

Mark sat up, rested the receiver on the cushion and went to the door. Bernie, sitting at her desk and checking a carton of supplies against its invoice, looked up at him. She'd been wearing her new makeup all week, and she'd had her hair styled at a beauty parlor during her lunch hour. Now it feathered around her face, made her eyes appear even wider and the shape of her face more delicate. She had on khaki pants today, and a green-and-khaki blouse tucked into them that made her curves obvious and appealing. He was going to die of wanting her.

"My mother's on the phone," he said. "She wants to say hello to you."

For just an instant she looked disappointed, then she smiled and said cheerfully. "Great! Thanks."

He went into the darkroom to process film. In his current mood, it was a good place for him.

"WHAT'RE YOU GOING TO DO with the kids all weekend?" Mark asked, holding Bernie's coat open for her.

"Tonight we'll watch television, tomorrow we'll spend shopping, then picnic on the beach..."

"What if it rains?"

She headed for the door. "Then we'll come and take shelter in your studio."

He followed her. "I'm living at my mother's until she comes back, remember?"

She smiled at him. He drank it in. He felt starved for their old rapport. "You gave me a key, remember?" she said.

He leaned against the door frame as she stepped out onto the porch. A cold wind blew and she turned her collar up.

"So it's only shelter and not me you'd come in search of?" he asked.

She shouldered her purse and gave him a dry grin. "As though you'd want to spend a weekend with two kids and a woman who won't put out."

The next two and a half days without her spread out before him, dreary and threatening, like the sky.

"Don't be nasty," he admonished quietly. "Might rain. I'd better drive you," he said, patting his pants pockets for keys.

"No," she said firmly. "It's only four blocks to the school, then Sister Camille is going to drive me and the kids home. We'll be fine. You know," she said, her expression softening but confused as she smiled at him, "for someone who doesn't want to commit to a relationship, you certainly are protective."

He couldn't prevent the trace of a smile. "I would commit to a relationship, just not the same one you want."

She studied him one long moment, and when he would have expected angry words or at least a mild condemnation, she simply smiled. "No, thanks," she said. "I love you too much to do that to us." She ran down the steps, turning at the bottom to wave before heading down the Prom to her weekend with the Flynn children.

Mark shook his head at her, leaning sideways out the door to keep her in sight until she disappeared up Broadway. She loved him too much to give him what he wanted? He was going to have to think about that one. And she was going to have to develop a little armor if she was going to make it in the world, he thought, closing the door and heading toward the darkroom. He stopped in the middle of the studio as it occurred to him that she seemed fine. He was the one who'd been upset by their disagreement—and he was the one with the armor.

He slammed the darkroom door behind him. The whole world was going to hell. He just didn't understand it anymore.

Bernie knew something was wrong the moment she approached the playground. Laurie ran to her, jumping up and down with excitement. She held up a child's overnight bag with a picture of Barbie on it. "I've got new socks and perfume and..."

As Laurie carried on, Bernie looked around for Buster. She finally spotted him at the top of the monkey bars, staring forlornly into space. She smiled at Laurie and admired her bag and all its contents.

"What's the matter with Buster?" she asked, drawing her toward her brother.

"He doesn't like Sam," Laurie replied.

"Who's Sam?"

"A friend of Mom's. They're gonna get married."

"Ah."

Bernie guessed that Buster, who couldn't let go of his father, was faced with a possible replacement and he didn't like it.

"Do you like Sam?" Bernie asked.

"Sure," Laurie replied. "He's very nice. He took us for Happy Meals. Buster wouldn't eat his, and he broke the toy in it."

"Well." Bernie approached the monkey bars, reminded that her life wasn't the only one that had grown complicated. She leaned back to look up at the top bar. "Hi, Buss," she called. "You ready to go?"

With a heavy sigh, the boy swung his way down in a complicated method of cross swings, twists, stopping once to hang by one knee, twist and slide down a perpendicular bar. Bernie didn't draw a breath until he landed at her feet in a spray of sawdust.

"Did you bring a bag?" she asked.

Buster snatched a Teenage Mutant Ninja Turtles backpack propped against the bottom of the monkey bars and shouldered it.

Sister Camille, in her late sixties, drove twenty-five miles an hour in the ancient station wagon that belonged to the local convent. Laurie sat in the front seat, talking her ear off, while Bernie and Buster occupied the back in silence. All Bernie's efforts at conversation were met with nods, shakes of Buster's head or—when she asked about Sam—a stiffening of his bottom lip that she was sure was meant to prevent its trembling. She dropped the subject.

Sister Camille left them in the apartment parking lot, wished them a happy weekend and drove away at a snail's pace, other cars braking and swerving to miss her as she started happily home.

Laurie ran toward the stairs. Bernie had to tow Buster along behind her. "We'll have macaroni-and-cheese for dinner," she promised, "and we'll make popcorn and maybe even caramel corn, if I've got the stuff. Then we'll watch all kinds of great shows on TV until we can't stay awake any longer."

She fitted her key in the lock while Laurie waited patiently, then pushed the door open.

Laurie's scream was immediate. Bernie's froze in her throat as she looked down in disbelief at the water cascading over her shoes, then running off the edge of the gallery.

It was coming from the river of water standing in her apartment.

For a moment, she could only stare at it. She had a vague memory of Mark telling her when he'd fixed her stopped-up sink that the flow "felt funny" and suggesting she ask the landlord to have a plumber look at it. She'd never gotten around to it.

She began to realize that whatever the problem was and however it had happened, her apartment was uninhabitable and she was responsible for the care of two small children for the weekend.

She took each child by a hand and took off down the stairs to knock on the manager's apartment. He did not take the news well. His brother-in-law, a plumber, arrived in ten minutes. He waded into her apartment in hip boots then returned to the gallery to announce, "Pipe's busted in the kitchen. I can get right at it, but I have to go into the wall. And it's going to take a week to dry this place out."

The apartment manager stood under the gallery, separated from Bernie by the waterfall, and glared at her as though she was personally and deliberately responsible.

She walked the children to the public telephone in front of the convenience store across the street. She dialed Mark. She was about to give up on the fifth ring when he answered.

"Mark!" She heard the desperation in her voice and tried to calm down. "Mark," she said more calmly. "My apartment's flooded. The water pipe broke in my kitchen. Do you think...? I mean, since you're staying at your Mom's, do you think the kids and I could stay at your place for the weekend?"

"Where are you?" he asked.

"In front of the little store across from my apartment. But I'm going back to see if I can wade in for a change of clothes."

"I'll be right there."

It was only after Bernie cradled the receiver that she realized he hadn't answered her question.

MARK HAD SELDOM SEEN Bernie upset, but as he pulled up in front of her apartment building he could tell by the line of her shoulders that she was rattled now. No wonder, he thought, watching water trickle over the gallery. She had very little to her name, and right now most of it was under water.

The children ran to him as he crossed the parking lot toward her. Laurie took his hand and Buster began to climb his leg. In self-defense, Mark pulled him onto his hip.

"There's a flood in Bernie's apartment!" Laurie exclaimed with more excitement than distress. "Now we don't have any place to stay."

Bernie turned as he approached, momentarily startled by the sight of Mark with the children hanging on him. "Hi," she said. "Thanks for coming."

He gave her a look that told her she should be ashamed for ever considering he wouldn't.

"Would you stay with the kids," she asked, "so I can run in and get a change of clothes?"

He glanced at Buster who had a death grip on his neck, then at Laurie who now held his hand in her two while she jumped up and down. He'd stopped fighting their unconditional friendship. He turned to Bernie with a bland smile. "Do you think I could get away without doing myself severe bodily harm?"

She smiled reluctantly. "Probably not." She started for the stairs, then turned back to him, blinking against the lowering sun. "Is it okay that we use your place?"

He didn't hesitate. "No," he said.

She stared at him for a moment, uncertain precisely what he meant. It didn't seem likely he'd rush to their rescue only to let them sleep on the beach. But he didn't owe her anything, and seemed to be trying desperately to keep things that way.

Then he smiled at her with warm amusement. "We're all going back to Mom's." When she opened her mouth, he added, "We can argue the fine points later. Get your things so we can make the kids comfortable."

That was the priority, she told herself, as she climbed the stairs, stopped to pull her sneakers and socks off and pull her pant legs up as far as the narrow cut would allow.

The water was cold and rusty, and the carpet felt like sponge as she walked through the living room to the bedroom. She tossed her sweatpants, a sweater and a skirt and blouse over her arm, then went to the dresser for underwear. She retrieved her makeup bag from the bathroom and had to slide by two workmen with a giant drum-like vacuum cleaner who were attacking the water. She picked up her shoes and socks from the arm of the sofa where she'd left them, then hurried down to Mark and the children.

"Stop," he said as she stood on the last step in her bare feet. He put Buster down and handed him the makeup bag, then lay the clothes over Laurie's extended arms. He put his shoulder to Bernie's waist, locked an arm across her legs and carried her across the graveled lot to the van. The children trailed behind them, giggling.

"There are so many experiences one misses in the convent," Bernie said as her chest bumped against his back and she watched the movement of his tight hips with fascinated admiration.

Mark pulled open the passenger side door. "Happy to broaden your horizons. Watch your head."

Everyone settled, Mark put the key in the ignition. "Pizza or burgers?"

The vote for pizza was unanimous. Mark headed off in that direction. "But don't tell my mother," he warned Bernie. "She's horrified by the thought of anyone *buying* pizza."

Bernie glanced at him worriedly. "How's she going to feel about three strangers living in her home?"

He frowned at her. "You're not a stranger. And she's crazy about anybody's children."

When Bernie did not seem appeased, he turned to the subject he knew was the real cause of concern. "Look, my place has only one bed and lots of marinara sauce and beer and not much else. Mom's got more food than Safeway, and a yard full of playground equipment for the grandkids. You'll all be much more comfortable there." She sighed. "There are four bedrooms there, Bernadette. Four." He held up four fingers. "Count them. One for each of us."

She sighed again and pursed her lips at him. "I wasn't worried about that."

"Then what are you worried about?"

She tried to analyze that and wasn't sure. Herself, perhaps?

"I guess I'd feel better about it," she said finally, "if you'd call your mother and make sure she doesn't mind."

"All right," he agreed. "But by the time we get home it'll be about eleven, New York time. A call at that hour will probably scare her to death."

"In the morning, then," Bernie conceded.

Mark nodded. "In the morning."

They stopped at the video store after dinner and picked up cartoons and several Disney movies for the children. He grinned at Bernie. "Mom's got lots of tapes, but most of them are forties musicals or family stuff that would bore you to tears. You want *Going My Way,* or something?"

She peered at the shelves. "I love pirate movies."

"Pirate movies, huh?" He pulled her into the next alcove. "There you go. Being carried over my shoulder give you a taste for that?"

She looked at him in surprise for a moment, then elbowed him in the ribs with a little laugh. Then she made a dash for Buster, who was trying to climb a shelf.

With the children settled on the floor in front of the television with a bowl of popcorn and *Jungle Book* in the VCR, Bernie hung the few things she'd brought in the empty closet in what had been Mark's room.

The room was blue-and-white and held a beautifully kept old maple dresser that matched a maple bed. A trunk with a needlepoint seat stitched in a federal eagle design stood at the foot. The view out the window was of a tree-shaded yard filled with playground equipment. This was the perfect family house, Bernie thought. The perfect grandmother's house.

She went into the room across the hall, which had been Angie's, and found the children's bags on the bunk beds. Though there was room for each child to have a room, she'd thought it best for them to be together in a strange house.

She folded their small things in the white provincial dresser and closed the lavender-and-white curtains.

She found Mark in the kitchen making espresso.

"Cream?" he asked without turning.

"Please," she replied.

"Feeling better?"

She raised an eyebrow at his back. "Was I feeling bad?"

"I don't know." He poured the cream in and waited while the machine noisily frothed it. "You've been avoiding me since we got home."

He turned to hand her a delicate white demitasse, his eyes and his tone chiding. "Would I try to take advantage of a woman who can throw me through the window?"

She accepted the cup and made herself look into his eyes. "I told you I wasn't worried about that."

"You lied."

"Okay." She held the cup with its fragrant brew and looked at him evenly. "We've discussed cohabitation and ended up snarling at each other. I don't want that to happen."

He picked up his cup. "Then loosen up and do it my way," he taunted.

She sighed impatiently and opened her mouth to rebuke him when he laughed softly. "I'm sorry," he said. "I guess that wasn't funny. You just looked so worried I couldn't help myself. Relax, will you?"

Buster burst through the kitchen door at a run, grabbed Mark's hand and pulled him toward the living room. "You've gotta come. Ka scares me."

"But..." Mark dropped his cup on the counter just before he was tugged beyond it.

Buster, feeling the need for adult reassurance, wasn't interested in excuses. He pulled mightily. "Mowgli's in trouble. Hurry!"

"To Be Continued," Mark called to Bernie just before he disappeared through the door.

Bernie found a plate of Italian cookies and the small tray Mark was presumably going to use to carry their cups and the plate into the living room. She piled their things onto it and hipped her way through the door.

On the television screen, Ka, the snake, was slithering down the tree, venomous tongue flicking the air threateningly as he silkily pleaded, "Trusssst in me."

In a corner of the sofa, Mark sat with Buster in his lap and Laurie as close to him as she could get. He seemed reasonably relaxed, she thought, as she put the tray down on the coffee table. The Kids' Kingdom shoot had gone a long way toward helping him get over his unwillingness to have children around. And he was developing a special fondness for these two, she knew. Buster, in particular.

"Ka's not going to win," Mark assured him. "Mean people—and snakes—always lose in the end. Good people win."

Bernie turned to him, eyebrow raised in surprise. His eyes widened just enough to tell her to keep her teasing remarks to herself. He was just trying to get the children through the scary part of the story.

The second time through was a sedative. Bernie led a sleepy Laurie up the stairs while Mark carried Buster.

Laurie awoke enough to giggle as she climbed the ladder into the upper bunk, a new experience for her. Mark raised the side and she snuggled into her pillow.

He leaned into the bottom bunk, some paternal instinct he'd thought long since dead rising in him to make him pull up blankets, tuck the sides in, stroke Buster's hair back as he stirred.

It wasn't until habit overrode memory and his mind superimposed an image of Christian's face over Buster's that he drew his hand back and left the room.

Bernie watched him go with a sinking feeling of familiarity. Maybe he was a one-woman man, a once and forever father. She felt guilty about having put him in this position. She'd grown comfortable with his friendship, but she shouldn't have abused it.

She found him warming his espresso in the microwave. With the children in his lap, he hadn't had a hand with which to drink it all evening.

"I'm sorry we've upset your weekend," she said.

He glanced at her over his shoulder. His eyes were dark and pained. "Don't be silly."

"I'm not," she denied. "I needed help and you were the first person I thought of, but I shouldn't have done that. I've come to depend on you and that isn't fair."

"Why not?"

"Because you don't want the responsibility. I—"

He turned on her, demanding, "How do you know what I want?"

"Well don't get mad at me!" she shouted, a calm corner of her mind thinking that a moment ago she'd accepted blame and now she was trying to push it off on him. "I only asked to stay at your place over the studio. You're the one who insisted we come here."

"Maybe I'm mad at myself!" he shouted back. "I wanted you around, all right? I didn't want to spend two days without you."

Bernie stared at him a moment, surprised by his honesty, then she covered the few steps between them and put her arms around him. She felt his close over her and hold her. Curiously, his embrace contained more anger than tenderness, but she understood that. She was angry with herself, too, and she didn't know why, either.

She drew away, smiling up at him. "I'm going to bed. The kids will probably be up early, but don't worry about anything. I'll fix breakfast and keep them out of your hair." She kissed him quickly on the cheek. "Good night."

She was gone before he could respond.

Chapter Thirteen

Mark was awake at the first small sound. It was a whimper, then a cry of uncertainty. He was at Angie's old bedroom door when the wail began in earnest. Bernie was already kneeling beside the bottom bunk, trying to pull Buster into her arms.

"I want my dad," Buster wept pathetically, pushing Bernie's hands away. "I want my dad!"

Mark grasped Bernie's elbow, pulled her to her feet and reached into the bunk for Buster. The child hugged him tightly. He was crying lustily, but the screaming had stopped. Laurie didn't even stir.

Bernie followed Mark into the hallway.

"I've got him," Mark said. "Go back to bed."

"Are you sure?" she asked doubtfully.

"I'm sure. Go to bed."

Because he was wearing only white briefs that she could see very clearly in the shadows, she complied.

Mark took Buster into his room and sat in the chair by the window. The boy's weeping quieted, but he called for his father again.

"Your dad's gone, Buster," Mark said gently, rubbing his back. "He can't come back."

"But I want him."

"I know."

"I miss him."

"I know," Mark said again, holding him close, understanding his pain. He imagined nothing was more difficult to accept than that a loved one was there one moment and lost forever the next. He couldn't even imagine a child being able to grasp it.

Across the hall, Bernie heard Mark's gentle murmurs of comfort. There were probably few people better qualified to empathize with Buster than Mark, she thought. He missed his family with the same intensity Buster missed his father. And she couldn't help but make the correlation between Buster's resistance to his mother's boyfriend, and the distance Mark tried to keep between her and himself. She closed her eyes and prayed that man and boy would help each other.

MARK AWOKE TO THE SMELL of charcoal. He propped himself up on his elbows and tried to make sense of that. He realized as he caught another fresh whiff that something was burning in the kitchen.

The kids! he thought, flying out of bed and into a pair of gray sweatpants. Maybe after being awakened in the night, Bernie had slept longer than she'd expected.

He stopped his headlong flight down the stairs when he saw both children lying on the floor on a plastic tablecloth eating pancakes and watching cartoons.

"Hi," they said without turning away from the screen.

"Hi," he replied.

He went into the kitchen to find it filled with smoke, the back door open and letting in the chill air of a rainy morning. Bernie stood over the stove, wielding a spatula while humming to herself and reading from a cookbook. Occasionally she swatted the smoke toward the open door. On a plate beside her on the counter were four hard black disks.

The woman who lived on frozen yogurt and fast food was preparing breakfast.

He wanted to laugh and he wanted to kiss her. His equanimity was restored this morning. He'd held Buster most of the night. He was coming along; he really was.

He picked up a black disk and pretended to examine it. "You're making brake pads," he said. "How thoughtful."

She gave him a reproachful look, barely concealing a smile. "Do you want breakfast or not?"

He looked for evidence of something besides the black disks. "Are they it?" he asked cautiously.

She sighed tolerantly. "There's a good batch warming in the oven. Don't you know anything about cooking? You burn the first batch to season the pan."

He folded his arms. "I've never heard that one."

Bernie let her eyes raise as high as his tight rounded biceps and taut pectorals. She'd planned to just allow herself a quick glance, but his chest was so formidable it was a moment before she could look away. And then she looked at the laughter in his eyes.

She laughed with him. "I thought it sounded pretty convincing."

The timer went off and she turned her attention to the pancakes, flipping them onto a plate. She dropped two irregular circles of batter onto the griddle and turned the timer on again.

"What are you timing?" Mark asked, leaning over her shoulder.

"The pancakes. Two minutes on each side," she said, pointing to the cookbook with her free hand. "See, it says right here."

He closed the book and pushed it aside. "You just watch for the bubbles," he said.

"What bubbles?"

"Those," he said, pointing to the small bubbles that rimmed the pancake batter. "When they pop, it means it's time to turn them."

She tried to hand him the spatula. "Then maybe you should finish breakfast and I'll take a bath."

He took a step back. "No. I kind of like you cooking for me. I'll set the table." He went to the cupboard for plates and cups.

"Chauvinist," she accused with a grin. Then she sobered and said quietly, "Thank you for getting up with Buster during the night."

"No problem," he said, though he had stared at the ceiling most of the night. "He cried for a little while, then went back to sleep."

Bernie slipped an oven mitt on her hand, took the platter from the oven and put it in the middle of the table while Mark poured juice. "If you had plans for today," she said, "don't feel you have to entertain us."

He pointed her to a chair. "Will you please stop trying to exclude me from this weekend? I invited you here because I wanted to. Stop worrying about what it's doing to my psyche and just relax."

She sat across from him and smiled sweetly. "All right, but don't blame me if all this domesticity gives you a taste for home and family you can't resist. If you end up on one knee by my chair, pleading with me to marry you, I don't want you groaning later that I in any way maneuvered you into it."

"A *Jungle Book* double feature, a sleepless night and brake pads for breakfast?" He smiled back. "Don't pick out the china yet."

Bernie tried not to betray disappointment. She'd been teasing and he'd replied in kind. But this was it, she thought with a pang in her chest. *This is what I want. A husband* helping me in the kitchen, children laughing in the other room, dogs asleep under the table.

Oh, Mark! she cried silently. *Can't you see it? Can't you feel it?*

The kitchen door burst open and Buster appeared carrying his plate, messy with syrup but otherwise empty. "More pancakes?" he asked hopefully.

Bernie started to push away from the table, but Mark gestured her back in her chair. He transferred the contents of his plate onto the boy's and received a distracted "thank you" as Buster raced back to the cartoons.

He poured more batter on the griddle.

"Just watch for the little bubbles," Bernie teased from the table.

He looked at her over his shoulder, his dark eyes amused. Then, as they settled on her, something subtle changed in them—softened and warmed. *He sees it,* she thought, hope fluttering inside her. *He feels it.*

He smiled and threatened her with the spatula. "Be quiet and eat."

THEY SPENT THE MORNING in downtown Seaside wandering from one arcade to another while the children tried all the games, thanks to Mark's endless supply of change. They bought Gummi Worms at Columbia Chocolates, rode the carousel at Heritage Square and stopped at the bakery to buy day old bread to feed the ducks and sea gulls off the Neccanicum River bridge.

They voted on corn dogs on a stick for lunch.

Mark fell into step between the children as Bernie stopped to look in the window of a gift shop.

"Keep moving," Mark encouraged them surreptitiously. "Maybe she won't make us go in and shop."

Buster looked up at him with an expression that spoke of male understanding. "Why do ladies like to look at all that stuff anyway?"

"I don't know, Buster," Mark admitted. "But all ladies are the same. And most men hate it."

"Our mom never gets to go shopping," Laurie said, hooking her hand over the one he rested in his pocket. With the other she waved her corn dog expressively. "She has to work all the time. But Sam says she can stop if they get married."

"I don't like Sam," Buster said.

"But he likes Mom, and they're gonna get married and have babies." She smiled up at Mark with a grin of delight. "I'd like to have a new little brother." She leaned around Mark to stick her tongue out at Buster. "A *nice* one."

"Hey! Hey!" Mark pulled them apart when Buster squirted his packet of mustard at Laurie. Fortunately he missed.

While Mark applauded Laurie's adaptability, he sympathized with Buster's sense of alienation.

"Maybe when you get to know him better," Mark suggested to the boy, "you'll like him after all."

"He yelled at me," Buster complained.

"Cause you yelled at Mom," Laurie squealed.

"Ah, well," Mark said, "that's never a good move. Moms should never be yelled at. They work very hard and you're supposed to do what they tell you."

Will you listen to me? Mark thought, wondering what was happening to him. *Mr. Psychologist.*

Buster's voice was tightening. "My dad never yelled."

Laurie, ever the editor of his statements, took a large bite of hot dog. "He did, too," she said around it. "But not all the time. Ushly he was nice and made us laugh."

"Sam doesn't make us laugh."

"He makes me laugh," Laurie corrected. "You always hide when he comes."

Buster stopped and handed Mark his half-eaten hot dog. "I don't want this anymore," he said quietly. "I'm thirsty."

Mark saw him swallow with difficulty and knew tears of frustration and possibly even self-confrontation were only seconds away.

"Right." He took it from him and tossed it into a nearby trash container with his own empty stick. "How about 'a sixteen-ounce Coke in a Ghostbusters Slurpee bottle,'" Mark read from an overhead sign that offered pop in a purple plastic bottle with a picture of Slimer on it and a permanent straw with an attached stopper.

"Yes!" Laurie endorsed the suggestion with her signature leap into the air.

Buster brightened. "Yeah."

Mark ordered two, put them in the children's hands, then turned to ask Bernie teasingly if she wanted her own and realized she was no longer trailing after them.

"Did we lose Bernie?" Mark asked Laurie, looking up and down the crowded street in concern.

Laurie frowned at him. "Can a grownup lose another grownup?"

Mark ignored the irony in the question and responded to what he knew she meant. "If they don't keep up and stay with the group. Let's—"

"Aha! Surprise!" Bernie leapt out from a crowd of people moving toward the Turnaround, and held out a white paper bag. "Tried to lose me, didn't you?"

"No," Laurie replied seriously. "Mark was looking for you to buy you a Slimer bottle, but you didn't keep up. You're supposed to stay with the group," she admonished.

"You're right," Bernie said gravely. "I'm sorry."

Then she noticed the large bilious purple bottles they held. Buster sucked from his greedily. She looked up at Mark. "So where is *my* bottle?"

"You wandered away," he said, his tone teasingly reproachful. "I didn't know whether or not you wanted one."

"Do you want any of my fudge?" She held the bag up invitingly. When he tried to peer into it, she withdrew it and offered it to the children.

He bought her a Slimer Slurpee bottle.

"Will you carry it for me?" she asked, on the verge of laughter.

"No." He took the bag of fudge from her and handed her the bottle. "You're harder to control than they are," he said quietly.

She smiled sweetly. "I hope so."

MARK FIXED STEAKS, mashed potatoes and carrots for dinner. While they ate, Laurie and Buster relived the pleasures of the afternoon and drank milk from their purple bottles.

As Mark and Bernie cleaned up, the children settled in front of the television. Bernie wandered into the living room half an hour later to check the silence and found them fast asleep, Buster lying on the carpet, clutching his Slimer bottle, Laurie's tidily on the coffee table as she stretched out on the sofa.

Mark carried them upstairs again, Laurie first, then Buster, a warmth and respect for them welling inside him. He found himself wishing Buster could absorb a little of Laurie's survival instincts and adjust to the inevitable. But the boy had a lot in common with him, he could see. He was stubborn, determined to show the world he was not going to take its tricks lightly, and gifts intended to pacify him would be thrown back in its face. He wanted what he wanted when he wanted it.

Mark pulled Buster's blankets up and stroked his hair back as he settled into the pillow without waking.

"That's a tough way to go, Buss," he whispered. "I think you're going to find you have to give a little."

Bernie heard the quiet admonition from the corridor as she retrieved another blanket out of the linen closet and felt the little flutter of hope gaining momentum.

Mark found her peeking around his bedroom door. "Dare I hope you're looking for me?" he asked.

She started in alarm. "I . . . I was wondering if your bathroom had a tub. The other one only has a shower and the one downstairs off the utility room has only the commode. I'd love to soak for a while."

Mark folded his arms and studied her. He'd been growing dangerous this evening, she'd noticed. The careful emotional distance they'd kept while confined in the same house was wearing screamingly thin. And the children were sound asleep now.

"There is."

She swallowed. "May I use it?"

"Depends," he replied quietly. "Do I have to leave?"

Bernie smiled. "It would be the gentlemanly thing to do."

Mark sat on the foot of the bed, took her hand and pulled her down beside him.

"Don't you ever get tired," he asked, his eyes dark and warm as they wandered hungrily over her face, "of this game we're playing?"

She felt his eyes on her like a stroke and leaned unconsciously toward him. "I'm not playing," she said softly.

"You keep dancing out of reach," he accused gently, putting a hand to her face.

She closed her eyes and leaned into it, feeling its warm tenderness and strength. "Because you aren't playing fair."

He frowned. "You're the one withholding the prize."

She opened her eyes and smiled gently at him. "You're doing the same thing."

"I'm talking," he said, leaning closer to nuzzle her cheek, "about all a man and a woman share when they make love. You can't understand love until you've shared that."

Bernie struggled to keep her mind working. He was kissing and nibbling the cord in her neck and sensation tried to overpower reason. "You haven't spoken of love."

Mark was taken aback for only a moment. He hadn't spoken of love. He didn't seem able to. He wrapped his arms around her and drew her back with him to the mattress. He braced himself over her.

"Because too much talking," he said, "spoils the mood."

He's good at this, Bernie thought. Lost in this gauzy facsimile of her dream, she studied the masculine perfection of Mark's face looking down at her, the solid width of his chest pinning her down and the erratic thrum of her heart in response to him.

Mark saw passion blossom in her eyes, felt a yearning breath part her lips. He lowered his mouth to take them. He showed her no mercy this time. He delved deeply with his tongue, sparring with hers as it did its own exploring. Her death grip on him was as exciting as an intimate caress would have been because he could feel her need in it.

He dragged his mouth away so he could gasp a breath. But she was kissing his ear, the line of his jaw, his throat, and he couldn't breathe at all. It didn't seem to matter. His heart was pumping out of control.

He turned again until she lay atop him. While she rendered him near senseless with kisses, he ran his hands over her body, feeling the warm perfection of the curves he'd watched move innocently around his office for weeks. He'd wanted to touch her for so long. So long.

Bernie felt her blood rush, her pulse race, her nerves grow fevered and frantic. As Mark's hands traced her body she felt it come alive. He left heat and clamoring nerves wherever he touched. And still, she thought in wonder, despite the frenetic quality of her body's reaction, her soul seemed to quiet under his touch. All the loneliness she'd experienced, all the confusion and guilt she'd felt, all her concerns for her future smoothed away when he touched her.

Though he wouldn't speak of it, she felt love in his hands. She knew love guided her own. This, she knew, was what the desperate women she'd counseled had sought in their relationships with one wrong man after another—the peace under the raging physical storm. They hadn't understood that it wasn't the touch that brought it, but the love behind the touch.

Bernie felt Mark's hand slip under her sweater, felt the new, exquisite sensation of his large, warm hand closing over her lace-covered breast. She closed her eyes for a moment, helpless to protest. For an instant, vitality ran through her, touching the tips of her fingers and the tips of her toes. Then as his hand moved and sensation grew, vitality fell away and a thick, languid warmth began to fill her.

"Mark," she whispered, close to slipping under its spell. She had to call on every thread of self-control to remember that this was only a facsimile of the dream. It had many of its most pleasurable elements, but none of its foundation. He'd offered nothing, promised nothing.

Mark put his lips to her bare ribs, inhaled the clean, soapy scent of her. He rubbed his cheek in the little hollow there, further weakened by the silkiness of her skin and the thunderous pulse under it. He lifted his head and looked into her slumberous eyes.

He opened his mouth to ask her to come to bed with him. Then he saw the change take place in her eyes.

Tears slid from Bernie's eyes to the bedspread under her. She knew how much he needed her, how desperately she needed him. On the surface, it looked so simple. They wanted each other. But he wanted her without condition, and she wanted him with reservation. And she didn't seem to be winning.

Mark felt angry, confused, frustrated—but he couldn't do anything to hurt her. He sat up and pulled her into his arms. "Don't cry," he said, rocking her back and forth. "That's a sign of despair. That's against the rules, isn't it?"

She held him, absorbing the security he offered, wanting to believe it would be all right. But she couldn't see how. "It's not despair," she said. "It's just frustration."

He laughed softly, grimly. "I can certainly relate to that."

"I want to make love with you," she whispered, her cheek wet against his, a little sob punctuating her words. "I'd like to lay with you right now, to learn what's inside you and show you all the love inside me. But . . ."

His clamoring heart plummeted. He wanted to make love to her with a desperation he hadn't known in so long. He wanted to know her—really know her in the way only physical bonding could reveal her. But...the deadly word fell like a hammer.

"But . . ." he prodded.

"But I don't think it's time," she said, the words so quiet he had to strain to hear them, even though he held her in his arms.

He tried to make sense of that, and thought he knew what she was telling him. "You mean, we're not married."

She looked into his eyes, unwilling to hurt him, but knowing that either choice, making love with him or not making love with him, would hurt. She opted for the choice she thought wise. "I mean, I don't think it's time."

"If you want it," he said patiently, "and I want it, how can it not be time?"

The truth would make him angry, she knew, so she evaded it. "Because I have two children in my care who deserve my undivided attention even when they're asleep."

Marked looked into her eyes and knew she wasn't telling him the truth. Her answer was certainly valid, if a little overly cautious, but it wasn't at the heart of her refusal to make love to him.

She stirred in his arms. "I'll just take a shower," she said.

He got to his feet and pulled her up, staving off the hunger for her by closing his mind. After so much experience, he was now able to do that with an ease that frightened him. He drew her farther into the room and turned her toward the open bathroom door.

"Take your time. I'll leave fresh towels on the bed. How about Coke and popcorn and your pirate movie when you're finished?"

He didn't know where the generous offer came from. He heard himself speak with the same startled wonder he saw in her eyes.

"Please," she said.

"All right." He kissed her lightly and left her.

Immersed in a tub of warm water, Bernie drew her knees up, wrapped her arms around them and sobbed. Her body ached for all it didn't know and now longed for, and her heart ached for what she was beginning to feel sure she'd never have.

She had Mark's unqualified friendship and his deepest affection. She even had a part of his love, but not its entirety. It was still all bound up in Kathy and Christian, because he never spoke of love. He was always there for her on the moment, but in his heart forever was reserved for his dead wife and son.

She tried to imagine what was left for her. Historically women in her position entered the convent. That was out, she thought with gallows humor. She'd already tried that. Maybe she'd meet someone else. She considered that possibility and found it didn't even interest her. She wanted Mark. She would probably always want Mark.

Bernie dried herself off, pulled on the nightgown and robe she'd brought and made her desultory way downstairs, thinking grimly that she was proving to be a failure at everything.

MARK STARED OUT the rain-spattered kitchen window into the night. Nothing moved on the quiet suburban street, and the prisms of rain took the porch light across the street and made it into a thousand tiny stars. He didn't notice.

If he was ever going to have Bernie Emerson in his bed, he was going to have to marry her. The most frightening part about that was, he could no longer imagine a future without her in it, without the two of them on deeply intimate terms.

She'd want a wedding in the church, with vows made to a God in whom he no longer had faith. He would have to compromise all he'd come to feel to honor her beliefs. He acknowledged grimly that he was faced with an unsolvable problem.

He plugged the popcorn popper in and pulled a bottle of Coke out of the refrigerator. He looked heavenward. "Nice work," he murmured. "You're going to manage to stiff me twice. And I thought I was so smart."

She came down looking as hopeless as he felt. In the ugly pale green robe he guessed was a leftover from her convent days, she tried to smile. It hurt him to see her with that vacant look in her eyes.

He handed her the bowl of popcorn. "I'll bring the drinks," he said. "Your tape's on the television."

He'd just built up the fire, but its warmth hadn't penetrated yet and the room had grown cool. Bernie, the ends of her hair still damp from the tub, huddled in a corner of the sofa, obviously chilled. He took the afghan from his mother's chair and put it over her. She smiled at him, and he turned away to put the tape in.

When he came back to the sofa, she held a corner of the afghan open.

For just an instant he considered the danger of accepting her invitation. He wanted her so badly, being that close to her under a blanket would torture him. But she was wearing that smile that always made him feel he had to respond. Strange, he thought, how she really asked so little of him, but the things she wanted cost him so much in emotion and commitment. He got under the blanket.

She fell asleep during David Letterman, her movie long over. She had curled her feet up on the sofa so that her entire body rested against him, her face in his neck, her breasts against his chest, her waist in the crook of his arm. He'd tried valiantly not to notice the rightness of holding her that way, but he'd long since given up.

He should put her to bed; they'd both be more comfortable. But she slept so soundly, and he knew how empty his arms would feel without her. He simply wasn't willing to endure that tonight. He eased himself sideways until he'd made room to put his legs up, then tugged on the blanket until it was free.

Bernie opened heavy, unfocused eyes. "What...?" she began to ask.

"Nothing. Shh." When he pulled her down beside him and drew the afghan over them, she settled instantly. He stretched an arm out for the remote control, turned the television off, planted a kiss in her hair and closed his eyes. For tonight, he would pretend he could have her like this forever.

Chapter Fourteen

Mark drifted from sleep to awareness feeling the pressure of another body against his. He smiled, remembering that he'd fallen asleep with Bernie in his arms. But this couldn't be Bernie; the weight was too slight for an adult.

He opened his eyes and found Buster staring at him, blue gaze sparked with temper. He knelt astride Mark's waist, his arms folded belligerently.

"I'm not going," he said firmly.

Mark tried to gather his faculties. He had a feeling he was going to have to be sharp for this one. He put a hand behind his head. Sometime during the night someone had propped a pillow under him.

"You're not going where?" Mark asked.

"To church." When Mark didn't react immediately, Buster explained, "It's Sunday."

Mark closed his eyes. Come on, he said silently. Don't set me up for this. I'm not going, either.

"If you don't have to go," Buster said, indicating Mark with his index finger, then himself with a thumb, "then I don't have to go."

"But I'm an adult," Mark pointed out. "I can do what I want to do. You're a little kid. You have to do what people tell you."

"I have to do what my mom tells me," Buster corrected. "And she's not here. I don't *have* to do what Bernie tells me."

As though on cue, Bernie appeared, garbed in a soft pink sweater. She leaned over the back of the sofa and smiled at Buster. "You're supposed to be getting ready for church."

"I told you I'm not going."

"And I told you you are."

"You said *he* didn't have to go." Buster pointed at Mark as though he were guilty of some betrayal.

Mark looked at Bernie, whose eyes lingered on him with such sweetness that he knew instantly she'd valued the night in his arms as much as he had. But they had another problem at the moment. Her expression became carefully stern.

"I'm not taking care of *him* for the weekend," she told Buster patiently. "I can't tell *him* what to do. You're a different story." She glanced at her watch, then said firmly. "And if you don't get moving in about a minute, I'll carry you to church just the way you are."

Buster looked down at his white T-shirt and tiny briefs, then into Mark's face with indignation. "Can she do that?"

Mark sighed, defeated. "'Fraid so. The law's on her side. Tell you what." He bracketed Buster's waist and put him on his feet beside the sofa. Then he swung his own legs over the side and took a moment to brace himself for what he was about to do. "I'll come, too. We'll pick up some doughnuts afterward and the Sunday paper."

Buster looked at him, caught between holding firm and capitulating. "She can't carry *you* to church," he said.

Mark cast an innocent-looking Bernie a wry glance. She seemed to be doing just that. He got to his feet, caught Buster's hand and pulled him toward the stairs. "Come on. It'll be fun. I'll lend you a tie."

Buster ran up the stairs with Mark, giggling at the thought.

MARK TRIED NOT TO NOTICE where he was. At first it wasn't difficult. He was too busy pulling Buster out from under the pew, preventing him from making an airplane out of the church bulletin or from wearing the hymnal on his head to pay much attention to the church.

Then as the boy settled down, Mark remembered how much he'd come to love Sunday mass as an adult, particularly after Christian was born. He'd felt such pride in his family and enjoyed the admiring glances he got when he carried Christian to communion, Kathy moving serenely ahead of them.

Sometimes Tony and Becky and Hal and Angie and their children would crowd into their pew, Cecelia tucked in between her grandchildren, beaming. There'd been such warmth and sense of family, and a spiritual presence he'd trusted and in which he'd taken comfort.

Buster tugged on Mark's suit jacket. "I can't see," he whispered loudly enough that the people in the four pews in front of them turned around.

Mark hoisted Buster onto his hip. The boy watched, apparently fascinated, as the ritual continued. Mark resisted the pull of the music, the comfortable familiarity of the ancient traditions, though he hadn't participated in them in over a year, the softness that stole inside him and threatened to undermine his neutrality.

The real problem came at communion. Bernie started to leave the pew with Laurie, while Mark stayed behind with Buster.

"I want to go!" Buster whispered loudly. "I want to get my blessing."

"I can't go," Mark said softly. "Let's just wait here."

"Why can't you go?"

How did he explain to a child a soul not fit to consume the Body and Blood of Christ? It occurred to him to wonder why he felt that way when he attested to a general lack of belief to anyone who would listen.

"Go with Bernie," Mark suggested.

Bernie, aware of the quiet altercation, slipped back into the pew. "What's the matter?"

Quickly, quietly, Mark explained.

Buster held Mark's hand and refused to let go. "I want to go with you," he said stubbornly.

"You can come up and just get a blessing," Bernie whispered to Mark. "It's something new since . . . since you left. Just put your hand over your heart." She placed her hand on the left breast of her pink sweater in demonstration. "Buster knows how. He comes with his mother all the time."

"Come on." His hand already over his heart, Buster led the way out of the pew, towing Mark behind him.

Mark followed, thinking privately, *Okay, this is it. You've gone too far. I'm not doing anymore. You will never see me here again. Never.*

All the other communicants had passed them up and Mark and Bernie and the children fell in at the end of the line. Father John put the host on Laurie's tongue, then Bernie's, and they moved aside to the Eucharistic Minister who offered the wine.

Mark and Buster moved up. Father John placed a large hand on Buster's head and blessed him, then turned to Mark, his eyes widening in surprise when he recognized him. The smallest smile parted his lips as he placed a hand on Mark's head and said, "God bless you in the name of the Father, the Son and the Holy Spirit."

BERNIE RAN FOR THE RINGING telephone as Mark unlocked the front door. He was encumbered by a large box of doughnuts, the Sunday paper and Buster's hand. The boy was becoming permanently affixed to him.

Mark handed Laurie the paper and Buster the doughnuts. "You guys get comfortable on the floor while I make cocoa. Remember to save a few doughnuts for Bernie and me."

He went into the kitchen, pulling off his jacket.

"I'm sorry we missed you the first time, Cecelia," Bernie was saying. "We went to mass."

Mark heard the shriek on the other end of the phone line. Bernie rolled her eyes at him, grinning. "Yes, Mark took us. No, he didn't drop us off, he stayed."

As he filled the kettle, he gave her a warning look.

"He even took Buster up," she said with a defiant smile, "to get a blessing." She frowned suddenly, asking, "Cecelia? Hello? Yes, he's right here. Hold on."

Mark took the phone from Bernie with one hand and wrapped his fingers around her throat with the other and mimed throttling her. She laughed, pulling at his wrist, and escaped to get cups out of the cupboard.

Cecelia was crying.

"Mom, don't get excited," he said. "I went to church because Bernie needed a ride."

"But you stayed! You stayed!"

"Because I had to. So, how are you doing? You and Aunt Theresa still having fun?"

"When's the wedding?"

"We haven't talked about a wedding, Mom."

"You went to church. You must love her. I know you. When I get home, we'll talk about a wedding."

Mark closed his eyes and felt his life spin out of control. Between Bernie and his mother he was being ripped into the future, ready or not.

"Did you call Tony? Is he still coming to the airport for you?"

"Yes," she replied. "Day after tomorrow. Marco, I'm so happy."

It was pointless to argue or try to correct her impression. "I'm glad you're happy, Mom."

"Wait a minute. Aunt Theresa wants to talk to you."

"Mom, I..."

"Marco! You're getting married! I'm so happy..."

"Aunt Theresa..."

She wasn't listening. She was carrying on about what a relief it was for his dear mother, bless her, to know he was coming back to the fold.

Mark put a hand over his eyes and listened politely, wondering just where he'd dropped his guard and allowed this to happen.

"THAT WAS COOL," Buster said. He had most of a jelly doughnut on his shirt, his upper lip and the comic section of the newspaper he shared with Laurie.

Bernie, sitting on the floor near the children, her back propped against the sofa, looked up from the magazine section. "What was cool?"

"Mass."

Bernie cast a smiling glance at Mark. He lay stretched out with the sports section, Dot and Dash asleep on either side of him. He caught her eye with a silent scolding that lost its impact when he burst into laughter.

A WATERY SUN PEERED OUT in the afternoon and the children hurried out to try the playground equipment. Bernie sat in the glassed-in sun porch with a book, to keep an eye on them.

Mark worked on a sticky cupboard his mother had complained about, moving on to other self-imposed projects when he was finished. He stopped finally, to forestall Bernie's efforts to start dinner.

"I'll do it," he said.

"You don't trust me," she accused.

"That's right," he admitted. "If you can't pump it out of a frozen-yogurt machine, you're not too good at it, my love." He kissed her cheek. "It's a hard truth, I know."

My love. She repeated the words to herself, wondering if they had any real significance for him. She didn't deal well with subtlety. So she asked. "My love?"

He looked at her over the open refrigerator door. "We'll talk about it tomorrow night," he said gently.

She frowned. "The kids and I will be gone tomorrow night."

He shook his head. "The kids will be gone. Your apartment's still uninhabitable."

"Your mother will be home."

"Not until the day after. We've got a night alone together." He looked at her significantly. "Think about that, Bernadette."

She thought about nothing else. She stared at the ceiling most of the night, and poured cereal into Laurie's juice glass while thinking about it the following morning.

Mark watched Bernie's distraction and knew she loved him as much as he loved her. He could do this. It was going to work.

Bernie was in the living room helping Laurie with a broken shoelace while Mark finished a second cup of coffee and read the morning paper. He had ten minutes before they had to pile the kids into the van for school. Buster climbed into his lap.

"I'm not going," he said.

Mark rubbed a hand between the boy's shoulder blades. He'd developed a genuine affection for this child who fought everything.

"I thought you liked school."

"I mean, I'm not going home."

"Sam, right?"

When Buster nodded, Mark wrapped both arms around him. "You know what I think you should do?"

"Yeah, and I'm not going."

Mark laughed softly. "You've got to go home. That's your mom, Buster. She gets you everything you need, she takes care of you, she works hard to give you all the things your father used to help with when he was alive."

Buster nodded glumly. "I love her. I just don't like him."

"But he loves her, too. You have to find a way to be a friend to him. You know how hard it can be to live with women in the house."

Buster nodded heartily.

"Well, he'll need another guy who understands, to kind of help him out. And I'm sure if you're nice to him, he'll be nice to you. And if you don't yell at your mom, I bet he won't yell at you."

Buster absorbed all that in silence, then hooked an arm around Mark's neck and sighed. "I wish Mom would marry you." He sighed again. "But you belong to Bernie, dontcha?"

Mark didn't even have to think about that. "Yeah. I belong to Bernie." He tightened his grip on Buster. "You think you can try to be friends with Sam?"

"I guess." Buster leaned his cheek against Mark's chest. "You think my Dad would get mad?"

Mark stroked his silky blond head. "I think it would make him happy. He knows he can never come back to you. I think he'll like it that you're getting a new dad. You don't ever have to forget the old one, just kind of put him away and let Sam have his place now."

Bernie heard the words as she and Laurie trooped into the kitchen, coats on and ready to leave. His tenderness didn't surprise her, but his insightful, beautiful handling of Buster did. She wondered if he'd absorbed his own words and related them to himself.

THE DAY WAS INTERMINABLE. The entire board of Coastal Bank came to the studio to look over their proofs. When they failed to agree on the photograph for the front of their annual report, which had to be taken to the printer by Wednesday, Mark gave Jonathan Phillips the telephone number at Cecelia's so he could call him after hours. The owner of Waterworks was so pleased with his brochure, three merchants he recommended came in to look at Good Impressions' portfolio. The phone rang incessantly.

Bernie's nerves were frayed to fringe. Her relationship with Mark would be sealed or die tonight—she knew that with a certainty that made it difficult for her to concentrate on the simplest tasks.

As he passed through the office with clients, his eyes always found a moment to sweep over her, velvety and turbulent, as though he, too, could think of nothing but tonight.

He's going to let me in at last, Bernie thought. *I'll help him put away the pain that's plagued his life and open the future for him. We'll have babies and we'll love each other like no one in this world has ever loved.* She prayed silently, *Please, God. Let that be what You have in mind.*

It's time, Mark told himself. *I can do it.* He watched Bernie from the far corner of the darkroom, the door open just enough that he could see her talking on the telephone to Angie.

I want her forever. I want her beside me, beneath me, within me. I want to give her everything she wants, and take everything she offers. I can't live without her. I can hardly function, knowing she's still free to walk away from me if she chooses to. Tonight I'll take that option from her forever.

"DANCING?" Bernie allowed Mark to help her into her coat, wondering if she'd heard him correctly. The bank board had lingered an hour past closing to discuss the possibility of photos for a network-wide promotion and it was almost seven.

"Dancing," he confirmed, pulling her toward the door, flipping lights off as they went. "An orgy of French food, followed by a little light stepping..." He put a hand to his heart, held the other out as though it enfolded a partner's hand, and mimed a turn and a dip.

As Bernie, laughing, tried to walk past him out the door, he shot a hand out to bar her way, leaning over her until she thought she could feel the heat from his dangerous dark eyes. "Followed by," he went on, leaning even closer, "the seduction of your dreams."

She sobered instantly and touched her lips to his in lingering assent. "Then let's go," she said.

Gerard's at the south end of the Prom was decorated in pink and green and chintz, and reminiscent of a French country inn. The brochette was reminiscent of heaven.

Bernie closed her eyes and savored the subtle, succulent flavors. "We had a sister who cooked like this one summer at the motherhouse," she said. "But someone must have discovered her because she was with us just a month. She's probably basting game hens at the Vatican at this very moment."

Mark topped her wineglass from the carafe. "Lucky for me you aren't so gifted in the kitchen. If the Vatican had asked for you, I'd never have met you."

She met his eyes with an uncertain smile. "There've been days when I thought you'd have preferred that."

He acknowledged that with a tilt of his head. "Those days are gone forever. You going to eat the skewer, too, or do you want to dance?"

Bernie looked doubtfully at the small dance floor beyond the tables, where three couples took up most of the space and a violin and a piano filled the air with sweet music. "Mark, I haven't danced in twelve years. When I went into the convent, disco was in."

Mark rolled his eyes and took her hand. "Come on. There isn't much room to do anything fancy anyway."

He pushed her gently ahead of him toward the stone-tiled square. At the edge of the floor, he pulled her loosely into his arms.

"Just relax," he said, his hand at the back of her waist pulling her against him. "Your body will follow mine instinctively."

She looped both arms around his neck and leaned her forehead against his chin, knowing he was right. Her body had been waiting to do that for some time now.

She thought later that she'd never really heard the music. Once she'd turned into Mark's arms, sight and sound seemed to desert her. Eyes closed, she simply let her body feel. Until Mark, it had never known this onslaught of sensation that rippled over and over her as though magnified by some magic force.

She felt the smoothness of Mark's chin against the sensitive skin at her temple, felt the wool blend of his jacket under the inside of her arms. Against the tips of her breasts, highly sensitized by his closeness and her own finely tuned emotional receptors, the armor plate of his cotton-covered chest chafed a delicious friction. His thigh bumped hers once, then slipped between them causing a little frisson of sensation to the roots of her hair.

He held her as though she were precious and fragile, a gift he intended to treat with great care.

She sighed against him, wishing she could sustain the moment forever.

Mark felt as though he was ruled by nerves and desire. *It's ironic,* he thought, *that I went to Durban, to Palestine and to Ulster with relative fearlessness, and I'm standing here on a dance floor with a small woman who frightens me. If I commit myself to her she's going to expect totality, and I've hidden so much.* This afternoon when he'd watched her from the darkroom with twenty feet between them, this had looked easy. Now, feeling her melted against him, loving him, trusting him, it was proving to be the most difficult thing he'd ever done.

"So you're sure about the convent," he said abruptly. *That was cool, Costello. Suavely put.*

He was not surprised when Bernie looked up at him with a frown. "In what way?"

"That you're no longer considering going back."

She shook her head. "That's a strange thing to ask now."

He sighed. He was not doing this well at all. Bart Simpson had more style. "No, it's not. Would you answer me, please?"

"I am not going back to the convent," she replied dutifully. "I finally decided that what I missed were my companions and my work, not the life. I have a new life now."

He drew a breath. "Then will you marry me?"

She stopped dancing and stared at him, her lips parted in a gasp. She'd hoped to hear those words, had even expected she might. Still, the sound of them was the awesome shock of a dream come true. The real dream, not the facsimile. Everything trembled inside her.

"Yes!" she said a little too loudly. The other couples on the floor turned to look at them. "Yes," she repeated more quietly, more firmly. "Yes."

Happy beyond anything he'd ever hoped to feel again, Mark leaned down to kiss her. The others who shared the dance floor now looked discreetly away, smiling at one another in understanding and a little jealousy.

Mark took Bernie's hand and led her off the dance floor, pausing at their table only long enough to grab her coat and purse. Two steps into the parking lot, he stopped her in the rainy darkness to pull her into his arms again and seal his proposal and her promise with another kiss.

He felt new, he thought, young, fresh. He drank from her mouth like a man who'd been lost in the desert. She gave like a fountain in an oasis.

"Mark!" She finally pulled away from him, her light laughter feathering against his cheek as he refused to let her go. "We've got to go back," she said, "or we're going to be celebrating our engagement in jail."

Finally distracted from the consuming vision of love in her eyes, he refocused his attention with a small frown. "Why?"

"Because we left," she said, "without paying the check."

"FORTUNATELY GERARD WAS understanding," Bernie said as she preceded Mark into Cecelia's living room.

Mark tossed his keys onto the coffee table, pulled off his jacket and Bernie's coat and dropped them in a corner of the sofa. "Of course. He's a Frenchman." He wrapped his arms around her and fell with her onto the sofa cushions. "He understands that love blinds you to even the basic proprieties."

Pinned under his chest, Bernie thought she'd never felt more wonderful in her life. She wrapped her arms around his neck as he dotted kisses along her collarbone. She kissed his ear. "I feel as though nothing else exists in the world tonight but you and me."

Mark raised his head to look at her, intoxicated with the depth of his feeling for her. "I love you, Bernie," he said. "I love you so much."

"Mark!" His name came from her in a high whisper, filled with emotion and the dusky desire he saw in her eyes. "I love you, too. I've wanted you for an eternity."

He kissed her hungrily. "I've wanted you at least as long," he said hungrily. "And now we'll have eternity."

Bernie closed her eyes and just held him, afraid to believe this was happening. The man who just days ago didn't believe in tomorrow was promising her eternity. She said another prayer of thanks.

Mark felt her tremble in his arms and sat up. He gave her a quick kiss. "Why don't you change and I'll build a fire," he suggested.

She caught his sleeve as he tried to stand. "Because I don't want to leave you."

"You're shivering," he said. "The house is freezing." He nuzzled her ear and ran his hands promisingly over her back. "I'll build a fire, and we'll drink Mom's wine and plan the number of babies."

Bernie drew back to look at him, her eyes softening with a yearning that threatened to melt his composure. "Do you really want babies?"

"Yes," he said, kissing her again. "Yes."

She changed into a skirt and sweater in three minutes flat, running back downstairs in her bare feet, her body humming wildly with anticipation.

The fire was just beginning to catch as she sank down beside him on the hearth rug.

The sudden, jarring jangle of the phone drew a loud groan from both of them.

"I should have put Mom's answering machine on," Mark grumbled, sprinting to the kitchen to answer it. "Sit down. Relax. I'll pour the wine while I'm in there."

Bernie sat cross-legged and stared into the dancing flames, hunching her shoulders in delight at the thought that her life was taking off at last. She was going to have everything she wanted. She was going to have Mark.

She basked in contentment for a few moments, then went to peer into the kitchen to see what was keeping him, hoping it wasn't a problem with Cecelia or someone else in the family.

"No, it's all right, Mr. Phillips," he was saying, the phone cradled on his shoulder as he poured zinfandel into two tulip glasses. He caught Bernie's eye and pointed to the telephone with a forebearing roll of his eyes. "No, I meant it when I told you to call me tonight if you were all able to agree. I know how difficult it is for an entire board of executives to come together on anything." He made a helpless gesture with his free hand, indicating, Bernie guessed, that he might be a while.

She blew him a kiss and went back into the living room to wait. She spotted the pirate movie they'd rented the other night, and groaned as she realized she'd forgotten to return it today. Her eyes wandered to the cabinet beside the television where Cecelia kept her private stock of videotapes and smiled as she recognized all the Fred Astaire and Ginger Rogers titles. Then she saw a lineup of tapes labeled

"Family." *Her* family now, she thought happily. She pulled one of the tapes out, fed it into the VCR and turned the television on quietly, prepared to wait out Mark's phone call with "Anthony's Fourth Birthday."

The tape began with a shot of Becky tilting an enormous sheet cake toward the camera. It was decorated with horses and large frosting flowers. In blue gel was written, "Happy Birthday, Anthony—4 years old."

Bernie smiled as the birthday boy appeared for the camera in full cowboy regalia. The shot then took in a table set in the backyard with a large balloon bouquet in the center. Children ran around in the background and were corralled in family groups to smile at the camera.

Tony, wearing a chef's hat and a barbecue apron that said "Hot Stuff" in large red letters, turned away from his work to put an arm around Becky, who carried Cece on her hip. Janie stood in front of the trio and waved. Paul, Bernie realized, hadn't even been thought of yet.

The camera then panned to a sunny patch of grass where Hal blew up an inflatable swimming pool. He made hideous faces to indicate the extreme effort and Bernie laughed aloud. Then Angie, holding the baby Cameron, gave Hal a punitive shove and he put the pool aside to smile. Anthony pushed his way between them from behind and waved madly.

A tall, elegant blonde appeared next, holding a plump, laughing toddler in her arms. She looked uncomfortable in front of the camera and grimaced at whoever was handling it. It was a moment before Bernie realized who she was.

That she was Kathy, Mark's wife, struck Bernie like a jolt of electricity. Emotion swelled in her, threatening to choke her. Still sitting cross-legged, she stared at the screen unable to move.

Kathy was beautiful. Angie had mentioned that she'd been a model, and Bernie thought she'd have known that without being told. As she walked across the yard to point at a table covered with presents, she moved with a grace that was unmistakably professional yet somehow very honest. Her hair was golden and luxurious, her smile sweet. The baby reached toward the camera laughing, and Kathy made a beckoning gesture.

The picture jostled as though the camera was changing hands, then Mark ran into the picture, turning to pose beside Kathy. Christian kicked and reached for him and Mark took him, settling him on his hip.

Bernie's eyes devoured the beautiful picture they made, tears falling into the hands in her lap.

"What are you doing?" Mark's harsh voice startled Bernie to her knees.

She looked up at him guiltily, waving a hand toward the screen. "I was . . . I saw the tapes and you were . . . still talking, and I . . ."

Mark wasn't listening to her, he was watching the screen with a horror she could almost feel. She watched it burst in his eyes before he slapped a hand to the VCR to turn it off.

MARK HELD THE SCREAM of rage back with sheer willpower. He'd made a point of putting all photographs of his wife and son away and hadn't looked on a likeness of either of them since the accident. The pain he'd thought he'd conquered came back with deadly freshness. But even that was nothing compared to the anger that billowed inside him. How dare Bernie do that to him? She was always taking him where he didn't want to go. He ejected the tape and reached toward the fire to toss it in.

"No!" Bernie caught his hand and pulled it back.

He shook her off and tried again but she stopped him a second time, her fingernails digging into his wrist.

"They were mine!" he shouted at her.

"The tape is your mother's," she said, forcing herself to speak calmly. "You haven't the right. They belonged to her, too."

"Isn't that what you want?" he demanded. "For me to put them out of my life? Now they'll be gone for good."

"Mark..." she pleaded.

"You wanted to talk babies, didn't you?" Mark heard himself in a kind of trance. A small corner of his mind that still functioned despite the crushing hurt and fury wondered what he was saying. But it had no power to send out behaviour impulses in the vicious onslaught of anger overpowering him. "Well, let's get things out of our way."

He tossed the tape into the fire and Bernie lunged for it, screaming as the flame burned her hand. She drew back instinctively and the plastic housing sizzled and cracked, then twisted in on itself as it was destroyed. She watched it with a curious sense of fatality, feeling that same crack and twist within herself.

Mark turned her toward him with a biting yank. "There. It's gone. They're gone." He tried to pull her toward the sofa, but she resisted. She could see that he was wild with pain, but so was she. "Stop it!" she screamed at him.

He ignored her, or he didn't hear her, she wasn't sure which. He pulled her forcibly with him and tried to sit her on the sofa. "This is what you wanted, Bernie," he said, his tone ripe with bitterness. "You and everybody else are impatient for me to be done with the past. You've got your cozy little dreams and you want me to fit in. All right. I'm ready. Let's start planning. Three kids? Four? We'll have to do at least as well as Tony and Angie. Of course, I had a head start..."

She couldn't bear another moment. She caught him off balance as he shifted his weight to push her onto the cushions. She caught her foot around his ankle, leaned her hip into him and dropped him on his backside, his elbows propping him against the sofa.

Anger raging in him, he was on his feet in an instant, grabbing for her as she ran for the door. He caught her halfway across the carpet and pulled her back. Had her mind been functioning and not her heart, she could have broken his hold easily, but all she was aware of was pain— his and hers. She was sobbing now.

He pushed her onto the sofa and fell on top of her. "You've been riding me for a month. It's time you knew what it was like to be manipulated."

"I've never manipulated you!" she denied, pushing futilely at him.

"Come on," he said. "Every move you made was calculated to bring me around to be the man you were looking for after leaving the Convent."

"That isn't true and you know it!" she shouted at him. "You're angry with yourself, not me!"

"I'm not angry at all," he said smoothly.

"I told you before," she said, breathless with sobs, "I wasn't playing. But you were, weren't you? I suppose the proposal was just a way of getting sex out of Sister Simple!"

That gave him a moment's pause. His expression didn't soften, but he focused his attention on her eyes. "That's what marriage is all about. You're just afraid of it because you've never had it."

"I'm not afraid of it," she denied, desperately trying to make herself think, make sense. "I no longer want it with you."

Her words finally penetrated his pain and anger and he let her go. The cold sincerity with which she'd told him she no longer wanted to make love to him jolted him to reality. But anger still had enough of a hold on him that he considered this entire thing her fault. She was the one who'd made him believe he'd gotten over Kathy and Christian enough to plan a new life with her. She'd put the damn tape in the VCR.

"Safer to remain the little virgin?" he asked.

She suddenly understood what he was doing. She'd thought his reactions had been governed by pain and rage, but there was really a very insidious cleverness under his threatening behavior. It was calculated to push her away.

"Don't play games with me," she said, taking advantage of his momentary distraction to sit up. "I'm not the one backing out of this relationship, you are."

He leaned an elbow on the back of the sofa and regarded her as though she meant nothing to him. That, too, was calculated, she was sure, but it frightened the hell out of her. "You're the one," he said brutally, "who refuses to give anything to it."

"If you mean sex, say it."

"I mean sex."

Her throat closed and her heart tightened because now they were getting to the marrow of the matter and she wasn't sure she was strong enough. "Mark," she asked, her voice ragged, "how can you expect me to make love with you when you've still got a death grip on Kathy?" She waved a white-knuckled fist in front of him to show him how strong his grip was. "You don't want me, you want a body that'll assuage the pain for half an hour, then you want to be left alone with your memories. Talk about holding back. Sex is *all* you're willing to give. All right." She stood. "I leave you with your memories."

"And you just walk away?" he asked coolly while she searched for her purse. "At least I've remained committed to something. You've left the Convent, and now you're leaving me. This must be that hit-and-run ministry you told me about."

She picked up her purse off the floor near the chair and turned large, sad hazel eyes on him. "That's it," she said mercilessly. "Hold on to your victim status. Let yourself wallow and no one will expect anything else of you. You can hide in your darkroom and the whole world can lament the wasted life of the once famous Mark Costello." She took her coat off the back of the sofa and started for the door. Then she turned and came halfway back to him. She stopped in the middle of the room.

"And another thing," she said, "just for the record. The last thing I would have done as your wife was push Kathy and Christian out of our lives. I know they'll always be a part of you and I could live with that, but not if you insist on putting them between us." She swallowed with difficulty and drew a breath that held a sob. "You'd better call a temp service tomorrow morning," she said.

Cecelia would be back tomorrow, she thought. She thought about his family and realized with black, ugly certainty everything she was walking away from. For one panicky moment she wondered if there was any way she could settle for the facsimile if she couldn't have the dream. Then she looked into Mark's face, knowing what he could be like when he shed the anger and realizing anything less would turn out to be a nightmare. She made her voice strong. "Goodbye, Mark. I won't be back."

"Your apartment's uninhabitable," he reminded, his voice calm to hide his desperation. "Where are you going to go in the dark?"

She walked to the door, pulled it open and looked back at him pityingly. "The sisters will take me in. And I'll never be as deep in the dark as you are."

The door closed behind her with a slam of finality.

Chapter Fifteen

Mark slapped his hand against the door of Our Lady of Victory Church and was half surprised to find it give under his hand. He pushed his way in, irrespective of the early morning hour. In a turmoil of pain, rage and loss, he'd stormed around his mother's house for hours after Bernie left, trying to make sense of what he felt and what she'd said, but he couldn't pull it together. He'd decided to come to what he considered the source of the problem.

The only light in the church was the sanctuary light, the red cylindrical lamp near the altar that was kept burning day and night. Mark headed for it with a determination that made him ignore the holy-water font, the genuflection of adoration he should have offered when he stopped at the sanctuary steps, the prayerful attitude expected in a house of worship. Instead, he glared at the large crucifix behind the altar.

"Where are You!" he demanded. "All of a sudden You want all kinds of things from me. Well, where were You when I needed *You*? When Kathy and Christian were killed? You're supposed to be everywhere and You let a drunk run them over!"

He didn't hear Father John until he appeared beside him, garbed in his simple black cassock. Mark had no idea where he'd come from. He rounded on him. "Sent from heaven to drive me out of the temple?" he asked.

Father John smiled. "Not from heaven. Just from the sacristy." With a thumb over his shoulder he indicated the small room attached to the church where the vessels and vestments were kept and where the priest prepared for mass. "I was preparing for 5:30 mass. Let's sit down."

With a hand on Mark's arm, Father John guided him back to the first pew.

The priest sat beside him and smiled again. "Correct me if I'm wrong, but it doesn't sound like you came here to pray."

"To whom, Father?" Mark asked. "For what? If He's there, He looks the other way, He doesn't answer."

Father John studied him a moment. "Then why are *you* here?" he asked.

The question was pithy, direct, serious. Mark considered that for the first time since he'd raced out of his mother's house and gotten in his van. He tried to think back. He'd had no destination in mind, then, just a need to get out of the house, to move. When he'd found himself in front of the church, he'd reacted with the only emotion he seemed to have left—anger.

Unable to answer the question, Mark posed one of his own. "What kind of a God lets an innocent woman and child die and a drunk walk away from the accident?"

Father John nodded. "You're not the first to ask that kind of question. I wish I had an answer that would comfort you, but I haven't, except to tell you that the same God that allows you to be hurt, is the same God that heaps blessings on you. His plan is a mystery to us."

Mark made a cynical sound. "I thought the church had all the answers."

"No," the priest corrected. "It claims to have the path to follow to reach God and learn the answers. Only God has them."

"Good lives shouldn't be wasted."

"Good lives are never wasted. The only thing Christ promised, Mark, was that good people who obey his commandments will spend eternity with Him. He never said they wouldn't suffer while they were here." He put an arm around Mark's shoulder, his eyes gentle and empathetic. "I'm sorry about your wife and child, Mark. It doesn't mean God's got it in for you. It means we don't understand His plan. We know He's a just and merciful God."

Mark looked at him. "His plan has destroyed my life. Twice."

Father John frowned, taken aback. "Twice?"

"Bernie and I..." Mark couldn't put it into words; it hurt too much. "She's gone."

"Gone?"

Mark shrugged, desolation washing over him as the heat of his anger abated. "Back to the Convent, I think. She said the sisters would take her in."

"Why? I thought she was happy with her life here. I know she'd had some doubts about leaving the Convent, but I thought she'd resolved them."

Quickly, with only the necessary details, Mark told him what happened.

Father John listened, then tightened his grip on Mark's shoulder. "Okay," he said. "I'm not as good at this as I'd like to be, but let me tell you what I think. I don't believe your relationship needs more from her, emotional or physical, to make it work. I think it needs more from you."

"I love her," he said frustratedly, waving a hand in anguish. "I told her that. I asked her to marry me. Then I saw the film and…'' He shook his head powerless to explain how he'd felt.

"I know. It must have been like a punch to the gut. But you've got to stop letting it hurt you."

Mark gave him a wry glance. "No, you aren't very good at this. How in the hell do I do that?"

Father John patted his shoulder. "You *decide* to do it."

Mark looked at him.

"I'm not sure what's done this to us," the priest went on, "but we've all come to think love, grief, anger, happiness are cosmically visited upon us, that they just wash over us with vast amounts of emotion and we're swept along in their tide." He smiled. "That isn't true. Granted, the seed of all those things is dropped on us without our consent and much of the time without our knowledge, but how we deal with them is a decision we make.

"No one is lovable all the time, yet there are marriages that last fifty years because those people *decide* they will always love one another. Temper flares in us, but we have to *decide* to let ourselves behave angrily. Laughter doesn't make us happy if we don't want it to." He patted him again. "And grief will live with us forever if we let it."

Mark sighed. "You're telling me I'm a malingerer."

"No. I'm telling you you've had a right to your grief, but if you want Bernie you've got to get over it. There are a lot of things she wants in life that your grief won't allow her. Is that fair?"

"Father," Mark said earnestly, "I'm trying to rebuild my life. I've started a new business, I don't mope around, I've tried to be what she needs. I even came to church with her."

"Did it do anything for you?"

He tried to remember. As he recalled, he hadn't exactly been receptive. "No."

"I think your anger is choking you," Father John said. "It blocked your grief so that it kept a grip on you longer than it should have, and now it's blocking your love. Let it go."

Mark put his elbows on his knees and leaned forward, a turbulence in his chest rising into his throat, stinging his eyes. To let his anger go, he'd have to let Kathy and Christian go. Much as their memory hurt, it was all he'd ever have of them again. He put his hands over his face.

Father John leaned forward with him, his arm still around him. "Decide to be done with your anger. Let yourself love Bernie. If you think God owes you one, I'll wager this is it. Let it happen. Tuck your wife and son away where all the beautiful things in our lives we wish would never change but always do should go."

A sob rose from the depths of Mark's chest, filling the quiet church with anguished sound.

Father John held him a little tighter. "Let it go. Be done with it."

Mark leaned against the priest and wept, amazed that ridding himself of grief could hurt as much as living with it had.

BERNIE STOOD ON A child's chair in Sister Ann's classroom, helping her replace the tattered construction-paper alphabet that ran around the room above the chalkboard. It was late afternoon and Sister Camille had after-school playground duty.

"You should be resting," Sister Ann admonished, tacking up the bumblebee next to the letter *B*. "You mustn't have slept a wink last night."

"I'm fine," Bernie assured her tacking up a fuchsia letter *M*, her burned right hand wrapped in a bandage. *M* is for Mark she thought. *N* is for never. *O* is for over.

"You want to talk about it?"

"We have."

"You told me how Mark reacted to seeing the video of his wife and child. That he got angry and accused you of foolish things. You didn't tell me what you intend to do about it."

Bernie looked at Sister Ann over her shoulder in surprise. "Nothing. He doesn't want me. Anyway, you should have seen Kathy. She'd be hard to replace."

Sister Ann leapt off her stool and went to stand near Bernie. "I can't decide if you just got your feelings hurt or you're afraid of the competition?"

Bernie looked down at her with a sigh. "Annie, the competition has been gone for more than a year and she still means more to him than I do. Wouldn't that give you pause?"

"Yes," Sister Ann admitted, "but you've always been braver than I am."

Bernie snicked. "That must be why you're still in the Convent and I'm not. Pass me the *N*, will you?"

"Get down from there." Sister Ann tugged on Bernie's pant leg until she stepped off the stool. "And you talk about Mark and his unresolved past," she scolded. "Sit down."

Bernie tried to resist her friend's efforts to push her into a second grader's tiny desk, but was finally forced to comply. "I'm probably going to walk away wearing this," she complained of the tight squeeze.

Sister Ann looked severe. "Don't try to change the subject. Listen to me. God doesn't chain us in place. We take our vows with the sincerity of who and what we are at the time. But we can be dispensed from them because the Church is wise enough to know that, like everything God created, we grow and change. Can't you see what God wants you to do?"

She thought she'd known, the tears that were always so close to the surface since her fight with Mark now brimming in her eyes and spilling over. She'd been so sure. But he couldn't love her enough. He would never love her enough.

Sister Ann reached across the small space that separated them and closed her hand over Bernie's. "He wants you to love Mark. He's giving you that dream you used to tell me about, Bernie. He's just not making it easy for you."

Bernie pulled a tissue out of her pocket and dabbed at her nose. "I've tried. I can't make it come true."

"Then call in help."

BERNIE WASN'T AT the motherhouse. Running the studio by himself all day, closing time was the first opportunity Mark had had to dial Information and make the call. He replaced the receiver in surprise and considerable relief. He frowned. But she'd said the sisters would take her in.

A light went on in his brain. Could it be that simple? Could she be right here at the local convent? He doubted it, but he prepared to dial Information again.

A knock at the studio door forestalled him. Since he'd turned the "closed" sign, he intended to ignore it—but he glanced up just on the slim chance it was Bernie.

It wasn't. He saw a man and woman he didn't recognize, and two pairs of blue eyes peering into the bottom of the window. Those eyes had looked closely into his several times recently; he'd recognize them anywhere. They belonged to Laurie and Buster.

He pulled the door open and found the family clustered on the front porch. The woman, small and blond and dressed in a conservative suit, stepped forward. She offered her hand.

"I'm Susan Flynn," she said. "Laurie and Buster's mother. I was thanking Bernie for taking care of my children over the weekend, and she told me about her plumbing disaster and how you came to their rescue."

Mark's heart thumped against his ribs. If she'd talked to Bernie when she picked her children up at school, Bernie had to be staying at the parish convent.

Susan tucked her arm in that of the man beside her. "This is Sam Bradley, my fiancé." Mark nodded. He was short and stocky and had a firm handshake.

"We apologize for coming after hours, but Buster wanted to show us his routine on the monkey bars and...well, we lost track of the time."

Sam laughed. "Actually," he said, indicating Susan with a tilt of his head. "She had to be revived twice. Buster's routines aren't for the fainthearted."

Susan groaned and Buster looked proud of himself. Mark forced a polite smile. "I've seen him in action."

"I just wanted to say thank you," Susan Flynn said. "The kids have been raving about what a wonderful time they had, and we wanted you to know how much we appreciate your giving up your time and privacy like that."

"We brought you a present," Laurie said, both hands behind her back.

"I picked it out," Buster said, giving Mark his gap-toothed grin.

As Mark began to deny that a gift was necessary, Laurie produced a purple bottle with Slimer on it. "The other day," she said, "you were the only one who didn't get one."

Mark studied the bottle, embarrassed and touched.

"Can we show Sam the dogs?" Buster wanted to know. There was a little sparkle to his quiet demeanor today, Mark noticed. "He says we're gonna get a dog. Maybe we could have a damnation, too."

"Dal-matian," Susan corrected with a laugh.

"You know where they are," Mark said.

Buster and Laurie each took Sam by a hand and led him through the kitchen to the back door. Mark turned to invite Susan to join them, but she suddenly wrapped her arms around him. He stood still, confused.

"Thank you also," she said, stepping back, "for talking to Buster about Sam. Bernie told me that, too. She didn't tell me what you told him, but whatever it was, it's made our lives a lot more pleasant in just two days. Sam's tried so hard, but . . ." Her lip quivered, but she went on resolutely, "Buster loved his dad so much. It was hard for him to think of anyone else in his place. But we all need Sam. Life has to go on, you know?"

Mark had to clear his throat before he could get the words out. "I know." He thought with grim determination if Buster could go on, so could he.

Dot and Dash accompanied Sam and the Flynns to their car, then trotted after Mark as he leapt the Promenade wall, then wandered toward the water's edge. He wanted to run to Bernie immediately, but he also desperately didn't want to blow it.

He looked up at the stormy sunset, billows of purple cloud catching the dying light of a crimson sun. He prayed with a humility with which he still wasn't completely comfortable, "Please tell me what to say to her. Help me tell her how much I love her, how much I need her, how desperate I am to spend the rest of my life with her. And . . ." Emotion tightened his throat and stung his eyes, but was completely devoid of anger. "Thank you for the time I had with Kathy and Christian. And, please . . . forget most of the things I said."

HANDS JAMMED in the pockets of her gray coat, Bernie walked from the playground to the southern edge of town, then headed for the beach. It was deserted now, no walkers, no kite flyers, no children and dogs running off steam. Just her and her doubtful future.

She couldn't decide between walking past Mark's studio to see if he was still there, or packing her few belongings and taking the next bus out of town.

For the past eighteen hours her mind had played over and over what he'd said to her in his mother's living room. "You've got your cozy little dreams and you want me to fit in."

At first she'd been hurt that he could think such a thing about her. Then as she thought about it, she wondered if he hadn't hit upon the real truth. She'd told herself she was trying to coax him back to life, back to the church in a spirit of Christian caring. But in reality she'd recognized him almost right away as everything she wanted in a man—except that he'd alienated himself from God because of an anger he couldn't reconcile. It had been in her own best interest to help him. And hadn't she grown just a little impatient with his grief because it left so little room for her?

It was difficult and painful to admit to such a motive. She crossed the sand and headed for the water's edge with a heart so heavy she wondered that she could carry it. Maybe she had been selfish, but what prompted her was a love for Mark so strong, so enduring she knew it would live with her always.

Bernie looked out at the vastness of the brooding purple sky and the narrowing band of orange light on the horizon. The churning metallic gray of the ocean seemed to spread out forever, filling her with a humbling sense of insignificance. She stopped to look at it, longing for the sense of peace she always felt here, but experiencing only emptiness.

"You want me to leave, don't You?" she asked. "If You'd meant Mark and I for each other, You'd have made it work out. I don't understand it, but I'm sure You do. So where do You want me to go? North to Seattle? South to Lincoln City? You remember what Mother Catherine said. I like clear orders. It'd be so much easier for me to do what You want if You'd just lower a sign with six-inch letters." She could see it in her head. The sign would be white, the letters red. It would read, "Bernie, you will go to..."

She threw her head back to feel the wind in her face, to inhale a deep draft of air and clear her mind, and she saw him.

He was more than a hundred yards away and wandering along the water's edge in her direction. Dot trotted along beside him, carrying a stick, while Dash barked at the waves, chasing them as they receded, running from them as they flowed toward the sand.

Bernie's heart began to thud. She forgot how much she would have liked a sign with six-inch letters. Her heart, fully involved, knew precisely what she had to do. Bernie, it told her, you will go to Mark.

"YOU'RE NOT GOING to be happy until I throw that, are you?" Mark took the stick from Dot, who immediately tensed, waiting for the toss. Mark raised his arm, reared back and let the stick fly. Dot and Dash both shot after it. It wasn't until he brought his arm down that he saw the figure walking lazily in his direction, face lifted to the wind. Bernie.

He stopped, everything inside him crackling like a piece of equipment shorting out. *Oh, God.* It was a prayer, not an exclamation. *Please. I need her. Tell me what to say. Tell me what to do.*

At that moment, even from the distance of the length of a football field, he saw her head move, knew her eyes had focused on him, and she stopped. He felt only one moment's indecision, then everything became crystal clear. He needed her, and he was going to make her need him. He was going to get her.

He started to run. Dot and Dash, catching her scent on the wind, were already ahead of him. She seemed to hesitate a moment, during which time his heart almost stopped but he didn't. He kept running.

She started walking, slowly at first, then picking up speed. She ran through Dot and Dash, who circled around her from opposite directions and turned to follow her. She ran faster and faster.

He could make out her face, but he couldn't tell if she was laughing or crying, then he could hear the sound and he still couldn't tell. He saw her arms open, heard her say his name, heard hers explode from his burning lungs.

They flew into each other's arms with a force that would fuse them forever. Mark turned, swinging her off her feet to lessen the impact, to hold her high against his heart, to whisper desperately in her ear, "Bernie, I love you! I'm sorry! I'm sorry! God, I love you. Don't leave me. Tell me you're not leaving me."

Laughing, crying, Bernie absorbed the love words while she clung to Mark's neck, unable, unwilling to let him go. "I love you!" she shouted. "I love you. I'm not going anywhere. I'm sorry I pushed you, but I love you so much. I didn't think. I..."

"God, don't apologize." He put her on her feet and framed her face in his hands, staring at her a moment as though to reassure himself that she wasn't a figment of the sunset light. Then he crushed her in his arms again and just held her. "Tell me you still want to marry me."

He'd left her little air with which to speak at all, but she did her best. "Yes, I still want to marry you."

"Saturday.'

"I don't have any—"

"Whatever you need, we'll find it."

She laughed, so happy she wanted to scream. "Saturday." Then she wedged a space between them so that she could look into his eyes. She needed to rectify something between them.

Mark looked down at her worriedly, concerned by her sudden frown. For the first time, he noticed her bandaged hand.

"I would never—ever—try to make you forget Kathy and Christian. It may have sounded like I—"

Mark put a gentle hand over her mouth and pulled her into his chest. Then he drew her burned hand to his lips and kissed it. "I know. That was my anger and my guilt talking. I apologize for that."

"Guilt?" she asked.

"Because I wanted so much to give you more, but it was hard for me." He smiled. "Anyway, I had a long talk with Father John and he straightened me out on a few points. He heard my confession…" Mark sighed and Bernie could see in his eyes that the darkness that had lived there since she'd known him was gone. Kathy and Christian would always be with him, but he'd shed his grief and his anger. He could now be hers, and she could be his. "I'm ready for life to begin again."

Bernie clung to him, too happy to speak.

"You ready to tell the family?" he asked.

"I suppose if we're getting married Saturday, we'd better tell them."

"Tony's driving Mom back from the airport right now. We're all invited to Angie's for dinner to welcome her home." He put an arm around her shoulders and started across the sand toward the studio.

She reached down to fuss with Dot and Dash who whined for her attention, then straightened and wrapped her arm around his waist. "Your mother won't even be surprised."

"I know." Mark pulled her close and kissed her temple. "Whatever she prays for she usually gets, so be warned."

She looked up at him with a smug smile. "You be warned. She's not the only one that happens to."

Chapter Sixteen

Bernie stood in the vestibule of the church in Angie's tea-length wedding dress and a white lace picture hat she'd seen in a shop window and fallen in love with. Becky in fuchsia satin and Angie in plum fussed around her, adjusting this, fluffing that. Cecelia bustled about importantly, greeting the guests she'd all telephoned personally.

"They'll think she's pregnant," Cecelia had warned Mark when he'd insisted the wedding be that weekend.

He'd laughed and kissed her cheek. "She's going to be, so what's the difference?"

"The difference is we..."

"It's this weekend, or we're going to the Wed-O-Rama in Las Vegas."

Cecelia had capitulated, half afraid he'd meant it. Since then she'd abandoned concern over what people would think, to concentrate on the special blessing of the marriage of the son she'd begun to fear would never find happiness again.

The church was full now and she came to hug Bernie and take her hands. "You know how happy we all are to have you in the family."

Bernie nodded. "I feel so lucky to have all of you."

"Do you have any idea," Cecelia whispered, her voice filled with emotion, "how much it means to me that you've brought Marco back to us."

"He came back himself, Cecelia."

"Because you loved him." She squeezed her hands, then released them. "I prayed so long and here you are." She took a step back and gave Bernie a look of indulgent affection. "Marco's miracle."

Hal peered between the double doors. "Mom, you ready?" he whispered.

"Is it time already?" Cecelia asked.

Hal nodded. "I have to walk you up the aisle, give Bernie away, then serve as groom's man. There's no time to waste!"

As Hal disappeared with Cecelia, Becky smiled at Bernie. "Nervous?"

She was surprised to discover that she wasn't. "No. I feel very calm."

Angie looked doubtfully at Becky. "She's marrying a Costello and she's calm?"

"Let her enjoy it," Becky said, pushing Angie into position in front of the doors. "She'll get over it soon enough." As Becky got in line behind Angie and Bernie fell into place behind her, Becky turned with a smile and whispered, "Incidentally, we voted, and it's your turn to make Thanksgiving and Christmas dinner this year."

Bernie laughed. "Obviously Mark hasn't told you about my cooking."

The joyful sound of the organ intoning the Wedding March put a stop to their teasing. Hal hurried through the side door and took his place beside Bernie as the double doors opened and Angie started up the aisle.

"Sure you don't want to back out?" Hal whispered, patting her hand bracingly as Becky moved into position and they advanced behind her.

"Thanks, but no," Bernie whispered back.

"I've got a hot Ferrari by the side door."

Bernie frowned at him. "They're not going to come and arrest you in the middle of my wedding, are they?"

"The motor is hot," he said softly, "not the car. Look, I'm the comedian in this family. Could we get that straight now?"

She smiled sweetly at him. "Sorry. Now you're going to have competition until you're a very old man."

MARK WATCHED BERNIE come up the aisle with a sense of disbelief. He hadn't expected to ever feel this happy or this hopeful again. She looked pristine and elegant and, he thought, might almost look unfamiliar if it weren't for the hat. The sassy quality of the angled brim was so her.

Hal put Bernie's arm in Mark's and took his place beside Tony. Father John smiled at Mark and Bernie as they climbed the few sanctuary steps to stand before him, Becky and Angie on one side and Tony and Hal on the other.

Bernie felt every word of the ceremony in her heart. "Father," the priest prayed, "bind Mark and Bernadette in the loving union of marriage; and make their love fruitful."

They made their promises in clear voices. Mark placed a gold band with three diamonds on her finger and she slipped a simple gold band on his. Her eyes locked with his as they became husband and wife.

The nuptial mass followed, then Father John turned to offer the final blessing.

"May the peace of Christ live always in your hearts and in your home. May you have friends to stand by you, both in joy and sorrow. May you be ready and willing to help and comfort all who come to you in need. And may the blessings promised to the compassionate be yours in abundance.''

He smiled at the gathering. ''Ladies and gentlemen, I present to you Mr. and Mrs. Mark Costello.''

IN CECELIA'S BEDROOM, Bernie changed into the pink going away suit her mother-in-law had insisted on buying for her. A light rap on the bedroom door was followed by Mark's entry into the room. Changed from his tux into jeans and thick, wheat-colored turtleneck, he looked large and dark and romantically dangerous. Without a word, he came to take her in his arms and kiss her.

''I know this is real,'' he said after a moment, ''but I almost can't believe it.''

''I know.'' She gave him one last kiss as he straightened. ''It's a little scary when your dream becomes your reality.''

''You ready to go?''

Hal's family had offered them the use of their cottage at Arch Cape farther down the coast.

She snatched up her purse and slipped her hand in his.

The family and guests gathered in front of the house to wave them off. Everyone hooted and cheered, Cecelia wept, and Mark and Bernie drove away, trying to see through the JUST MARRIED written in shaving cream on the windshield.

THE SMALL COTTAGE PERCHED on an outcrop of rock far above the ocean. The furniture was comfortable odds and ends forming a happily eclectic whole. The walls were covered with treasures apparently garnered beachcombing; a small shelf of shells, a battered oar, an interesting coil of frayed rope from which someone had hung beads and a glass float. On a stone fireplace was a ship's wheel and a glass bottle with oriental characters on the label.

While Mark built a fire, Bernie put away the groceries they'd brought in the small yellow kitchen. Her task finished, she turned to find him leaning against the door frame, watching her. She went into his arms, drawn there by a power beyond her control.

"You hungry?" he asked, stroking her back with wide, firm sweeps that told her he wasn't.

She smiled up at him. "Only for you."

God, he loved her for that. He kissed her hungrily, then drew back. "Then we have two choices here," he said. "The bed, which is very soft, has a down comforter but is in a frigid room. Or the floor in front of the fire, which will be toasty and romantic, but will probably leave us requiring orthopedic surgery by morning."

Bernie laughed, her arms tight around his neck. "How difficult would it be for us to move the mattress and the down comforter in front of the fire?"

Mark kissed her soundly. "Brilliant!"

Moving the double-bed mattress required shouted orders, much laughter and almost superhuman effort by the time they reached the carpet in the living room. It resisted all Bernie's efforts to pull, and Mark's to push. He finally put Bernie aside, flattened himself against the mattress, arms outstretched, letting it fall onto his back. Then he turned his hands, closing them over the corded edge, and inched his way to the fireplace.

"Okay, okay, stop!" Bernie directed, when he was directly in front of the fire. "Right there."

Mark let the mattress fall. It landed with a whoosh that made the fire sputter. He went back to the bedroom for the comforter. When he returned with it, Bernie had turned off the lights and sat on the edge of the mattress closest to the fire, pulling her flat shoes and knee-highs off. The flame lit her profile and put redwood highlights in her hair. When she turned to him, her green eyes were fathomless and lit with the fire's reflection.

He put the comforter on the foot of the mattress, then knelt in the middle. Bernie moved to pull her sweater over her head, but he reached out to stop her. "Let me do that," he said softly. He hooked a hand around her bent knees and turned her toward him.

Sitting beside her, facing her, thigh to thigh, he reached under the hem of her sweater. Her lashes swept closed as he made contact with the silky skin at her waist. A small shudder went through her. He wondered if it was nervousness, but she opened her eyes and he saw a suggestion of tension and beside it longing and the beginning of passion. He smiled, happy for her and what she was about to discover. Happy for himself that he'd been given the gift to explore with her, learn with her.

He ran his hands up her sides, over her bra, then along the insides of her arms as she raised them to let him remove the sweater. He tossed it beyond the mattress. Her bra was pale pink lace and cupped only the underside of her small breasts. Peeking from the top were the dark moons of her nipples. He felt her nervousness, and he laughed softly to give her time to relax, and himself time to go slowly.

"What have we here, Bernadette?" he teased, running a finger gently over the lace edging one cup. He felt her small shudder again. "I expected something white and functional."

She put her hands on his arms as he reached around her to the hooks. "The panties match." She grinned with a teasing tilt of her chin. "The set was a gift from Angie and Becky. They said the strongest weapon in a woman's arsenal is surprise."

He laughed and kissed her neck. "You've put me into shock more than once since I've met you."

But never quite to this degree, he thought an instant later as he tossed the lace atop her sweater and filled his hands with her cool, silken, bead-tipped breasts. She uttered a little gasp of pleased surprise as he rubbed a thumb across one nipple. He caught the gasp in his mouth as he freed one hand to cup her head and kiss her, lowering her upper body to the mattress.

Everything inside her was trembling. Her body had never known anything like the feelings his touch effected. It was her body, all right, but it was doing things of which she'd never known it to be capable. The tremors seemed to lie over a heat that spread through her from head to toe. But she was becoming aware of the turbulent center of it in a part of her body she'd paid little attention to until this moment.

"Cold?" Mark asked in concern.

She ran her hands along his shoulders and shook her head. "No."

He smiled, encouraging her to be honest. "Nervous?"

She thought about that a moment. Nervousness seemed to have fled. "No," she said in some surprise. "Just . . . I don't know."

He leaned down to kiss her, pleased with her answer. "I do." He put his fingers in the waistband of her slacks. "Let's see the rest of this gift."

Despite her denial of nervousness, her cheeks flushed in the firelight as she lifted her hips to allow him to tug the slacks down. "Believe me when I tell you there isn't much to see."

She was right. The scanty scrap of lace lay like a thin vee across her hipbones, exposing her flat stomach, long, slender thighs and suggesting the shadow between them. Like a man in a trance, he pulled them down and off of her.

They'd been a gift to her. What their removal revealed was a gift to him. He felt at once weak with wonder and inspired beyond bearing. Bernadette Costello was his. God. He'd lost everything, and now everything any man could ever want waited to be made his. He knelt over her, at a loss for words.

Bernie reached up for him with a loving smile, and that was the moment his life changed. He knew it with certainty, would remember it later and forever. He would make her his, but in doing so made himself hers. He went into her arms, feeling the change within himself. He was no longer his first priority.

Bernie reached under his sweater, then tugged at his T-shirt to find his broad, warm back. She expelled a little sigh of pleasure when her palms made contact. *Just follow his lead,* Becky had told her this morning in a completely unself-conscious effort to help her be at ease on her wedding night. *Just trust him, love him and give yourself over to it. Nature is wonderful. Love is wonderful.*

Bernie brought her hands around between them, running her fingers over his strong rib cage as high as she could reach. Mark sat up astride her waist and pulled the sweater and T-shirt off. It joined the growing pile beyond the mattress.

Bernie welcomed him back with a little groan of pleasure; his hair-roughened chest chafed a delicious friction against her breasts. The heat in the center of her being began to make her lightheaded and vaguely anxious.

She pushed gently at Mark's shoulders until he lay on his back beside her. Then she knelt over him and worked at the buckle of his belt. He smiled indulgently at her bent head and touched her face.

She looked up at him anxiously, not sure what the gesture meant. "Stop?" she asked.

"Of course not." He spoke with such sincerity that she relaxed. "I'm just admiring your adventurous spirit. I realize you're a grown woman, but I expected you to feel a little helpless."

She met his eyes frankly, still wondering if she was committing a faux pas. "I was at first," she admitted. "But now you've made me..." She smiled in self-deprecation. "'Eager' is such a naive word, isn't it?"

He shook his head, thinking that she was indeed a miracle. "I can't imagine a man in the world being distressed to find the woman he was making love to eager to continue. Go on. You're doing beautifully. You might start with the shoes first."

Giggling at the thought of what might have resulted if he hadn't pointed that out, Bernie pulled off his leather loafers and socks, then tugged his slacks and briefs down and removed them.

Mark pulled her down beside him, cradling her in his arm and leaning over her. He kissed her tenderly, then with passion billowing inside him. Her eager response began to blur his determination to proceed with care, but her wide, loving eyes on him sharpened it again.

He moved his hands and then his mouth over her breasts until he felt the tremor rebuild in her. Then he traced a line down the center of her with kisses, not stopping where she expected he would. He felt her little start of concern, but ran a soothing hand along her thigh and she relaxed. He nuzzled and kissed until he felt her move fretfully. Then he lay beside her again, tucking her into his arm, pulling her thigh across his hip.

Bernie felt his first touch inside her like a little shock that seemed to reach all the way to her heart. Clinical knowledge was nothing, she thought, clinging to him in wonder as his fingers explored. The body had its own knowledge the mind could not explain. Such an invasion should seem so foreign, yet her body molded itself to it, tightened around it, welcomed it—and waited.

She felt the sudden tension in herself with some surprise. Almost instantly the surprise became anticipation. She felt it begin as a little spin of unease that widened its course and its intensity with the movement of Mark's hand. She couldn't move, couldn't think, couldn't feel anything but the spiral of sensation growing inside her.

Just as she began to wonder if it could make a woman mindless, pleasure struck, hovering one awesome, delicious instant before showering her with wave after wave of glorious well-being.

Mark didn't notice her fingernails in his shoulder. He held her as her body convulsed against his and felt as though he knew almost as much pleasure as she did. When she drew her head back to look at him, her eyes wide with awe, her lips parted in wonder, he kissed her, weak with love.

She put a hand to his chest, stroking gently. "Mark," she whispered. "Tell me what to do for you."

Smiling, he brushed the hair from her face. "What do you want to do?" he asked.

"Touch you," she said.

"Then do," he encouraged. "I'm yours."

Bernie remembered his tender, careful stroking and copied it, moving over his ribs, over his flat stomach, bravely over his manhood, and down his thighs. She worked her way back up again, pausing to explore him this time, awed by the warmth and the strength of him. He groaned, allowing it for only a moment before pulling her up beside him again and positioning himself over her.

He smiled at her concern. "No. You did nothing wrong. But if I'm not to hurt you now, that'll have to wait until next time."

Cupping her hips in his hands, he entered her as gently as he could, moving easily to help her accommodate him. He felt her body's resistance, her slight stiffening to prepare, and forced his way past it. She gasped and he hastened to comfort her, covering her face with kisses.

"Try to relax," he said. "It'll be all right."

"I'm all right," she whispered, kissing his shoulder. "I'm wonderful. You're wonderful." She moved a little, encouraging him to go on. The pleasure he felt at that slight movement startled him. She clasped her legs around him and followed his careful lead, staying with him as his movements became stronger. But he wasn't leading, he thought in a kind of disbelief. This was new territory, beyond any pleasure he'd ever experienced.

The power of it stunned him so that he felt the delicious wonder of it as though it were the first time. Bound together, allied in the pursuit of their mutual fulfillment, they came together, each confounded—Bernie, because a new world had opened for her—Mark, because the old one would never be the same.

SUZANNA'S SURRENDER
Nora Roberts

The final novel featuring The Calhoun Women.

Suzanna remembered Holt Bradford as a dangerous teenager with a bad attitude and she didn't feel that after ten years as a Vice cop he would have mellowed. So she wasn't pleased when her family decided that as she knew him — having once knocked him off his bike — she should be the one to talk to him regarding his grandfather and her great-grandmother.

Holt wasn't interested in any romance their relatives might have had or the missing emeralds, but he was interested in Suzanna. She made him hungry…

BUNDLE OF JOY
Barbara Bretton

Caroline Bradley and Charlie Donohue avoided each other by mutual agreement. She was a knockout but out of his league, and he was built on a heroic scale but was more of a beer and peanuts sort of guy. Who would have thought their points of view would change in just one night?

One night locked in a storeroom and nine months later they were going to be parents. Charlie thought a kid's parents ought to be married; how could Caroline argue with that?

Silhouette Sensation

COMING NEXT MONTH

FLASHPOINT
Patricia Gardner Evans

The forces of good were out to trap a killer and
Ariel Spence was the bait. No one knew exactly
how involved Ariel might have been in her late
fiancé's lucrative but illegal business. So, Ariel had
been placed in a small Montana town where she
could be watched and strangers would be noticed.

Ryan Jones was a burnt-out rather battered warrior,
but he was intrigued by the case and had agreed to
keep an eye on Ariel. They became uneasy
housemates and, as their intimacy grew, so did
Ryan's worry that Ariel was innocent and that
somebody wanted her silenced permanently!

RAFFERTY'S CHOICE
Dallas Schulze

Rafferty Traherne was looking for a housekeeper.
Someone who could cook, clean and care for his
ten-year-old daughter, Becky. *You may remember
meeting Becky in* Tell Me a Story.

Amanda Bradley had obviously exaggerated on her
application form but Becky liked her. So how bad
could she be? In fact, Amanda was a domestic
disaster — different calamities lurked around every
corner. But she *was* good to Becky. She was also
very pretty — too pretty…

COMING NEXT MONTH FROM

Silhouette

Desire

*provocative, sensual love stories
for the woman of today*

THE MOLLY Q Lass Small
NO LIES BETWEEN US Naomi Horton
LEATHER AND LACE Ryanne Corey
A WOLF IN SHEEP'S CLOTHING Joan Johnston
MORNINGS AT SEVEN Sally Goldenbaum
TALL IN THE SADDLE Mary Lynn Baxter

Special Edition

*longer, satisfying romances with
mature heroines and lots of emotion*

OBSESSION Lisa Jackson
FAMILY FRIENDLY Jo Ann Algermissen
THE HEALING TOUCH Christine Flynn
A REAL CHARMER Jennifer Mikels
ANNIE IN THE MORNING Curtiss Ann Matlock
LONGER THAN... Erica Spindler

From the author of Mirrors comes an enchanting romance

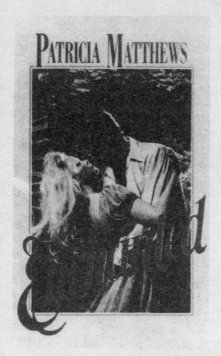

PATRICIA MATTHEWS

Caught in the steamy heat of America's New South, Rebecca Trenton finds herself torn between two brothers – she yearns for one, but a dark secret binds her to the other.

Off the coast of South Carolina lay Pirate's Bank – a small island as intriguing as the legendary family that lived there. As the mystery surrounding the island deepened, so Rebecca was drawn further into the family's dark secret – and only one man's love could save her from the treachery which now threatened her life.

W♥RLDWIDE